A Bend in the Snake

A Brenda Tower Mystery

*For a dear friend
Gary London,
I hope you enjoy this
read*
LaMar

LaMar A. Palmer

A Bend in the Snake

by LaMar A. Palmer

ISBN 1490498265

978-1490498263

Cover photo by Larry Ridenhour, courtesy of National Scenic Byways Online www.byways.org

Acknowledgements

Roger Burke, a high school classmate and the author of numerous novels, encouraged me to write and read and commented on the manuscript.

Joan Palmer, my beloved wife, listened patiently to my ideas for the story, read the drafts, and gave me feedback.

Lola Fish, Carol Wildman, and Cathy Carling read the initial draft and provided numerous recommendations for improvement.

The Knoxville Mystery Writers' Group contributed their reactions and valuable comments.

A special thanks to my editor, Cathy Kodra, *Kodra Editing Services*, whose professional editing made this book possible.

Craig Alexander designed the cover.

A Bend in the Snake

Main Characters

Carlos Mendoza –Illegal alien, Ramiro Sanchez's cousin
Ramiro Sanchez –Illegal alien, harvest worker
Lin Stone – Columba County Sheriff
Brenda Tower – Portland Oregon Police Detective

Supporting Characters

Cliff Abbott – County Coroner
Don Barber – Sheriff's Deputy
Ned Carver – Sheriff's Deputy
Jack Duval –Truck driver
Rusty Gates – Criminologist
Ken Gear – Harvest worker
Sam Hardesty – Sheriff's Deputy
Kathy Johnson – Art Sabin's daughter
Ron Johnson –Tab Johnson's father
Tab Johnson – Art Sabin's grandson
Christina Lopez – Art Sabin's harvest cook
Calli Mendez – Art Sabin's live-in housekeeper
Steve Packer – Brenda's companion while on vacation
Ed Pearson – Volunteer Deputy
Emily Robbins – Melody Robbins' daughter
Melody Robbins – Housewife
Angela Sabin– Art Sabin's wife (separated)
Art Sabin – Prominent wheat farmer
Tony Sabin – Art Sabin's son
Everett Schuster – Art Sabin's Lawyer
"Squeaky"– Art Sabin's long-time friend
Brad Summers – Retired, widowed trekker
John Talbot – Sheriff's Deputy
Melba Townsend – Owner of Huber's Café
Joey Valentine – Harvest worker
Carol Wannamaker – Owner of Aunt Jennies B & B
Sheila Wattenburger – Wheat farmer's daughter
Chet Weber – Sheriff's Deputy
Chauncy West – Geology expert

July 10, 2007

Portland, Oregon

The detective approached the woman's hospital bed and felt the contents of lunch rise in her throat. She breathed deeply through her nose, swallowed, and managed to keep them down. The RN backed quickly away from the bed and the visitor's pale face, saying she'd be right outside at the nurse's station should the detective need her.

The unconscious victim had been placed on her back with the head of the bed raised. White sheets covered a slender body to the base of the neck. An IV dripped steadily into one arm, and a blood-pressure cuff hissed and inflated on the other arm as the detective leaned in for a better look. The woman's sallow complexion, what the detective could see of it, was mottled with ugly, purple-black bruises covering her cheeks and left temple. The area below the blood-crusted hairline looked like a child's finger painting gone awry—bright red and darker red gouges ran horizontally above her eyebrows, and bluish-black welts blotted the surface like inverted craters. Both eyes, sunken and closed, were surrounded by crimson, puffy flesh that would turn black by tomorrow. Her attacker had pummeled her mouth, probably with a closed fist, until it swelled into an odd, misshapen cluster of split lips and dried blood. Finger-shaped abrasions marked the woman's slender neck. The detective couldn't see below the hospital gown draped over the victim's shoulders, and she wasn't sure she wanted to.

She steeled her stomach and called the nurse in, and when she saw the rest of what had been done to the hooker, the detective turned quietly, vomited into a bedpan on the nightstand, and left the room.

Detectives James Collins and Brenda Tower had been on the hunt all day for a pimp named Claude Jennings, wanted for the brutal beating of one of his street girls. They entered the Lost Horizon in a seedy downtown section of Portland around 7:00 p.m. and went directly to the bar. Collins showed his badge to the longhaired bartender wearing a red shirt. Tower laid a mug shot on the bar. Tapping her finger on the photograph, she leaned close, looked the man in the eye, and asked, "Seen this guy today?"

The bartender answered flatly, "No, I don't think so."

"He's in his forties, thinning brown hair, sports a beard, and he has a missing pinky finger. You're sure he hasn't been in here?"

The bartender cleared his throat. "Wait a minute! Look back there—he's the guy in the far back facing this direction."

Collins turned to see a man stand, run to the back door, and fling it open. Chasing after him, Collins ran between tables to the back of the room and through the open door into the alley. He looked left and right, but the man had already disappeared. Collins went back inside.

"That's the man with the missing finger," the bartender said. "He's in here quite a bit."

"We'll get him," Tower said over her shoulder as the two detectives hurried out the front door.

Back on the sidewalk, a scowling Collins asked his partner, "Where the hell was our backup?"

"I don't know, Jim. I only know it's been a long day. But—but look, we've got the make on Jennings' car. It's probably along the street here somewhere or in that lot at the end of this block. He's not going to leave that baby in this neighborhood at night."

"It's a dark-blue Lexus LS 430, right?"

Tower nodded. "You got it. I'll look along the street if you want to check in that lot."

"Sure, I'll radio you if I see it, ditto if you do."

As she moved down the street, Tower checked for the car along both sides with no luck. Entering the next block, she spotted the Lexus parked on her side of the street about halfway down.

"Jim—Jim, it's in the middle of the 700 block," Brenda spoke quietly into the shoulder mic.

"Good! I'll be right there. Sit tight."

Tower crouched behind a black Dodge pickup parked close to the back bumper of the Lexus; from there, she could keep an eye on the street and not be seen easily by passing autos. Shadows from buildings across the street offered additional cover.

A young teen in jeans and a Portland Trailblazer tee spied Tower from the sidewalk and came close, hands jammed in his pockets. "Hey, what ya doin', lady?" he asked.

Tower turned and scowled at him. "I'm waiting for someone—now get out of here."

"But this is where I live," he said, pointing to a second-story window above the flower shop.

She lunged toward him. "I don't want you to get hurt. Now get!"

The kid retreated hastily down the street.

A short rain earlier had left the street wet. Tower could hear the *swish* of passing tires. After a few minutes had passed, a silver Mercedes crossed the intersection and crawled along the street in her direction. She drew her weapon as it slowed to a stop. Jennings emerged from the backseat, looked around furtively, and darted toward his car. Tower stood and rounded the pickup as the Mercedes sped away. She ran up behind Jennings just as he reached for the door handle.

"Jennings, you're under arrest. Put your hands on the car and spread your legs." Tower yelled.

Jerking his head around, the pimp smirked. "What, my parking meter's expired?" He quickly turned away from the car and leaned forward, poised to bolt.

Tower slammed the barrel of her Glock into his ribs, and Jennings gasped.

"You think I don't mean business? Now turn around and get those legs spread!"

Groaning, Jennings shifted back around and spread his legs, clapping his palms on top of the car. "You can go to hell," he muttered under his breath.

3

"You're under arrest for the assault and battery of Jodie Evans."

"I don't know any Jodie Evans." he growled.

Tower heard footsteps, and Collins strode alongside Jennings, grabbed his arm, and slapped on a cuff. "Turn around, you, so I can get your other wrist."

Jennings turned. Tower heard the second cuff click shut.

"I knew it would take two of you," the pimp said, his lips curling in a sneer.

"Can it!" Collins barked, his hand gripping the cuff chain. Turning to Tower, he said, "I'll stay with him—you bring the car around."

By this time, a few curious onlookers had gathered. They watched while Collins and Jennings waited for the cruiser to arrive. When the patrol car squealed to a halt beside the Lexus, Tower leaped out and opened the back door. Collins eased Jennings into the back seat and shut the door.

A young male in the crowd stepped forward and asked, "Why'd you arrest that guy?"

"Let's just say his conduct has been disorderly," Tower said, recognizing the teen she had sent away from the scene a short while ago.

"Oh." The boy nodded.

"You've got some quick glide to those feet of yours, Brenda. You stopped that turkey before he had time to squeal out of here," Collins said as they climbed into the cruiser.

"Thanks, partner, but I'm not feeling fast on these feet. I'm tired—I need a rest."

"We've got court in the morning—the Marlow case."

Tower sighed, laid her head back, and closed her eyes.

1

Portland, Oregon wasn't a bad place. It boasted a good climate, pretty scenery, great shopping, and plenty of homicide to keep a disarmingly gorgeous detective employed. But it wasn't in the rearview mirror where it belonged. The world was a messy place, and it was no different for Brenda Tower as she gripped next week's duty roster, ready to tear it to shreds. It was mid-July, 2007. Iran and the International Atomic Energy Agency were in a heated dispute over the country's nuclear program, Al-Qaeda was rapidly regrouping, and American soldiers were battling and dying in Iraq and Afghanistan.

Also ready to do battle, Brenda ran through the poorly lit hallway, flew into Chief Lowery's office, and slammed the door behind her. Surprised by her clamorous entrance, Lowery flinched and dropped his pen. His brows drew together over dark eyes, and he glared at the woman across from his desk in the windowless room.

"This is wrong, Chief!" Brenda blurted out, as she waved the duty roster in his face. Her green eyes didn't lie. "Tile eyes" they called her, after the shiny floor tiles in police headquarters. They were emeralds in the tall, slender brunette whose sassy jewelry box housed them.

"You got that right," growled the Chief. "Barging in here and practically spitting in your superior's face should be a crime."

"Chief, you approved my vacation for next week, and now my name's back on the duty roster. What the flip's going on?" Brenda suspected a clerical screw-up.

Lowery brushed his hair back with his hand and stared momentarily at her. "I guess I forgot to tell you, Tower. I got to have you next week."

She heaved a disgusted sigh, and her arms flew to her hips. "You forgot to tell me, Chief! Look, you approved my vacation a month ago. You can't go back on it now—I've got plans."

"We're falling behind, Tower—two detectives are out. And the Mayor's on my ass every day."

"Tell him to get you more people. I can't keep up this pace. I'll call in sick."

Lowery leaned back in his chair and placed his right foot on top of a partly opened desk drawer. His face was as hard and immovable as granite. "I need you here next week, Detective. We'll work something out for you later."

Brenda moved closer, slapped her hands down on his cluttered desk, and stared Lowery directly in the eye. "Later, it's always later with you. I've put off my vacation month after month to support your schedules." She shook her finger at him. "We had a deal, you and me. This time Chief, you better stick by it—fix this damn duty roster."

Shocked by his detective's pushback, Lowery jumped to his feet and cleared his throat. "Don't you come in here unannounced and bark orders at me!"

Brenda didn't respond. She stepped back, pulled open the door, and slammed it behind her. Heart pounding, she returned to her office. She hated confrontation, but she knew this couldn't continue. I have to look after my health, she told herself. I've got to have some time off, mid-year reviews be damned. It doesn't matter anymore what the Chief thinks of me.

The vacation Brenda longed for and so desperately needed had almost slipped through her hands. If the Chief failed to act, she could still be in trouble. Well aware of the department's manpower shortage and the corresponding spike in homicides in recent months, she had always played the good soldier, submitting to the Chief's requests to roll ahead her vacation. It's not going to happen this time, she thought.

Brenda's new partner, James Collins, eagle-eyed her when she returned and plopped into her chair. "What's going on partner? I've never seen you like this."

"Lowery's trying to screw me out of my vacation again. I'm so tired I can hardly get out of bed in the mornings. I have to get some time off."

"You must have talked to him."

"We yelled at each other. I told him I wasn't responsible for his manpower shortage and I couldn't keep working at this pace. I nearly died years ago from overwork and exhaustion."

"Want to tell me about it?"

"I was going full-time to Colorado State University while working twenty hours a week and helping out on the ranch. My mother died that winter and left me with two younger sisters to look after. Dad was an alcoholic—he couldn't do much. They found me passed out on the kitchen floor during finals week that next spring. I hadn't been sleeping, my nerves were shot, and my stomach bothered me. The doctor said I'd lost over twenty pounds. I vowed then I'd never, ever again allow myself to get into such a wretched physical condition."

"Do you want me to talk to Lowery?"

"Not now. I'm going to give him the afternoon to correct the duty roster."

At five feet nine in her stocking feet, Brenda worked hard to maintain a trim figure, partly out of vanity, and partly because of her work. In the last year or so, she'd let her hair grow to shoulder length to soften her appearance. A certain country quality set her apart from the other women on the force: how she stood, walked, carried herself, and smiled in that friendly, eager way. Her smile, friends said, drew people to her like hummingbirds to sugar water. She could be most disarming when interrogating a suspect or questioning an eyewitness.

Brenda made a final check before leaving the stationhouse that Friday. To the Chief's credit, and to her considerable relief, he had crossed out her name on the duty roster and initialed and dated his correction. At last, her vacation would go forward as planned. Monday she would begin a week away with Steve Packer, a man she had come to know through her cycling club. Packer had invited her to vacation with him at the family cabin on Lake Coeur d'Alene in the Idaho panhandle. During the day, they could water ski, jet-ski, boat, fish, hike, and enjoy the countryside. He had made a point about the cabin having two bedrooms, assurance she'd have her nighttime privacy. There would be no pesky alarm clock, no log-jammed freeways, no pointless meetings, no overloaded schedules or worrisome deadlines, and no homicides. Lake Coeur d'Alene was less than five hundred miles from Portland; the two would be at the cabin by Monday evening.

2

Carlos Mendoza crossed the border into the United States from Mexico in the first part of July, 2007. He sat at a table in a truck stop outside of El Paso, Texas, where the taste of good coffee and a heated cinnamon roll refreshed his spirits. Straining hard to hear the conversation among three over-the-road haulers at an adjacent table, he heard one of the men say he had a load going to Los Angeles. It was music to Mendoza's ears. He swallowed the last of his coffee, raised himself from his chair, grabbed his duffel bag, and headed for the exit. From there he waited for the California-bound trucker to come out and walk to his rig. When the man did come out, Mendoza followed him. "Hey man, can you give me a lift to California?"

The trucker looked him up and down. "My company doesn't allow . . ." He stopped. "What's it worth to you?"

"I'll give you this gold chain," Mendoza said, pulling it from his jeans pocket and dangling it in front of the man. From the look on his face, Mendoza could tell he'd struck a deal.

"I won't put up with no foolishness. Don't slow me down. You buy your own food, you hear me?"

"Yeah, I understand. I'll do what you say."

"Give me the chain and climb up."

Several hundred people entered the country illegally from Mexico in early July. Each one of those border runners came with a purpose; most were honorable, some not so much. Each came leaving behind a past, some not so pleasant. Few, if any, could match the past Carlos Mendoza was leaving behind.

Riding shotgun in Trucker John's Kenworth across southern Arizona gave the twenty-nine-year-old Mendoza ample time to think about what he'd done in the years since he left home. He remembered his interview with Caesar Estevez, the powerful drug lord in Ciudad Juarez, who hired him as his personal bodyguard.

"How'd you get that broken nose, the scar above your right

eye, and the long, jagged scar on your arm?" Estevez wanted to know.

"Protectin' turf, you know. I had myself a gang in Chihuahua City some time back. After a while, man, nobody messed with the Jaguars," Mendoza had bragged.

"Tell me about that mayor's daughter, the one in Madera."

Estevez peeled an apple and ate it with a knife while they talked.

"No matter what her old man said, I knew it wasn't me. Shit, three of my gang members banged her that summer."

Estevez sat up straighter in his chair and questioned Mendoza with steely eyes. "Carlos, what makes you think you can do this job?"

"I know the drug trade, I been in it for years. I had a string of whores for a long time. I know how to handle them, and how to protect them. You heard about me probably 'cause I'm an armed gunman in a drug racket south of here. I'm damn good, too."

Estevez called Mendoza his "man of steel." "He's fearless," he boasted to other employees, "like Poncho Villa, storming a wall lined with Federales. The man completes assignments with great skill: always thorough, on time, neat and clean, never any incriminating blowback."

Nothing in his line of work caused Mendoza pause. He shot men down the way another man would swat flies. He could strangle or stab a man with little more effort than that required to take out the trash. Mendoza flourished as a notorious killer until the day the federal police raided his *cuarto*. He remembered a neighbor girl had spotted the uniforms as they gathered on the street below, and she alerted him. Fleeing out the back way and down the stairs, he hid himself under the canvas covering a motorcycle. The police missed apprehending him by seconds. After running wild in Mexico for several years and killing twenty-three men, his game was finally up. His name hit the most-wanted lists.

"Where did you get the gold chain you gave me?" Trucker John asked, as Mendoza looked out the window at an overhead sign for Tucson.

"In Guatemala."

Mendoza had fled south across the border into the Guatemalan mountains five years earlier. There he found sanctuary with a band of guerilla fighters battling to protect the Mayan farmers against their own government. He threw in with them, a perfect setup. He spent his days fighting Portilla's troops and saved the nights for marauding, looting, and raping.

"Live there long?"

"Long enough, I guess." Mendoza had rat-holed a substantial cache during those years.

Trucker John spat a chew out the window. "Where're you heading, young fellow?"

"My sister wants me to come and stay with her in Meridian, Idaho. Sort of start over. But first I'm goin' to see a cousin in Bakersfield."

The ride to Los Angeles across Interstate 10 brought Mendoza to within a hundred miles of his destination. It took him a few more hours to hitchhike the distance to a landmark south of Bakersfield. A phone call followed. His cousin, Ramiro Sanchez, picked him up and drove him to his rented trailer, a twenty-year-old, silver and blue single-wide. Although the two men had grown up as friends, ten years had passed since they'd seen each other.

On Thursday, July 11, the day Sanchez left town, Mendoza washed his new truck and purchased floor mats, a dash cover, a steering wheel cover, and a GPS.

Late that evening he heard a knock on the door and recognized the woman on the landing. "You're Lily, right?" Mendoza smiled broadly.

"You remembered me."

"You were here with Ramiro's girl. Come in, come in." He stepped back from the door and bowed, sweeping his arm in a wide arc like a matador in the arena.

Lily, a tall brunette with long hair, dark eyes, and a body men braked to stare at, sashayed into the living room.

"You missed Ramiro, you know. He left this morning."

Lily flashed him a generous smile. "I didn't come to see Ramiro. You busy?"

"Nah. Come and sit?"

The two sat close on the turquoise velour couch. "What have you been up to, Carlos?"

"I bought myself a truck. I'm gettin' it ready to travel."

"Travel! You just got here. Where're you off to, anyway?"

"Ramiro's got himself a job in Washington in the wheat harvest. He invited me up. Say, you want a beer?"

"Sure, I'll have one."

Surprised Lily came to see him, he welcomed her presence. She's a *mamacita*, he thought, very hot in her cut-off jeans and low V-neck black tee. He grabbed two beers from the refrigerator, popped the tabs, and walked back to the couch. Lily took the beer he handed her and, for a few moments as he stood over her, he enjoyed the view. She smiled and took a drink.

"This is so good on a hot night," she said.

Mendoza sat back down next to her and put his hand on her bare knee. "What have you been up to, Lily?"

"Not much. I'm a cashier at a Safeway. Same ole, same ole every day, you know."

"Can you stay?"

"I'll stay if you want me to."

"I'd like that. I haven't talked to a pretty woman in a long time."

"Sure, I'll stay and talk with you."

He inched his hand slowly up her leg. She made no effort to block his advance. "Ramiro told me you lived in Guatemala. What'd you do down there?"

"I was a freedom fighter." He slid his hand up under her shirt and fondled a breast. Smirking, he asked, "Got anything you want freed?"

In short order, the two moved from the couch to the back bedroom. Mendoza planned to teach Lily a thing or two about sex with a near stranger. Surprisingly, it was Lily who turned out to be the teacher. She wore him out with her sexual gymnastics and Olympic endurance. When their time together ended late and Lily left, Mendoza presumed he would never see her again.

Early the following morning, Lily banged on the trailer

door. Afterward, he lay back, panting and spent. The small hand on the bedside clock hadn't reached eight when she started pulling on jeans and a standard, grocery-store smock. "I'll see you after work," she told him, playfully yanking his ponytail.

After work, he repeated to himself. He enjoyed the personal attention from Lily. But the thrill of being pursued had already started to wane. He usually took what he wanted from a woman and moved on. This reverse role with Lily both confused and annoyed him. What was her game, he kept wondering. The more he thought about what she might be planning for him, the more it unnerved him. Carlos changed his plans. He had not intended to leave Bakersfield on Friday, and Sanchez told him he was welcome to stay for a few days. The new tenant wouldn't show up until Monday the fifteenth. Nevertheless, he packed his truck and drove away Friday before noon, long before Lily returned from work.

After hours on the road, Mendoza pulled into a rest stop along Interstate 5 to stretch his legs and have a smoke. A biker couple in leathers drove in on a big Harley and parked as he walked near the curb. The bearded, heavyset driver yelled out, 'You bitch!' The man hurried to the restroom, leaving his female rider at the curb. Mendoza looked in her direction. The petite, attractive brunette removed her helmet and shook out her hair. She approached him at once. "Can you help me, friend?" she pleaded. "The man I'm with isn't right. He's on something. I don't feel safe with him. Would you take me with you?"

"Sure, why not? That gray pickup's mine," he said, pointing down the row of parked cars.

"Great, I'll get my things."

Mendoza walked to the front of his truck and waited. The woman approached him with her small bundle of belongings. "I'm Sally. I promise I won't be a bother."

"I'm Carlos, You won't be a bother. Get in. I'll put your stuff in the back."

The biker exited the restroom just as Sally put a foot on the running board. He hurried toward her, yelling, "Get the fuck out of there!"

"I'm not going with you, Mike."

"If you know what's good for you, you'll get your little ass back on that bike."

"Leave me alone!" she screamed.

Mike yanked on the handle, flung the door open, and grabbed Sally by the wrist. At that moment, he felt the sharp point of a blade press against the right side of his neck.

"The woman says she's had enough of you. Better let her be."

"Who the hell are you?"

Mendoza pressed his blade a little harder. "You don't want to know. Be on your way, Bud."

"Take the bitch, asshole. I've had enough of her, anyway," the biker said, releasing his grip on Sally's arm.

Mendoza and Sally watched him speed away.

"Please wait for me? I need to use the sandbox," Sally said. Within minutes, she returned to the truck with her leathers over her arm.

Mendoza took them and placed them in the back. It was close to 8:00 p.m. when the two pulled onto the freeway. "I plan to stop for the night someplace."

"You're the boss. By the way, I'm glad you had the knife. Mike could have been a real problem."

"No, you're wrong. He'd never be a problem for me."

3

Three young harvest workers leaned over the hood of a dusty black '89 Impala in a field near Elam's Crossing. Their conversation often turned to women: how to find them, win them, keep them, and lose them. This night it would be different. There'd be no talk about women, not even about Sheila Wattenburger, the sexy, hot-blooded daughter of the wheat farmer they worked for. Away from the rental they shared with a fourth man, they could talk uninterrupted about something that had been on Ramiro Sanchez's mind for some time.

At twenty-five, Sanchez was older than the other two men. He had run the Mexican border at age eighteen and found work at a feedlot in Hereford, Texas. Later, he wandered west into California's San Joaquin Valley where he worked in the orchards and the packinghouses for several years, losing the smallest finger on his left hand in a conveyer pulley. For the past two summers, he worked the wheat harvests in Washington and Montana.

"It'll be a cinch, man," Sanchez told the others. "We'll get in, grab the money, and get out fast."

Ken Gear removed his baseball cap and scratched a full head of thick, dark brown hair. A tall, slight built, dark-skinned American, he had grown up poor in a large, dysfunctional family in rural Arizona. Tired of seeing his father beat on his mother with his fists, turning her black and blue, he lit out on his own at seventeen, making a living in Washington State cutting asparagus and picking cherries, peaches, and apples. He worked in the packinghouses in the off-season and had followed the wheat harvest these past two summers.

Gear's eyebrows rose into skeptical twin peaks. "You figure they'll invite us in nice-like 'cause we knock real pretty?"

Sanchez took a long drag on his cigarette, exhaled hard, and shot Gear a disgusting look. "Sabin's an old fart, man. We'll push him aside."

Gear scratched the inside of his ear with a wooden matchstick and continued to press Sanchez. "What makes you think there's money in the house?"

"He keeps it in the office, man. I saw a tall stack of hundreds there last year." Sanchez's voice rose a notch.

Joey Valentine, the Gringo-Mexican, had grown up in Sunnyside, Washington. A little younger and smaller in size than the other two men, he was the only one among them who graduated high school. He carried the sports letters he earned in basketball and track among his belongings. Spitting out the wheat stalk he'd been chewing on, he asked, "Anyone else live there, Ramiro?"

"Sabin had a teenage grandson with him last year."

"The kid could give us a hard time," Gear said.

"He's a wimpy gringo whelp, man. We won't take no shit from him." Sanchez smacked his right fist into the palm of his left hand.

"We got an old man and a kid to deal with. What about the woman you mentioned?" Valentine asked.

"Calli won't be no problem, trust me, man." Sanchez nodded to punctuate his statement.

"We're not going to hurt nobody, right?" Gear asked.

"We're jist goin' to pick up some easy money," Sanchez said, shifting his weight from one leg to the other. "You guys don't need no money, maybe?"

Gear pushed back. "You kidding? Hell yes, I need money."

"I need money like crazy—my car's down," Valentine said.

Sanchez stood up straight, stretched, and looked hard at Valentine.

"All we're doing is taking some of that rich man's cash," Valentine said. "He'll hardly miss it."

Sanchez turned and smacked the palm of his hand down hard on the hood of his dusty car. "I don't give a damn if the old bastard misses the money we take from him or not, man. He treated my people *bad* over the years. He worked 'em hard on crap jobs for no kind of wages. Screw him, man. It's time we get some of that bread back he cheated from them."

"Just going to be us three, right?" Valentine asked.

"Us three, man." Sanchez pointed to Gear, Valentine, and himself. "You guys in or out? 'Cause if you're out, I got someone else lined up."

"Okay, okay, I'm in," Gear said.

"Me, too," came from Valentine.

They shook hands to seal the deal.

"We'll go in the morning," Sanchez said.

Gear and Valentine nodded agreement.

"Tomorrow we'll have some real money, won't we, Ramiro?" Gear asked.

"Tomorrow, man, you'll have more money than you've ever seen at one time."

4

Brenda and Steve Packer left Portland Monday morning before dawn for a week together at Lake Coeur D'Alene. They witnessed the morning light break, unveiling the splendor of the Columbia Gorge, a protected area of diverse geologic landscape and extraordinary beauty. Packer opted to travel through Pendleton, Oregon, over to Lewiston, Idaho, and north on US 95 to Lake Coeur d'Alene. It would be a slower drive than taking the freeway through the Tri-Cities and Spokane.

The silver Explorer left Interstate 84 at Pendleton and crossed into Washington near Walla Walla, where Packer picked up US 12 for Waitsburg and Dayton. The Palouse country would be a far more picturesque drive with its rolling wheat fields, old farmhouses, grain elevators, and small country towns. He pulled into a Maverick station in Dayton to refuel and give them both a little time to shake their legs. Brenda went into the store to use the restroom and purchase a bottle of water.

The sounds of a whimpering child caught her ear as she left the building. Rounding the corner, she came upon a young girl sitting against the wall, arms wrapped around her knees and cradling her head.

Brenda crouched down, touching her lightly on the arm. "What's the matter, sweetie?"

Dressed in a tee, jeans, and sneakers, the girl lifted her head and offered a blank stare through watery, bloodshot eyes.

Brenda guessed her to be eleven or twelve years old. "My name's Brenda, sweetie, what's yours?"

"Patty."

"Why are you crying, Patty?"

"Don't know," the girl said as she wiped her nose on her shirtsleeve.

Brenda smiled warmly. "I'm a police woman." She took a moment to show the girl her badge. "I talk with girls every day. Patty, I want to help you."

"What do you care?"

"Sweetie, did someone hurt you?"

"Not really."

"Won't you tell me what's wrong?"

"I had to get out of my house."

Brenda glanced over at Steve leaning against the car, arms folded across his chest. She waved to him. He waved back. "Patty, why did you have to leave?"

Patty lowered her head and almost whispered, "Because of the party."

"You didn't feel safe there?"

The girl shook her head.

"Where'd you go?"

"No place."

"Have you been out all night?"

"Uh-huh."

The girl rose to her feet and Brenda stood next to her.

"Where was your mother during the party?"

"At work."

Brenda shook her head, drawing in air through her teeth. "Patty, your mother's got to be sick with worry."

"Do you think?" Patty asked, brushing the last of the tears from her eyes.

"Let's go into the store. You can wash your hands and face." Brenda pointed. "That's my friend over there. We can take you home if you need a ride."

Patty looked over at Brenda. "You'll go to the door with me?" she asked.

"Sure I will."

"Okay, I'll come."

While Patty washed up, Brenda bought her a soda and a chocolate-covered donut. When she met Brenda outside, the girl downed the donut as they walked toward the car. Now sitting behind the wheel, Steve watched the girl climb into the back seat as Brenda eased in beside him.

"Steve, this is Patty. She needs a ride home."

Hesitating for a moment, he said, "We'll take you. Show me

where to go, Patty?"

She pointed. "Go straight till you come to the courthouse. Then go right. I'll show you our house." Patty reached up and touched Brenda's shoulder when Packer stopped in front of her home. "Come with me?"

Brenda nodded. The two exited the Explorer and walked to the small, brown bungalow. Brenda rang the doorbell and peeked at her watch while they waited. It was 10:15. The sun was just rising above the tall oak tree in the yard. A woman opened the door and burst onto the porch. Patty stepped back, but the woman lunged forward and caught her up in her arms.

"Baby, I'm so happy to see you."

Patty flung her arms around her mother and began to sob.

A sweet aroma flooded the open doorway. "French toast?" Brenda asked. The woman nodded.

Brenda wondered if there were other children, or a husband.

"Thank you so much for bringing Patty home."

"You're welcome. She can tell you why she left last night."

The mother held her daughter's chin in her hand while looking into her eyes. "Randy's gone, honey, for good." To Brenda, she said, "When I got home and saw the mess with what they'd done to my home, and my girl missing, I kicked him out. He won't be back."

A wide smile spread over Patty's face when she heard this.

"You'll be safe here now," Brenda told her.

Patty held Brenda's hand a moment longer and looked up at her. "Thanks," the girl said, and then she stepped into the house and out of sight.

Patty's mother offered Brenda her hand. "Thank you again for returning my daughter."

"She's a lovely girl. I wish you both the best." Brenda turned and walked to the street, content she had taken the time to help the girl.

Back in the Explorer she told Steve, "I think she was afraid to go home. Afraid of what her mother might do to her for running off."

Packer nodded as he adjusted his seatbelt. "We need to be on our way. I want to take that little detour I was telling you about earlier."

"I know. Thanks for being patient back there."

5

A few miles out of Dayton, Packer turned left off Highway 12 onto Highway 261 West leading to Elam's Crossing, a village about eight miles from the junction. Packer's great- grandfather worked on the railroad there in the community's glory days. He planned to hunt down his ancestor's headstone and take some photographs. They'd be on their way within an hour, he promised Brenda.

Moments after making the turn, Brenda noticed a man walking in their direction on the far side of the highway. He wore a baseball cap, shouldered a backpack with a sleeping bag, and sported orange-trimmed walking shoes.

"Wonder where he's off to?" she asked, pointing in his direction.

"The Snake River isn't too far from here. Could be he's been fishing and camping," Parker said.

"I don't see any fishing pole, Steve."

"Maybe it's a collapsible in his backpack, along with his catch."

Brenda turned to look back as they passed, following the man with her eyes. "Must be lonely for guys like that."

"You don't know, Brenda. He could be on his way to see his girlfriend."

Before long, Brenda's eyes caught hold of a little country lane making its way through the meadow on Packer's side of the car. It crossed over a narrow, one-lane wooden bridge and meandered off through a canyon to the south. "Steve, look at that white, two-story farmhouse on the bluff up ahead. And there's an octagonal barn. This scene reminds me of a photograph in my *Country Living* magazine."

"Want to take some photographs on our way back?"

"Let's do." Turning back to her side of the road, something in the wheat field caught Brenda's eye. She thumped Packer on the thigh with the back of her hand. "Quick! Stop the car!"

Packer flinched, startled by her unexpected brusque command. The vehicle slowed to a turtle's pace. "Why stop here?"

"Pull off into the weeds."

He pulled off the road and cut the engine. "I don't get it. There's nothing here."

Ignoring his comment, Brenda opened her door and slid out. "Come over here, Steve."

"Okay, okay, I'm coming." Packer stepped out and walked around to where she stood. "What is it?"

"Look at the pickup in the field." Brenda pointed.

"I see it, but so what? It's not exactly photo worthy."

"No, it's not that. The driver's slumped over the steering wheel."

"How can you tell from here?" Steve squinted.

Without a word, Brenda walked over to the barbed-wire fence, pushed the second strand down, bent over and thrust one leg between the wires, and slipped through. Negotiating barbed-wire fences and tramping through grain fields was second nature to the one-time cowgirl.

"Where are you going?"

"Out to the pickup, of course. Coming?"

Packer looked at his watch, heaved a sigh, and hurried after her. City to the bone, he had grown up in an apartment complex in Oakland, California. Roughing it as a youngster meant shooting hoops without a net. Negotiating a barbed-wire fence and tramping through a dusty wheat field would be a whole new experience. "We're getting behind on our schedule," he said.

"Uh-huh," Brenda answered, remembering he wanted to be at the lake before sundown. She cocked an eyebrow at him when he caught up to her in the wheat. "We've got time. I need to check on this man."

Packer sighed. None of our damn business, he thought, but he followed Brenda.

As they walked, the scent of near-ripe wheat and the dust it created teased Brenda's nostrils. She cupped a hand near her mouth and sneezed out loud as they approached the red Silverado.

"You were right, Brenda, he isn't moving."

She stepped closer and gazed through the open window at an older, gray-haired man dressed in jeans, a short-sleeved, printed shirt, and boots. The steering wheel cradled his head and his shoulders; his arms dangled down on either side of the wheel. Packer hung back. "I wonder if he's passed out drunk or maybe from an overdose."

"I don't know," Brenda said, reaching over and feeling the man's neck for a pulse. Then she gently touched his eyelids with her thumb and forefinger.

"What's the matter with him?" Packer asked, irritation creeping into his voice.

"The man's dead, Steve. He hasn't been dead long, though; rigor hasn't set in."

"I'm calling 911." Packer reached for his cell, opened it up, and dialed. Silence. He dialed again. Nothing. "No service here." He shook his head in annoyance.

"Steve, we're in the boonies. We could have expected there'd be no service."

"This isn't our problem, anyway. Let's go." He twined two fingers through Brenda's belt loop and tugged hard.

Brenda knocked his hand away and scowled at him. "Give me a minute, okay?" She opened the pickup door. The man's right back pocket produced a wallet with a driver's license. She pulled it out and studied it. "His name is Arthur Sabin—he's sixty-six years old."

Packer stood back, slump shouldered, and said nothing.

Brenda replaced the license and the wallet. Then she noticed what appeared to be a bloodstain on the back of the seat. She moved around to the open window on the passenger side for a better look and said, "Oh shit, he's been shot! We've got a homicide on our hands."

"You're wrong, Brenda. This is *not* our problem. Let's drive to Elam's Crossing and tell the authorities, okay?"

"Just relax, Steve."

A look of growing exasperation spread across Packer's face. Brenda stepped back to survey the area around the vehicle. "The pickup wasn't moving when the shooter fired," she said.

"Can we go now?"

"Steve, will you drive into Elam's Crossing and call 911?"

"I have a better idea. Let's you and I drive there together. We can report this and be on our way."

"I need to stay. Something could happen to the body."

Packer figured he could argue with Brenda, or he could comply with her request. His refusing to go alone would only make her disposition more difficult.

"I'll go, if it's what you want."

"Bring back some lunch after you make the 911 call, will you?"

6

Packer nosed the SUV into the little town of Elam's Crossing at the Tucanon Street entrance. Traveling a quarter mile or so, he turned right onto Main Street and soon spied the post office up ahead on the left. Entering the small, brick-faced building, he stepped to the counter and watched for someone to come from the back room. A small, middle-aged woman with long, braided hair appeared at the opening and looked the stranger up and down.

"How can I help you?"

"I need to call 911."

"Just a moment." The clerk turned and stepped back to a small table in the corner. Lifting a black rotary phone on a long cord, she carried it to the window and set it on the counter. "You can use this."

Packer dialed.

"Sheriff's office, can I help you?" the dispatcher asked.

"Hello, this is Steve Packer. I'm calling to report a homicide. There's a dead man in a wheat field on Highway 261, about four miles east of Elam's Crossing."

"Who's this again?"

"My name is Steve Packer. My friend spotted a pickup in the field with a dead man inside."

"Where'd you say this happened, sir?"

Packer cleared his throat. "About four miles east of Elam's Crossing on Highway 261."

"What's in the pickup, you say?"

"A dead man, a body, a corpse," Packer blurted, his face flushing to a deep red.

"I'll send a sheriff's deputy right out."

"That'd be good." Packer hung up the receiver and smiled stiffly as he thanked the clerk.

"Your message startled the woman. She doesn't get many

calls like that. Who's the dead man?"

Packer knew better than to shoot off his mouth. "He's an older man, that's all I know. By the way, does the café up the street do take-outs?"

"Yes, they do."

~

Tired of leaning against the pickup, Brenda lowered the tailgate and sat down to rest her legs while she waited for Packer's return. It was almost noon. She mulled over the disagreement she'd had with Steve. He was right after all, she told herself. They were on vacation, and this homicide was someone else's responsibility. He would be back soon, and they could be on their way. It had been hard enough to get this time off— she needed to take advantage of it while she could.

Just then, Brenda noticed a gray Ford pickup creeping along the highway. The driver stopped. Was he eyeballing the dead man in the cab, or gawking at her with those binoculars, she wondered. As she slid from the tailgate and brushed off her fanny, he drove away. She decided to walk back to the fence near the road. From there, she could keep an eye on the Silverado and be ready for lunch when her partner returned.

The two were sitting on the tailgate of the Explorer eating their poor-boy sandwiches when a sheriff's car pulled up behind them.

"Don't tell this lawman I'm a police woman," Brenda whispered.

Packer chuckled. "Are you kidding? I don't want you to get involved here."

A tall, young deputy stepped out of his cruiser and approached them. Brenda and Packer set their sandwiches and Cokes aside and slid off the tailgate.

"Hello, folks, I'm Deputy Ned Carver.

"I'm Steve Packer—this is Brenda Tower."

"I assume you two discovered the body."

Brenda nodded. "Yes, sir, we did."

"Thank you for reporting it."

"Deputy, you've got a homicide out there," Brenda assured

him. Packer shot her a warning look.

"I'll go out in a minute. I notice your car has Oregon plates."

"We're on vacation," Packer responded.

Another sheriff's car approached from the east and parked across the road. "Don't leave yet—I need to talk with you two a little later." Carver walked across the road to meet with the fellow deputy. The two men crawled through the fence and walked into the field toward the pickup.

Packer and Brenda resumed eating. After a few minutes, Packer placed his empty Coke bottle and sandwich wrapper back inside the café sack and turned to Brenda. "You about ready to go?" he asked.

"We were told to wait." She continued to eat her poor boy.

Packer looked at his watch and scowled. Soon an ambulance pulled up across the road and parked behind the deputy's car.

"I'm going out," Brenda said, eager to talk with the deputies. "Want to come?"

"No," Packer responded. But a moment later, he slid off the tailgate and bounded after her.

The uniformed deputies talked a short time with the ambulance driver and his assistant before approaching the vacationers. Carver introduced Deputy Hardesty and then asked, "May I see your drivers' licenses?" After taking down the information he wanted, he handed them back.

"I overheard the two of you talking," Brenda said. "What can you tell us about the victim?"

"His name is Art Sabin. He's a big wheat farmer around here. In fact, we're standing in one of his fields," Carver said.

"Is his home near here?"

"The entrance to his farm is about two miles west of here on the right. Why are you so interested?"

"It isn't every day I find a dead man in a field. An unusual place to commit a murder, don't you think?"

"We've never seen anything like this in the county," Hardesty said.

"You did the right thing, folks, by reporting what you found here," Carver added. "Now you go on and enjoy your vacation."

Realizing Deputy Carver didn't want to prolong the conversation, Brenda turned and walked back out to the road, Packer at her side.

7

Brenda and Packer sat in the parked car after walking away from the murder scene. "I want us to be on our way," Packer said, as he started the car and swung it around, heading back to Elam's Crossing.

Brenda's mind raced. The circumstances surrounding Art Sabin's murder had ignited her curiosity. "Why would someone kill that man in his field?"

"Beats me."

"I'd like an answer to that question."

Packer turned off the county two-lane highway at the edge of Elam's Crossing and followed the narrow, bumpy street into town.

"Quaint little place, tucked in this valley," Brenda said. "The map shows a river running along the far side of the community."

"That's the Tucanon. This place isn't much anymore. It was a booming railroad town a hundred years ago when my great-grandfather lived here."

"So many old Western towns have gone this way."

"It's been on the skids for decades. A lot of nice homes here at one time, almost a thousand people."

"The sign says 135 now."

"The Corp of Engineers moved in here when it built Little Goose Dam in the 1960s. They bulldozed down a bunch of vacant houses to make room for construction workers' trailers."

"Our government at work."

"There are hardly any businesses here now."

"I can see that," Brenda said, as she gazed out at empty, boarded up or rundown buildings, many with for-sale signs.

"It's the only community near the Snake River for a hundred and fifty miles. Fishing on the river is good, so the bait-

and-tackle shop stays busy."

"Interesting."

Packer pulled in front of the post office and parked.

"I'll bet there hasn't been a homicide here in years. Know what that means, Steve?"

"I can't imagine."

"It means the sheriff won't have much experience to draw on. Look, while you're chasing your ancestor's gravesite, I'm going to nose around a little on my own."

"Go ahead—waste your time. I'll pick you up in an hour, tops. Then, we have to be going."

"Okay." Brenda glanced at her watch. "Two-thirty, then."

"Why don't I meet you at the little café?" Packer pointed up the street.

"I'll be there. Don't forget me, now."

Packer laughed. "How could I forget you, Brenda? See you in an hour."

She stepped out of the car and stood in front of the post office for a moment, uncertain where she would find answers to the questions gnawing at her. She had an idea of what to say to people to get them to talk about Sabin, but she had little time. She must find someone quickly.

She walked to a large brick building on the corner. Across the street, she spied a Varner's Tackle Shop sign and walked toward a faded white, clapboard, one-story building. From what Packer told her about the business, this could be a good location to meet someone. A weathered green bench out front looked inviting. Brenda walked over and took a seat. In the midst of her thoughts, she caught sight of a white-bearded man in a straw hat bounding toward her from across the street. Brenda stiffened, unsure of what the man wanted.

He came close, smiled, and tipped his hat. "Hello, miss."

"Hello back."

"I haven't seen ya before—new in town?"

Brenda relaxed. "Just visiting. My name's Brenda. What's yours?"

"You can call me Squeaky."

Curiosity tugged at Brenda. "Tell me about your name."

"Well, we had them desks with lift tops in grade school. Whenever I opened mine up, the hinge would squeak. Guys knew the squeaking annoyed the teacher. Someone started calling me Squeaky, and the name just kinda stuck."

"Interesting," Brenda said. "Have you got a few minutes?"

"Sure, I got a little time."

Brenda patted the space next to her. "Sit down and talk to me."

Squeaky's smile broadened, and he promptly settled next to her on the bench.

"I'm looking for someone who knows a farmer named Arthur Sabin."

Squeaky laughed. He reached out and touched Brenda on the arm. "It happens I know Art. Me and him went to school together."

"So, I'm in luck?" Brenda said.

"You are, for sure."

"I'm doing my mother's genealogy. We think Mr. Sabin is in our family tree. I'd like to learn something about him before I make his acquaintance."

"I'll tell ya what I know."

"Great! Give me the lowdown on him."

"Art was an orphan, you know. The old Sabin family lived here for years without any children. They adopted Art in about, oh, 1952. He inherited their farm when they died years later, you know."

"Uh-huh. What happened to the Sabins?"

"Killed in a damn auto crash."

"That must have been hard on their son. "Tell me about Mr. Sabin's family. He was married, I presume."

"He married Angela Cummings—she was a Dayton girl."

Brenda scribbled the information as she received it. "They have kids?"

"A girl and a boy raised by their mother."

"Art and Angela were divorced, then."

"They separated, all right, never divorced. Angela had

asthma real bad, you know. She couldn't tolerate the dust on the farm. She ended up in the emergency room several times. Art bought her a home in Walla Walla. She and the children lived down there."

"Mr. Sabin lived alone all these years, then?"

"Art live alone? Oh, no." Squeaky chuckled. "He's always had an itch for female companionship."

"Is someone with him now?"

"Calli Mendez, a Mexican woman."

"They been together long?"

Squeaky squinted and fingered his beard. "'Bout fifteen years now."

"Wow, that's a long time. Do you know anything about the children?"

"Kathy married young, lives in Salt Lake City. Tony lived with his dad in the summers when he got older. He worked on the farm for many years after he graduated high school."

"Any other family members you know of?"

"There's a grandson, Kathy's boy. He moved in with Art a few weeks back."

"Do you know his name?"

"Tab Johnson. Nice kid. I see him and Art together a lot."

"A teenager, I suppose?"

"He just graduated high school."

Brenda noticed Squeaky peeking at his watch. "Sorry I've taken up your time."

"I've gotta check on Mrs. Griffin, otherwise I'd stay and talk longer."

"Just one more quick question, then. Does anyone else in town know Art Sabin well?"

"Let's see now," Squeaky said, removing his straw hat and brushing back his hair as he pondered the question. "I'd go over and knock on Big John Edward's door. He's off work with a bad back."

The two stood up, and Squeaky gestured with his hand. "Go to the corner and turn right. The Edwards home is number 106 at the far end of the street. You can't miss it."

"It was nice to meet you, Squeaky."

"Yes, maybe we'll meet again." Squeaky raised a hand in farewell and hurried off in the opposite direction.

Brenda looked at her watch. She had plenty of time. It wasn't difficult for her to spot Big John. He was standing in his front yard, watering a small flowerbed crammed with petunias, pansies, and marigolds.

"Hello, Mr. Edwards? I'm Brenda Tower," she said, as she approached along the walkway. "Can I speak with you for a few minutes?"

"Uh, okay. You can come sit on the step here." Edwards looked surprised by the stranger's request. He dropped the hose, turned off the faucet, and took a seat on the concrete step next to her.

"I'm told you know Art Sabin."

"Yes, I know Art. I ran his harvest crew for seven years."

"I'm doing a little story. I'd like to ask you a few questions about Mr. Sabin."

"What kind of story?"

"It's my mother's history. I'm trying to add a little bit in the story about each of her cousins."

"Art's your mother's cousin?"

"We're pretty sure he is. I'll verify it with him later."

"Okay, fire away."

"How would you describe the man to people who don't know him?"

"Well, let's see. Art has always been a hard worker. He's smart too, takes care of his money. He knows when to sell his wheat and when to hold it for a better price. That's why he's so successful."

"We've heard he's quite well-to-do."

"When I worked for Art, he farmed six thousand acres of his own ground and rented another six thousand acres. He also owns his own grain elevator."

"I assume he was good to work for?"

"He was good to me, all right. He gave me one of his nice automobiles one year when we brought in a bumper crop that made him some real money."

"You stayed seven years, you said. Why'd you quit him?"

"Look, I'll answer the question, but be careful how you use the information, okay?"

"Off the record, you mean?"

"Yeah, off the record."

Brenda nodded her agreement.

"I left for two reasons."

"Are you willing to tell me what happened?"

"Sabin made it hard for me to manage the crews."

"He did?"

"Yeah, because he paid his local harvest workers one wage; the Mexican help he paid a lower wage for the same work."

"Hmm, I see."

"Then there was Tony, his son."

"Tony?"

"That's right. He was a royal pain in the butt. He couldn't stand taking directions from me. The man did everything he could to make me look bad in front of his father. He caused a lot of tension and unnecessary conflict."

"I know about those kinds of 'people' problems."

"When the Dayton Co-op offered me full-time work year 'round, I took it."

"Is Tony the foreman now?"

"Tony's gone. He and Art had a falling-out a few years back."

"Hmm. That's a shame. Is Mr. Sabin well thought of around here?"

"Jealousy in some about his wealth, I suppose. You must know about the Mexican woman living with him?"

"Yes, I do."

"That situation causes some to question his judgment, I suspect."

"Do you know his grandson?"

"Yes, we do. Our Suzanna is dating Tab Johnson some. He's a nice kid. You should talk with him."

"I will, thank you. He's on my list."

Brenda stood up and brushed off her jeans. Edwards stayed seated. "Thanks for your help. By the way, I love your flowers."

Edwards smiled.

8

Brenda walked back to Varner's Tackle Shop where she purchased a Diet Coke from the machine and sat out front for a minute. Thoughts of the boy, Tab Johnson, came to her mind. Was he with his grandfather when the man was killed? Could he have been abducted? Where was he now? Dead? She shivered slightly despite the warmth of the sun.

Brenda remembered her own abduction. She had been helping her father repair a fence one fall day when she was fourteen. When a neighbor came by and asked her father to go look at a horse, he told Brenda to have lunch and rest until he returned. She sat in the cab of the old Dodge pickup, listening to Patsy Cline's "Walking after Midnight" on the radio. She remembered seeing an eagle swoop down from the sky, rip a little gray rabbit from the field, and fly away. After a while, she dozed off.

The next thing Brenda recalled was the door flying open and a man grabbing her and pulling her out of the truck. He pressed one hand hard over her mouth. He took her to an abandoned shack, tied her to an iron stove, and rambled for hours about things she didn't understand. He wore dirty overalls and a sweat-stained shirt, the smell of which had gagged her. His face and hands were unwashed, and his long, straggly hair lay matted against his neck. She remembered how long nose hairs and bushy eyebrows added to his creepy appearance. He drooled, and at times his arms flung aimlessly about as though he couldn't control them.

A gray Ford pickup slowed and parked across Main Street in front of the boarded-up, redbrick drugstore, jolting Brenda back to the present. The driver stared in her direction. *That's the man who gawked at me when I was in the field earlier.* He wore large sunglasses and a baseball cap pulled low over his forehead. Was he waiting for someone, or was he following her?

Brenda stood up and walked to the corner, but the pickup sped away when the driver noticed her moving in his direction. She turned right toward Huber's Café at the north end of Main Street. Pulling open the screened door, she walked to the bar. A young waitress greeted her.

"Miss, do you know a man named Art Sabin?"

"No, I'm new here. I'll get the owner."

As she waited, Brenda admired an old iron, nickel-plated stove that reminded her of the one in her grandmother's parlor. A pleasant-looking, middle-aged woman in jeans and rolled up shirtsleeves emerged from the kitchen. A red-paisley bandana held back her hair.

"I'm Melba Townsend. You're wanting to know about one of our people?"

Brenda smiled. "Yes, you see I'm working on my mother's history. It includes a little bit about each of her cousins. A farmer who lives near here is one of them."

"You're in a pretty small sandbox when you're in Elam's Crossing. What's his name?"

"Art Sabin." Brenda rubbed her nose, covered her mouth, and sneezed. "Excuse me."

"I'm back there scrubbing tile with some strong cleaner. Maybe that's what's bothering you?" Brenda nodded, and the woman continued. "Sure, I know Art. He comes in here to eat with his grandson about once a week."

"How would you describe the man to people who don't know him?"

"Good as gold. Been up to the cemetery?"

Brenda shook her head.

"He's paid for the maintenance on the grounds up there for many years. Story is he committed to taking care of the place when his adopted parents were laid to rest."

"He's a good man, then."

"He's also caring for that grandson. They go everywhere together, just like two peas in a pod."

Yes, the grandson, Brenda mused. He's always with his

grandfather, people say. Thoughts that the boy may have been abducted swarmed over her. *He could end up like I did, tied up in an abandoned shack, dirty, hungry, cold, scared to death, under the thumb of a half-wit. Or worse, he could be dead.* The strongest sensation of foreboding flooded over her.

Brenda saw Packer's car pull up outside. "My ride's here. Maybe we can talk later. Thanks for your help."

"Come back, now, won't you?"

Brenda hurried to where Packer parked in the shade, and climbed in.

"I went up to the cemetery and located my great-grandfather's gravestone. Drove around for a while and snapped a few photos. I'm ready to leave. You ready?"

"Three people here told me Art Sabin has a grandson living with him."

"Well, the kid's going to be short a grandfather, isn't he?"

"I'm wondering if the boy was with his grandfather when he was murdered."

"Do we care? Look, we have to be on our way, Brenda. Enough is enough."

Packer released the emergency brake and pulled away from the café.

"The boy could have been abducted."

"Your imagination is running away with you."

"I'm serious, Steve, I want you to stop back at the truck for five minutes so I can look around."

"You've become obsessed with that damn shooting! You promised me we could leave after you had this hour in town."

"We'll stop for just a short time, I promise." Brenda smiled, tilting her head beseechingly.

Packer heaved a sigh. "I'll hold you to your promise."

"You got it."

The furrows deepened in Steve's forehead. No need to add to his aggravation, she thought, so she kept quiet about the details of Art Sabin's life.

Brenda wasn't certain what she would do with the information she'd collected. One thing for sure, though—she wasn't going to leave without telling the sheriff, or one of his deputies, that a teenage boy may have been in the pickup when Sabin was killed.

9

Brenda stared out the window, ignoring Packer during the drive from Elam's Crossing back to the crime scene. Once there, he eased onto the gravel shoulder and stopped across from the two sheriffs' cars. They climbed out of the Explorer and walked across the highway. Brenda slipped through the fence and, without looking back for Packer, walked toward the men in the field. Packer crawled through the fence and caught stride with her.

Seeing them approach, Deputy Hardesty nudged Sheriff Stone. "Here's the woman coming now who discovered the body."

Stone, who had bent over the passenger seat to peer at the dead man, looked up with some surprise to see an attractive tall brunette and a city slicker approaching. The tall, broad-shouldered sheriff, face bronzed by the sun, stepped back from the truck and moved toward the visitors. His dark eyes caught Brenda's.

"Sheriff, I'm Brenda Tower, this is Steve Packer."

He took Brenda's extended hand with mild reluctance. "I'm Sheriff Stone." A stern look crossed his face as he shook Packer's hand. "If you folks need directions, my deputy can help."

Hardesty flashed Brenda a big smile.

"We're not lost, Sheriff. I came across some information in town you should know about."

Stone removed his cap and pushed his hair back with one hand. "Something I should know, huh?"

"Yes. Art Sabin's teenage grandson moved in with him a few weeks back. The kid's name is Tab Johnson."

"So?" Stone said, cocking his chin and meeting Brenda's eyes.

"So, the boy could have been with him when he was murdered." She held Stone's gaze.

"Could have been, I suppose. But why are you sticking your nose into police business?"

"That's been my question, too," Packer interjected.

Brenda shot Packer a steely glance.

"Lady, you shouldn't be talking to anyone about this homicide."

"Sheriff, I didn't tell a soul about what happened here this morning."

"You shouldn't be asking questions at all. You could muck up a thoroughly good investigation."

Brenda's adrenaline spiked like a diabetic's blood sugar on donuts. "I didn't *muck up* your precious investigation, Sheriff. This information could save the boy's life. I didn't see any of your team in town asking questions."

Stone snorted as he dug his right boot into the ground. "Don't you worry about what my men are doing."

"I'd like to look around for a few minutes, Sheriff. I won't mess anything up, promise."

"Sorry, miss, I can't let you do that. This investigation's got to be handled by professionals. I can't afford to have you screw it up."

"I'm not going to screw anything up, Sheriff," Brenda snapped. Her hands flew to her hips as she strode one step closer to Stone and glared at him. "I'm an experienced detective with the Portland Police Department. I've worked nine homicides in the last year." She flipped open her billfold and pushed her badge in front of his face.

Stone's eyebrows arched. "Well, why didn't you say so?"

"All I'm asking is for you to let me look around for a few minutes. You may want to take advantage of my help for a day or two."

There, she'd done it, committed herself to a major change of plans, should the sheriff accept her offer.

Packer stiffened and glared in her direction. "You're willing to throw away our vacation just like that? The sheriff already told you this is none of your business."

She knew Packer was right. It wasn't reasonable for her to take on work, the very thing she'd left behind for the sake of her health. But she couldn't turn her back on what she knew about the boy. What if the volunteer who found Brenda years ago, tied to an iron stove in an abandoned shack, had turned *her* back and walked away?

Packer's hand shot out to grab Brenda's arm. Jerking back, she threw him a look that could wilt a man. Her eyes followed as he stomped out of the field in a silent rage.

Stone's jaws tightened as he considered his situation. The combined homicide experience of his nine deputies paled in comparison to this woman's background, and he knew Hardesty would never let him live it down if he let her go. "All right, I'll give you until the car hauler shows up to move this pickup."

"Good." Turning away, Brenda wondered out loud if the shooter had used a four-wheeler to track down the pickup. If the stand of wheat had been thicker, she could have spotted evidence of four-wheeler tracks along the gentle hillside. Closer examination on the ground would be necessary.

"Sam, give me some of your red markers," Stone said. "Walk back along the route the pickup traveled. Keep an eye peeled for smaller tire tracks coming off the hillside. Detective Tower and I will look up ahead."

"See you back here in a few," Hardesty said over his shoulder as he walked away. "Why does Stone take the detective chick rather than assigning her to me?" he grumbled in a voice too low for them to overhear.

"Come with me, Detective," Stone ordered. They walked side by side at a slow pace in a westerly direction. When they had traveled the length of a football field, Stone stopped and bent down.

"Tire tracks," he said, pointing.

"Here, too," Brenda commented. "Looks like a four-wheeler."

"Tracks from a second machine over here." Stone pushed the wire markers into the ground.

Walking carefully to avoid stepping on the evidence, Brenda pointed to the ground. "Boot heel prints."

Stone placed additional markers, then stopped and mopped the perspiration from his face with a red bandana.

Standing up straight, he stretched and looked over at Brenda. For the first time, he noted that the woman standing next to him was not just attractive, but uncommonly attractive. It made him feel a little uneasy, but he liked what he saw.

"We might have something here, Detective."

"I think so."

"By the way, my first name isn't Sheriff. Call me Lin."

Brenda smiled at the softer tone. "Does this mean you want me to stay and lend you a hand with the investigation?"

"That would be much appreciated."

"You'll have to pay my room and board and provide me transportation."

Stone felt at ease for the first time since he'd shaken her hand. "I wouldn't have it any other way, Detective."

"Okay, I'll stay. By the way, you can call me Brenda."

Stone's lips twitched at the corners, and then his mouth widened into a genuine smile. They walked back in the direction of the pickup.

"There must have been two perpetrators, at least," Stone said. "Let's examine this area." Spotting Hardesty approaching from behind the truck, he said, "Keep back, Sam, we're looking for footprints here."

"There's nothing back that way, Sheriff." Hardesty jutted his chin in the direction he'd just come from.

"We found tire prints from two four-wheelers up ahead," Stone told him.

"The ground's all churned up. There may have been a struggle here," Brenda said.

Stone bent down to take a closer look. "I think you're right, Detective."

The loose, sandy soil revealed several imprints. "Looks like a knee print here, and there's a hand print." Brenda traced the air above the ground with a finger. "The boy maybe tried to get away, and one of the perps put him on the ground."

After studying the area for a minute, Stone concluded Brenda was probably right—there had been a second person in the pickup.

The three heard the low rumble of the car hauler approaching, and Hardesty hurried out to the highway to meet it. Stone stood deep in thought, his shoulders slumped and his gaze troubled.

"Has anyone been to the Sabin place yet?" Brenda asked.

"Deputy Carver stopped there a couple of hours ago. No one was home. Carver said something about a Mexican woman living with Sabin."

"That would be Calli Mendez, his live-in housekeeper." Brenda wondered if Stone would get irritated at her again for asking questions.

Instead, he grinned. "You're good at acquiring information."

"I can't help myself—I'm a detective."

"Sure you want to stick around to help me with this case?"

"I wouldn't have offered to stay unless I meant it. My real concern is for the boy. I'll stay till we find him. I—uh—I was abducted once myself—I know how awfully frightening it can be."

"That must have been some experience."

"I've never gotten over it."

"Have anything to do with you wanting to be a cop?"

"I think it did." Brenda paused. "Well, you know, we've got to start looking for Tab as soon as possible."

"I agree." Stone eyed her as he considered what to do. "There's a little bed-and-breakfast called Aunt Annie's in Elam's Crossing. It's at the far end of Tucanon Street. Take a room there, and tell Mrs. Wannamaker the sheriff's office will pick up the bill." Stone glanced at his watch. "It's now 3:40. I'll stop by around 4:30. I'd like you to go with me to the Sabin place."

"I'll be ready." Brenda hurried out of the field and up to the SUV. Packer started in on her the moment she opened the passenger door.

"Come with me *this* minute or I'm leaving you here. I'm through screwing around!"

Brenda settled into the seat. She had known Packer would be infuriated. "Steve, I'm going to stay and help find the missing boy. You can drop me in Elam's Crossing at the bed-and-breakfast."

"You've messed up our vacation to take on something that's none of your damn business."

"There was someone in the pickup with Art Sabin. It appears whoever killed him also abducted his passenger. I think that passenger was his grandson."

Packer shook his head. "Why are you making this your problem?"

"I need to help find the boy. I've never told you, but I was abducted from my dad's pickup when I was . . ."

Packer broke in on her. "It's goofy, I tell you. You're goofy. If I knew you were going to do something like this to me, I would've never invited you to come with me."

"If I had any idea you were so self-absorbed and impatient, so disaffected by tragedy, I would never have accepted your invitation."

"Let's drop it. We're through, and that's it. Don't even think about calling me to take you back to the city."

"Believe me, Steve I'd hitchhike before I'd call you."

They rode in silence to Aunt Annie's. Brenda retrieved her belongings from the back of the car while Parker stared grimly out the front window. Brenda turned and walked away, looking once over her shoulder as Packer drove off.

10

Brenda pulled her roller bag to the front door of the two-story, blue and white Victorian B & B set on a large corner lot at the southwest end of town. From the front porch, she watched a woman put down her hoe, brush herself off, and cross the road. Brenda smiled as she approached.

"I'm Carol Wannamaker. Welcome to Elam's Crossing and to Aunt Annie's."

"It's my first time here. Your weather is considerably warmer than in Portland, but I love the countryside."

"Looks like you need a room."

"I do indeed."

"I have two rooms upstairs."

At that moment, a middle-aged man in carpenter's overalls stepped onto the porch. Nodding to Brenda, he asked, "Carol, where'd you put the key to the back door of the cottage?"

"Honey, it's on the nail inside the garage."

He turned and disappeared around the house.

"My husband is remodeling a place in the back to rent out."

"Must be nice to have a husband who's good with his hands."

"Please come in. You can see what he's done in here."

When the two women were inside, Brenda spent a few minutes admiring the man's handiwork and commenting on it. She loved the matching inlaid walnut that bordered the dining room walls. Then she turned to Carol and said, "I may be here for a few days. The sheriff's office is picking up the bill."

"That'll be fine."

Brenda registered and took her belongings up to the room. She unpacked and hung her clothes in the closet, freshened up, and changed her blouse.

Carol was relaxing in a gray mohair side chair next to a

black grand piano when Brenda descended the stairs to the living room.

"Is your room okay, Miss Tower?" she asked.

"Please call me Brenda. Yes, the room will be quite comfortable. I love how you've decorated it."

"Well, thank you. The television in the large center room is for your use. Let me know if there's anything you need. Uh, you're carrying a handgun, aren't you?"

"Yes. I'm a policewoman. Sheriff Stone has asked me to help him solve a homicide while I'm in town on other business."

"Someone here was killed?" Carol leaned forward in the chair.

"Yes, that's correct."

Carol covered her mouth. "Oh my, that's horrible!"

"I didn't mean to be so abrupt. Please excuse me."

"I'm just not used to hearing that kind of thing in our little town. I saw plenty of blood and my share of death working in field hospitals in Vietnam."

Brenda scanned the woman quickly and noticed a tattoo of a small American eagle on her upper arm. "Well, I can't say much more about it at this point. I came here to do some genealogy research on my mother's family. A wheat farmer living near here is one of her cousins. I've been asking a few people about him before I go introduce myself. You might know the man."

Carol leaned back in the chair. "My family has been here for over a hundred years. Yes, I probably know him. What's his name?"

"Art Sabin."

"Why yes, I know Art."

"May I ask you a question or two about him?"

"Sure, go ahead."

"We've heard from a family member that his wife left him many years ago and that he's living with a Mexican woman. Is that correct?"

"Yes it is. Art always was kind of a scoundrel, you know, in his younger days. After Angela left, he chased after every woman within fifty miles who'd give him the time of day. He had a thing for my oldest sister. Art even chased after Mexican women who came during the harvests."

"Was Calli Mendez one of those women?"

"She was, sure enough. It was Calli, actually, who settled him down."

"Does he have friends in town?"

"He's well known here because he's a rich man. I can't tell you about his friends. Other farmers could answer that. Those big dogs don't run with the work-a-day people in this little community." Carol peered out the front window. "Oh, Brenda, the sheriff's car just pulled up"

"That's my ride. I'd better go. By the way, I'm glad you had an available room. Maybe we can talk another time?"

"Sure, we'll do that. See you tonight," Carol said.

Brenda took her seat in Stone's Expedition with some difficulty. "This thing's like climbing up on a wagon box."

"Moves better, though. I was rounding up my team to start a search for the Johnson boy."

"Good."

"For the record, I verified your employment with the Portland Police Department."

"Phony badge, maybe?"

"Can't be too careful."

"What if you hadn't gotten verification?"

"I'd have to put you on a bus."

"Small chance," Brenda said.

Stone turned to her, smiling. "Kidding aside, I'm pleased you're here, Brenda."

"I hope I can be a help to you. Know the way to Sabin's place, do you?"

"I do now. Deputy Carver lives in Elam's Crossing. He knows the people up this way. My office is in Dayton, twenty-five miles from here. I don't know the Sabin family."

As Stone angled his vehicle away from the curb, Brenda said, "I heard some interesting things about the man."

"Case related?"

"Could be. Want a rundown?"

"Uh-huh."

"Sabin's been separated from his wife for decades. They had a daughter, Kathy, and a son named Tony. Tony worked the farm with his father for years, but something happened between them. Tony is no longer there."

"Family feud—it happens."

"Sabin was a womanizer. He also took undue advantage of his Mexican workers."

"You don't say."

Stone turned left off 261 onto Hidden Valley Lane. The gravel surface soon gave way to a dirt road. It led them up a long grade following the mouth of a narrow canyon for over a mile before it emptied into a small valley. They could make out the farmhouse and outbuildings up ahead.

The lane ended at a large, dirt-packed area about the size of a football field in front of the main house—a tall, two-story frame structure. To the left of the main house stood a smaller, one-story cottage. A string of five single sleeping rooms adjoined the far side of the cottage, and a three-car garage bordered the right side of the big house. A huge, unpainted horse barn from a bygone era stood across the central area, opposite the big house. A large, metal shop flanked the barn on one side and several grain storage bins on the other. Three eighteen-wheeler, wheat-hauling rigs hulked alongside the shop, and three combines waited on an asphalt pad in front, ready for work.

Stone parked the car, and they got out and climbed the stairs to the large front porch. He rang the doorbell while Brenda peered through the tall, oval glass in the door. Stone rang the bell again. After a moment, he knocked hard enough to shake the glass.

Brenda walked to the end of the porch and peered around the right side of the house. When she turned back, she caught sight of a black shepherd dog lying in the grass.

"A dead dog here," Brenda said, pointing over the railing.

Stone strode in her direction and looked down. "That explains the quiet."

Brenda eased her Glock from its holster. Stone stared at her as though she'd lost her mind. "This isn't the city, Detective.

We don't crash down doors with guns drawn unless there's a reason."

Skeptical, she re-holstered her weapon. They walked back to the front door, and Brenda tried to ignore her sense of foreboding. Stone tried the door and found it unlocked. He stepped inside, Brenda close behind him.

"Anybody home?" Stone shouted. His words echoed faintly.

"Seems we're alone here," Brenda said. "Better check?"

"Yeah, let's take a look."

A large living room spanned the entire width of the house in front. A walk-through dining room with an office to the right butted up against the back of the living room. The office had been ransacked, desk drawers pulled out and emptied onto the floor. The filing cabinet stood vacant, its drawers open and its contents thrown about. Books lay scattered all around. Chairs rested upside down, and an old Tiffany floor lamp lay smashed on the hardwood.

"A burglary," Stone said.

"Looks like it." Brenda felt something damp on the back of her hand when she picked up a pile of papers from the floor. Placing her load on the desk, she brought her hand up close, examined the spot, and smelled it. Her attention returned to the floor. Suspicious of what lay beneath more scattered papers, she moved them cautiously with her foot. Her heart sank as adrenaline shot through her system. "Blood, Sheriff!" she said, still staring at the floor.

Stone moved to where she stood and peered down at the stain on the hardwood. "Damn it all," he said, grimacing.

As Brenda headed back toward the kitchen to wash her hands, she noticed smeared blood along the oak floor in the dining room. "More blood," she called out. She could hear water running in the sink as she stepped into the spacious old farm kitchen. Stone hurried in as she scrubbed her hands. "Someone left the cold water on."

"Bloody fingerprints on this door over here," Stone said. Brenda dried her hands on a kitchen towel as he opened the door.

Stone spied the string for the downstairs light and gave it a tug. They eased down the steep, open stairway to a basement, their eyes adjusting to the relative darkness in the large, open room at the bottom. A single, dangling bulb lit the space.

"Damn." Brenda let out the breath she'd been holding. They peered down at a woman's body sprawled at the bottom of the stairs, one leg pinned under her lower torso. Dried blood stained the front of her shirt. Brenda noticed puncture wounds on the woman's right side where the flowered blouse had come untucked. Jagged cuts marred her right arm, and three slashes puckered the skin on the right side of her neck. Another deep slash extending across her face had severed the woman's right eye, split open her nose, and laid wide her left cheek. Terror was forever locked in the one good eye and across her twisted face.

Brenda covered her mouth. "This poor woman," she said, through splayed fingers. "Someone dragged her body to the open door and threw it down the stairs."

"Haven't seen anything like this since I left St. Louis," Stone said.

"Who in the world would do this?"

"Some crazy bastard, that's who."

The two tramped up the stairs and stood together at the kitchen table. "She must have been the housekeeper," Stone said.

"I suspect so. She looked Mexican, and Calli Mendez is a Mexican. No one else lived here except her and Art, and the grandson."

"I need to call an ambulance and grab my camera. Want to look for a photograph of the boy?"

"Shouldn't we clear the house first?" Brenda asked.

"From the dried condition of the blood downstairs, the murder took place hours ago. Whoever committed this crime is long gone. You just said three people live here? We've accounted for two of them—Art and Calli. My men are looking for the boy."

"All right, you go ahead. I'll try to find a photo. The boy's room has to be upstairs."

11

Stone knew this day would not be like any other since he had arrived in the county. It would be some time before he'd feel the full weight of two homicides on his shoulders. He walked out of the house and through the yard to his vehicle. *We should probably search the rest of the buildings. But who knows how long that's going to take. I'll get an ambulance out here now.* He made the call. Next, he called Rusty Gates, a criminalist in Walla Walla—fifty miles to the south.

"Sheriff Stone here. You busy, Rusty?"

"I'm always busy, Sheriff. What can I do for you?"

"I got two homicides: a man shot to death in his pickup, a woman stabbed to death at his farmhouse."

"Damn, you stepped in it with both feet, didn't you?"

"Yeah, it's a mess. Can you come in the morning?"

"Maybe ten o'clock. Best I can do."

"Take 261 toward Elam's Crossing. About three miles east of town, look for Hidden Valley Lane on the right. It's the Art Sabin farm."

"You'll be there, Sheriff?"

"I'll be here."

"Tomorrow morning then," Gates said.

Stone reached in through the open car window and replaced the receiver. He turned and leaned back against his Expedition, pausing for a few moments. Gates was right. He *had* stepped in it with both feet. Solving these murders and apprehending the killer was squarely on his shoulders, and he had no one experienced enough to be much help. *This volunteer detective could do me some good,* he thought, yet she might be more trouble than she was worth. Taking out a handkerchief, he mopped his brow. *At least she's got homicide experience, and she's not hard to look at.*

His eyes and ears searched for some sign of life on the property. The only movement was swirling dust in the field, kicked up by a small whirlwind. He heard the slight rustling of leaves in the trees and the distant call of a meadowlark. He made a mental note to check the shop and barn for the missing boy before they left. Who knew where the grandson was? *We assumed he was with his grandfather, but maybe not.* Grabbing the camera from a storage compartment, he sauntered back to the house.

Brenda was sitting at the kitchen table, drumming her fingers to camouflage shaking hands.

"What's the matter, Brenda?"

She felt weak, sick to her stomach, almost overcome. Her voice quivered. "There's another woman's body lying across a bed upstairs."

"What in the name of hell?" Stone barked, taking off his cap and slapping it against his leg.

Brenda shook her head. "Her clothes have been ripped away. Looks like rape. Her upper body is covered with knife wounds. The room's a bloody nightmare."

Stone closed his eyes and shook his head. "Son-of-a-bitch."

"I was wrong about the woman in the basement. I should have recognized her as too young to be the housekeeper. I knew Calli had been with Sabin for fifteen years. She's the woman upstairs."

Stone filled a glass with water and set it on the table in front of Brenda. He placed his hand on her shoulder. "I was wrong, Brenda; you were right. We should have cleared the house together before I left. I'm sorry for leaving you in here alone." He rubbed his chin with the back of his hand.

Tenting her arms on the table, she cradled her head. "I'll be okay. That took me by surprise, is all. I guess I'm still in vacation mode. And I've been tired lately. I need a little time to catch up." She stared at him, a hollow, distant look. "You'll be hunting a madman."

"I know. Wait here."

The kitchen and a large bedroom lay behind the dining room and office. A pantry and a laundry room ran across the back of the house. Along the inside kitchen wall, stairs led to the rooms above. Stone skipped every other step as he hurried up the stairs. The scene in the front bedroom was every bit the gruesome sight Brenda had warned Stone it would be. Multiple knife wounds covered the victim's upper body. Blood soaked the bed sheets. It was difficult for him to look at the woman, but he had to. He needed photographs. Calli Mendez had been an attractive, mature woman—close to fifty, he figured. Stone wiped his eyes as he left the room.

Grabbing two blankets from the second upstairs bedroom, he placed one of them over Calli's body. He descended to the kitchen and then on to the basement, snapping more photos and covering the second body. Blanketing the bodies, his small gesture of civility, could not hide the savagery committed that morning.

Back at the kitchen table, Stone made some notes while Brenda continued to regain her composure. "Covered the bodies, didn't you, Sheriff?"

"I had to."

"Good." Brenda paused. "Thank you for remembering to do that."

"Feeling any better?" Stone looked at her closely.

Brenda suddenly screamed long and hard at the top of her lungs. Startled, Stone didn't know what to think. The table took a pounding from her clenched fists. She stood up and moved to the opening of the utility room, turned her back to the door casing, and kicked it hard with the heel of her shoe. At the sink, she ran water over her face and dried it with a towel. "Sorry, Sheriff. I'm better now." She threw the towel on the counter. "We've got to catch the damn pond scum who murdered these poor, defenseless women."

"We will, Brenda, count on it. Listen, the ambulance will take a while. Let's hunt down some photographs."

"What if we try the built-in cabinet in the dining room?"

They discovered an old photo album next to a stack of *Washington Farmer* magazines. "Nothing in here of use to us," Stone said.

Brenda scanned the strewn books in the office, hoping to

find another album. No luck. She located three photographs of Art and the woman upstairs pinned to the far side of a large bookcase, not visible from the entrance into the room. She removed the pushpins securing them to the mahogany and returned to the kitchen.

Stone grabbed a small copy of the Johnson boy's senior yearbook photo found upstairs on top of a dresser and joined Brenda downstairs at the kitchen table. They briefly shared their finds before leaving the house.

Stone returned the camera to his car, and they proceeded through the yard to the cottage. Here, too, they discovered an unlocked front door. They stepped inside and ambled through the living room to the kitchen. "Fresh produce in the refrigerator," Stone said.

"A woman's clothes here in the closet," Brenda called out from the back bedroom. "There are aprons on hooks behind the door in here."

Stone joined her in the back of the little house.

"This is the cook's cottage, what do you bet, Lin? The woman in the basement could have been the harvest cook."

Stone noted that Brenda had called him *Lin*. He turned his head slightly so she wouldn't see the flush spreading across his cheeks. "Could be. Let's try to find out who she was."

"The place is pretty bare. It won't take long to go through it," Brenda said.

"I'll look up front."

Brenda found an envelope in the top dresser drawer addressed to Christina Lopez, Yakima, Washington. It held a letter from the woman's mother. Christina's purse contained only a bus ticket stub—no driver's license. Brenda found Stone in the tiny, sparsely furnished living room and said, "Her name was Christina Lopez. Here's a letter from her mother."

"Good." Stone took the envelope. "We now have a name and an address."

Once outside, Brenda and Stone found the doors locked to all five, single sleeping rooms. After finding the ring of keys marked 'singles' hanging by the back door in the main house,

Stone searched the rooms while Brenda waited for the ambulance. "Nothing more," he reassured her when he finished. Within a few minutes, the ambulance roared up in front of the big house in a cloud of dust. The driver and his assistant joined Stone and Brenda on the front lawn.

"I need to warn you men before you go in the house."

"What about, Sheriff?" the driver asked.

"There are *two* dead females inside. Both have been brutally stabbed to death." Stone indicated the window above them. "One is in this front bedroom on the second floor. She's naked—there's a blanket over her body. The other woman is at the foot of the basement stairs off the kitchen."

"Thanks for the heads up," the driver said. The men grabbed the stretcher and coverings, maneuvering them up the front steps and into the house.

Stone strolled to a large grey maple tree nearby, turned, and leaned against it, his gaze following Brenda as she paced back and forth along the sidewalk. *Strange how this detective showed up on the day I so desperately need help*, he mused. "This has turned out to be a whole lot more than either of us figured on, Brenda. Do you wish now you'd left here with your friend?"

"I'm not about to quit on you. Two innocent women have been viciously slain. I want to help catch their miserable killer. And we gotta find the boy."

"I know. My force is out searching for him now."

Shortly, the men brought the Mendez woman's body out and strapped it in the ambulance. The Lopez woman's body came next.

"Thank you for your work here this evening," Stone said, nodding to the men.

"Whoever did this is a real monster," the driver said, shaking his head.

After the ambulance left, Stone and Brenda made a visual sweep of the shop and both floors of the barn to be sure Tab Johnson was not lying dead in one of the two buildings.

Although late in the day, the mid-July heat forced Stone to mop his brow with his bandana. "My deputies will be searching the fields and the roadside away from the house. We'll have more people searching in the morning." Stone studied Brenda's face for agreement.

"Can we continue looking for a while longer?" Brenda asked.

Stone nodded. They walked the trail behind the shop in the direction Sabin's pickup had gone that morning. They searched all around the farm lot and between the buildings. There was no sign of the boy, and the sun had dipped behind the distant hills. As they climbed into the Expedition, Stone said, "It's been a long time since I've eaten. Go to dinner with me?"

Brenda closed the passenger door, slumped against it, and smiled. "That'd be nice."

"There's a little café in Elam's Crossing," Stone said as he drove away from the house.

"Sounds good. Do you know yet how you're going to proceed in the morning?"

"We'll keep the hunt going for the boy. We'll start an in-depth search for evidence out here. I've lined up a criminalist." Stone hesitated. "I know what I'd like you to do first thing, if you would."

"What's that?"

He looked away and then back at Brenda. "Break the news to Sabin's wife. You'd do a better job of that than I would."

Brenda frowned. "I stayed to search for the boy. Look, I'll go see Mrs. Sabin in the morning if you'll put me on the search when I get back."

"Okay, good. Deputy Carver will go with you. Find out where her son lives and pay him a visit, too, okay?"

"We'll do it."

Stone slowed the vehicle and stopped when they reached the search staging area off 261. Hardesty met them as Stone hit the button to lower his power window.

"I saw the ambulance go by," Hardesty said. "What'd you find at the house?"

"Two victims—Mexican women, both knifed to death. No sign of the boy."

Hardesty's face fell. "What the hell's going on here?"

"Some kind of rural Helter-Skelter," Stone replied.

Hardesty glanced at his watch. "Seven men have been searching for almost two hours. I've got a deputy stopping traffic to ask if anyone has seen the boy. Men on four-wheelers are searching the ravines and the roadsides. Two are walking the Tucanon River."

"That's good, Sam. Detective Tower and I searched the farm lot and went through the buildings. Keep me informed."

Hardesty's eyes followed the Expedition as its tires threw gravel. "Looks like Stone plans to keep the detective with him. She's a babe," he muttered to himself. "Maybe he'll assign her to me one of these days."

12

Stone selected the corner booth farthest from the counter and front door. There, he and Brenda could talk quietly without being overheard. Hubers'—a little western-style café—featured pine boards etched with cattle brands high above the windows on three sides of the room. Copies of famous western paintings added color to the paneled walls. The dining room carpet seemed out of place to Brenda, more like what she would expect to see in a fine restaurant in the city, but an old, upright piano and a disconnected nickel-plated iron cook stove, no stovepipe attached, added the right feel. A plaque near the door read: *Unattended children will be given an espresso and a free kitten.*

Stone ordered a steak while Brenda settled on a grilled chicken salad. Only one topic of conversation could hold their immediate interest.

"What're your thoughts about the house murders?" Brenda whispered, leaning across the table.

"A burglar could have overpowered those women, all right. He didn't have to kill them."

"Who in his right mind takes a break from a burglary to commit a rape?"

The waitress brought their drinks—lemonade and Diet Coke—and they both stopped talking until she moved away. Stone unwrapped his straw and placed it in his lemonade. Brenda found it interesting the county sheriff would even use a straw.

"If there were multiple perpetrators," Stone said, "the killer might have had the time to commit rape."

"Christina Lopez could have walked in on the burglars and surprised them."

"Could be. Brenda, we've been saying 'them' like we know there were more than one involved."

"Just feels that way to me," Brenda said, taking a drink of

60

her Coke. "Was Sabin killed first, do you think, and the house murders committed later?"

"Don't know." Stone knotted his straw cover two or three times and laid it back down.

"If they killed Sabin first, they had the boy to deal with," Brenda said.

"Maybe they saw Sabin and the boy leave in the pickup. They could have entered the house, committed the burglary, and killed the women. Later, they could have tracked Sabin down, shot him, and snatched the boy."

"How would they know where Sabin and the boy went? There must have been a lookout." Brenda swirled the melting ice in her glass.

"If the house murders occurred later, a lookout could have kept the boy subdued."

The two stopped talking again as they spotted the waitress carrying their orders. She placed heaping plates in front of them, giving Stone an opening to change the subject. "Your friend must have been furious with you when you ended your vacation."

Brenda hesitated. "It's a long story. Steve started getting pissy with me right from the start. He didn't want to get involved and kept trying to get me to leave. He wouldn't listen to anything I had to say. He threw out ultimatums—I finally had enough. I'm too stubborn, I guess."

"Well, I'm pleased you stayed. I can sure use your help."

"How could I not stay?" Brenda poured Ranch dressing on her salad, waiting for Stone's reply.

"I was a little rough on you at first." Stone reached across the table, picked up Brenda's straw cover, and proceeded to weave it into three knots. She wondered where he'd acquired this nervous little habit.

"You had every right to be leery about me. I neglected to tell you I was a policewoman."

Stone shrugged. "Those things happen—it's behind us now. Enough about work. Tell me a little about you."

Brenda briefly knitted her brows, but then her face melted into a smile. She smoothed her blouse and leaned toward Stone.

"Sure, I'll talk about myself a little if you'll tell me something about you."

"That's fair."

"I grew up on a small cattle ranch in Colorado. Dad put me on the back of a quarter horse when I was young. Earnings from competitive barrel racing helped pay my way through college." Brenda omitted how hard she had to work to keep the family together after her mother died and how her father's drinking got the best of him. By the time she left the ranch, she'd had enough of it: the drafty old house, the lack of pasture and winter hay because of droughts, falling cattle prices, rising taxes, and short nights.

She took a bite of garlic bread and another swallow of her drink.

"And then?" Stone asked

"I worked for the Loveland Police Department in juvenile for a few years while I completed my master's. Then the Portland Police Department recruited me ten years ago."

"Recruited you, huh? I'm impressed."

"I had a graduate degree in criminology by then. The department was adding officers to its homicide division, and the recruiter told me I fit the niche."

"Been a detective long?"

"Over five years. Okay, now it's your turn."

Stone cut two pieces of steak and placed his knife on the edge of his plate. "I'm from Jefferson City, Missouri. Dad was a guard at the Missouri State Penitentiary when I was growing up."

"Did you always want to be a lawman?"

"I think I went into law enforcement to please my dad." Stone went on to tell Brenda that he'd been a good student, a decent athlete—football and wrestling—and president of his senior class in high school. Finding a job had never been a problem for him, so he hadn't seen the need for college at the time.

"This is too sour," Stone said, sucking lemonade through his straw. He never had been good at talking to women about personal matters, but if he was to broach the subject of relationships, he figured he'd have to start somewhere. "Plenty of opportunity to date, I'd guess, living in Portland."

"Sure, I date, but I won't date men I work with. No blind dating or Internet dating for me, either."

"Ever been married?"

Brenda raised her eyebrows. "Do I look like a divorcée to you?"

"Well, I've always assumed attractive women are either married or have been. I'd guess you were married, once," Stone said.

"No, I've never been married, never even close. And you?"

"Yes, married once. Her name was Lena. We lived in St. Louis."

"Did your job get in the way?"

"It probably did. One day I came home to an empty house."

"That had to be hard."

"I went through hell, first trying to get her back, and then trying to get over her." Stone fell silent for a moment. Telling his dinner guest how he'd nearly torn their apartment to pieces didn't seem appropriate.

"How did you end up in Dayton, Washington?"

"Lena's leaving put me to drinking, and it got way out of hand. I knew I had to do something different."

"Threw a dart at the map on the wall, did you?"

"Not exactly. My dad worked in the pea harvests out here when he was in high school. He often talked about his time in the Palouse Country. He raved about the people, the land, and the weather. I got wind of an opening in the sheriff's department and applied for a deputy sheriff's position six years ago."

Stone studied Brenda, careful not to be obvious. She had a drop-dead smile, and dark, blue-green eyes met him squarely when he talked to her. And then there were the dimples, the way she wore her hair loose and soft on her shoulders, the clean, smooth complexion, and a figure he couldn't stop noticing.

Back at Aunt Annie's, Stone reminded Brenda, "Deputy Carver will pick you up here in the morning. Good luck with Mrs. Sabin." Stone held Brenda's gaze a moment longer than necessary.

"Dinner was nice, Lin. Thank you. See you later on

tomorrow."

In her room, Brenda mulled over the events of the day. So much had taken place, it seemed as though two days had passed since she and Packer left Portland. She smiled, remembering her experience with little Patty. Catching a glimpse of the dead man in his pickup was so coincidental. She'd been soaking up the scenery on the other side of the road, and she and Steve could have easily passed by the pickup without seeing it. Her day would have ended quite differently had they not stopped. And finding the bodies of the two Mexican women had been more than she'd bargained for. But she volunteered to help. She was committed—she wouldn't change her mind and back away.

The grandfather clock downstairs chimed eleven times, and an owl hooted somewhere off in the distance. She lay in bed gazing out the window, listening to the hum of the air conditioner. Her thoughts drifted to Elliot Hammond, the tall, forty-something man in her recent past. A Delta pilot with captivating eyes and an infectious smile, the charming man had been extremely attractive. She remembered standing at the window of his sixth-floor apartment when he asked her if she would like to move in with him.

His invitation had surprised her. She loved him, but did she love him enough to give up her independence? Two days later, Brenda gave him her answer. Excited about her future with Elliot, she started mentally arranging their life together. But the day before her planned move, a fellow pilot dropped the bomb—Elliot was married. The news had paralyzed her.

When she confronted Elliot, he had sheepishly admitted to a wife in Marietta, Georgia. To some women it wouldn't have mattered, but to Brenda it did. She broke off their relationship at once and returned the gifts he'd given her. She couldn't sleep and she wouldn't eat. Two days in a row she called in sick and wandered aimlessly about her apartment. Brenda promised herself she'd never trust a man again. She continued to date but only accepted invitations from men she wasn't attracted to—like Steve Packer.

How would she feel about Lin Stone if she hadn't bound her actions with this promise? Brenda wondered as sleep overtook her.

13

As planned, Brenda rode with Deputy Ned Carver to Walla Walla on Tuesday morning. Tall and slender with blond hair, clear blue eyes, and a fair complexion, he reminded Brenda of a Norwegian Olympic ski jumper. Angela Sabin lived alone in the Pinehurst area on a leafy street filled with custom ramblers built in the 1960s. The house, a white brick, hip-roofed design on a corner lot, featured large windows, black shutters, and bright red double doors.

A petite, brown-eyed woman with jet-black hair rolled into a bun opened the door. Her short-sleeved, white blouse stood out against a tanned face and arms. She carried a dishtowel in her hand. The years had been good to her, Brenda thought. *I wonder if there's a pool in the back yard.*

Carver removed his cap. "Good morning. Mrs. Sabin?"

"Good morning to you both."

"We're with the Columbia County Sheriff's Office. I'm Deputy Carver, and this is Detective Tower."

"I received a call early this morning about your visit." Angela Sabin stepped back and swung the door open wider. "Please come in." She gestured toward the living room. "Have a seat. Is Tony in trouble again?"

Sure enough, out of the corner of her eye, Brenda caught the diving board through a living-room window as she turned to sit down on the large sectional. Carver opted for the matching chair. Angela sat next to Brenda.

"We're not here about your son, Mrs. Sabin," Brenda said.

"What is it, then?"

"It's about your husband."

"Oh, no!" Angela cried out. Her hands flew to her mouth, and she shuddered. Did Art get hurt on a piece of equipment?" The words tumbled out, her voice shaky. "Did he have a heart attack? Tell me, what's happened to him?"

Brenda reached over and gently touched her on the

forearm. "I hate to be the one to tell you, Mrs. Sabin." Their eyes met. "Your husband is dead."

"No, no, dead! This can't be. Are you sure?" She began sobbing unashamedly.

Brenda moved closer and put her arm around the grieving woman. "We're certain, Mrs. Sabin. We found him in his pickup in a field yesterday. Take your time. When you're ready we'll try to answer your questions."

Once the initial sting from the numbing news of her husband's death subsided, the woman wiped her eyes with trembling hands and blew her nose on a tissue she dug from her apron pocket. "Tell me what happened," she said, crossing her legs and clutching her hands together in her lap.

"Someone shot him."

The woman clenched her teeth, jaw hardening. "Someone murdered him, you mean?"

"Yes." Brenda nodded. "I'm so sorry to have to deliver this news."

"Where's his body now?" Mrs. Sabin asked, taking a deep breath and smoothing her blouse.

"It's at the morgue in Dayton."

"You're needed there to identify the body as soon as you feel able," Carver said.

Mrs. Sabin nodded. "What happened? Why . . . who would want to kill Art?"

Brenda leaned back and turned toward her listener. "He was in his pickup in a big field about two miles from the house. It appears he may have stopped to talk with someone who was waiting there for him. The perpetrator opened the passenger door and . . ."

Mrs. Sabin's head fell into her hands. She said nothing for several moments. Looking up again finally, she asked, "Was my grandson with him?"

"We think so. Tab is not at the farm or anywhere we've looked," Brenda said.

"My poor Art, and young Tab. Who could have done this?"

"We don't know. Sheriff Stone and his deputies are

investigating."

"I need to call the kids." Angela covered her face with shaking hands and wept again. She swayed in her seat, and Brenda put out a hand to steady her.

Angela wiped her eyes with the dishtowel she had carelessly tossed on the couch when they first sat down. "Wait here. I need some cold water on my face." She left the room, walked to the kitchen, and steadied herself against the island. Brenda heard water running in the sink. A few minutes passed before Angela returned and sat back down next to Brenda. "Why would anyone want to kill my husband and take my grandson?"

"We just don't know, Mrs. Sabin." Brenda paused. "May I ask you a few questions?"

"I'll answer them the best I can."

"Your husband and son worked together for several years. Can you tell us what caused their breakup?"

"For nearly twenty years, actually. Tony got caught selling grain from our elevator and pocketing the money."

"He was stealing from you?"

"Yes, that's what Art told me, and he fired him. I was against the decision. We fought over it for the longest time."

"When did that take place?"

"About four years ago."

"Do you have Tony's address and phone number?"

"Why do you want to contact him? He wouldn't have anything to do with his father's death."

"We need to ask him a few questions—it's standard procedure."

"Well, Tony lives in Dayton. I'll get my phone book." Mrs. Sabin returned promptly with it, and Carver copied down the information.

"What is Tony doing now?" Brenda asked.

Tears continued to leak from Angela's eyes. "He's divorced—lives alone. He works at that little Get-N-Go quick mart in Dayton."

"When we came in, you asked if Tony was in trouble *again*. What kind of problems does Tony have?"

"Problems? Well, with his wife, Molly. She has a restraining order against him. He violated the order once or twice and got himself arrested."

"You have a daughter, too, we understand. We'll also need her name, address, and telephone number." Brenda glanced at Carver, whose pen hovered over his notepad.

"I have that right here."

Carver scribbled as Brenda continued the questioning.

"Are there other children in the family?"

"Tab is our only grandchild." Angela wiped at her eyes.

"Was your husband having difficulty with anyone you know of?"

"No, I don't think so. He's always gotten along well with people."

"I don't have any more questions right now, Mrs. Sabin. Deputy Carver, did you have anything more?"

"No more questions. I knew your husband, ma'am. Please accept my condolences."

Angela nodded.

"I'm sorry we had to meet under these circumstances, Mrs. Sabin. We'll contact you when we have something concrete to report," Brenda promised.

"I want the man who killed my husband behind bars. Please keep me informed. Call me anytime, day or night."

Carver and Brenda showed themselves out. They sat in the cruiser in Mrs. Sabin's driveway for a few moments.

"You didn't tell her about the other victims," Carver said.

"She'll find out soon enough."

"We need to contact Tony when we're in Dayton this morning."

"Let's go do it," Brenda said.

14

Tony Sabin lived on East Spring Street in a little two-bedroom, frame cottage with faded green paint. An old Buick Century sat on grass that needed mowing. Nearby shrubs needed to be trimmed. Carver parked the car in front of the house, and he and Brenda walked up the rickety wooden steps to the front porch. Excessive clutter allowed only one of them at a time access to the front door. Carver knocked with authority on the weathered black door. Following a long wait, the door swung inward.

A man in a maroon bathrobe and bare feet leaned against the open door, his uncombed hair a curtain over bloodshot eyes and a sleep-wrinkled face. He peered through the screen door. "What do you want?" he demanded.

"We're with the sheriff's office. I'm Deputy Carver, my partner is Detective Tower. Are you Tony Sabin?"

"Yeah, that's me. What do you need?"

"We'd like to come in for a minute. We have something to tell you about your father. We'd prefer not to discuss it here on the porch."

"My father sent you, huh? He still thinks I owe him something, I guess." Tony pushed the screen door open. "Come in." He moved some papers off a sofa in the crowded front room just left of the entryway. "Sit," he gestured. Brenda and Carver sat together on the couch. Tony plopped into an overstuffed chair.

"I work nights. You woke me up with your knocking. What does Mister Sabin want now?"

"Sir, your father was found dead yesterday," Carver said, removing a small notepad and pen from his shirt pocket.

"What? Dead? My father is dead? What happened?"

"He was in his pickup out in a wheat field when someone shot him."

Tony sank farther into the worn mohair chair, closed his eyes, and buried his head in his hands. He remained still for a time. Then he straightened and leaned forward. Elbows tented on his knees, chin resting in his hands, he asked, "It wasn't an accident, then?"

"Sir, your father was murdered," Carver explained.

"We're very sorry to bring you this news," Brenda added gently.

"I don't know what to say."

"Can you think of anyone who would want to hurt him?" Carver continued.

Tony raised his head, eyes distant. "No, I'm at a loss."

"Tell us what happened between you and your father that caused your falling out"

"Dad stopped paying my wages, damn it. That's what happened."

Carver nodded. "Go on."

"Dad had a large reserve of wheat in an elevator he owned. After months without a paycheck, I finally sold a little of that wheat and kept the money. I was a married man back then. I needed a regular income."

"Why'd he stop paying you?"

"Because he's a tight-ass," Tony growled. "Was."

"Your father discovered what you'd done?"

"Yes, he did. It was the year he built the new shop and bought a truck and trailer. I knew it was a difficult year for him, but he trashed me. He threw a fit. We had a terrible fight, and he forced Molly and me off the place."

"What'd the two of you do?" Carver asked.

"We moved in with her parents till we could find work."

"Two women were also murdered at the farm yesterday," Brenda said. "Calli Mendez was one of them. The other woman is Christina Lopez."

"Oh, crap! Rotten, dirty luck. Calli was a wonderful woman. I don't know the other one."

"So, I gather from what your mother said that you and Molly have divorced?" Carver said.

"A car accident about three years ago left me with some brain damage. I spent four months in rehab. We had lots of bills.

Too much for her, I guess."

"Your mother told us you work at a convenience store."

"It's not too stressful there. I don't have seizures when I take my meds and get plenty of rest."

"Your nephew may have been in the pickup when someone killed your father," Brenda said. "We think that same person or persons also abducted the boy."

"You're telling me everyone at the farm is dead." Disbelief spread over Tony's face.

"We hope Tab's alive," Brenda said. "Sheriff's deputies and volunteers are searching for him."

"We have to ask this, Tony. Where were you yesterday morning?" Carver locked eyes with the man.

"I've been working nights. When I got up yesterday morning, I went over to Sally's to help her paint a room."

"Who's Sally?"

"She's one of the women I work with."

"Do you have Sally's last name and address?"

"It's Matthews. She lives at 237 South Oak."

Carver scribbled the address and name on his notepad and turned to Brenda. "Detective, questions for Mr. Sabin?"

"No," she said, shaking her head.

"We won't take any more of your time. Call the sheriff's office if you think of anything we should know."

"I want to join in the search for my nephew," Tony said, rubbing his eyes.

"Call the sheriff's cell phone number. He'll know where the teams are working."

Carver jotted down the number on his notepad, ripped the sheet off, and handed it to Tony.

Carver and Brenda left the house. "What's your take on Tony?" Brenda asked, as they settled back into the cruiser in front of the shabby little house.

"He doesn't appear to be a ruthless, vengeful sort. I think he was telling us the truth."

"I agree with you, Ned. He's sure had his share of bad luck, though, hasn't he?"

"He sure has. Let's go check out his alibi."

15

Sally Matthews showed up at her door in an orange flight suit and a flowered bandana tying back a full head of thick, red hair. She spotted Carver's uniform and without hesitation started in. "You're here about the parking tickets? It's my daughter. She insists on parking in those no parking zones."

The three stood at the front door. No invitation came for them to enter the house.

"I'm Deputy Carver with the Sheriff's Department, and this is Detective Tower. We're not here about parking violations. Are you Sally Matthews?"

"Yes, I am. Have I done something wrong?" Her face turned chalk white and her hands began to fidget.

"No, you're fine. We're investigating a case, and we received your name from Tony Sabin. We understand you work with Tony."

"We're not always on the same shift, but we do work at the same place."

"Are you and Tony good friends?"

Brenda caught the beginnings of a smile at the corners of the woman's mouth.

"I'd say we're more than good friends." A little color came back into her cheeks. "We've been dating for nearly six months."

Carver brushed a buzzing fly away from his face. "Do you know where Tony was yesterday morning?"

"Why are you questioning me about Tony?"

"His father met an untimely death yesterday. Tony can tell you what happened. We're here to verify his whereabouts at the time it took place."

"Tony was here yesterday helping me paint my girl's room." She stepped back from the door. "Want to come in and see?"

Carver could smell the lingering scent of fresh paint from inside the house. "That won't be necessary," he said.

"Tony and me worked from about 10:00 till 1:00. I fixed us some lunch and after we ate he left. Trust me, he was here. Want to ask my kids?"

"That won't be necessary. Thank you for your time."

The two left the house and walked back to the car.

"Let's stop by the office," Carver said. "You can use the phone to call Sabin's daughter."

~

Carver pulled into a parking space alongside the courthouse. "It's going to be another hot one. I'm not used to this heat," Brenda said.

"The sheriff's office is on the ground floor—it's cool in there."

"This courthouse is a beautiful old building," Brenda commented, as they walked from the car to the sheriff's office. "I get a feeling I'm in another time."

"The building underwent a thorough restoration not long ago. She's the oldest operating courthouse in the state and on the national historical register. The cellblock came from a ship's brig. It was purchased back east, transported here by rail, and placed on the foundation. Workers constructed the building around it."

"That's interesting." Brenda stopped for a moment on the sidewalk and took in the whole structure.

Once inside the office, Carver laid his open notebook on the sheriff's desk in front of Brenda. Her eyes found the Johnson's number and she dialed.

"Hello, Mrs. Johnson? This is Detective Tower with the Columbia County Sheriff's Department in Washington State." She paused. "Did your mother call you this morning?"

"Yes, she did.

"You know about your father, then?"

"I'm still in shock. I don't know what to think."

"Did she tell you your son is also missing?

"Yes . . ."

Brenda heard Kathy Johnson's voice trail off. "The sheriff

asked me to call you and answer your questions about what happened here. We don't know much yet, but I'll tell you what I can.

"Mother said someone murdered Dad in his pickup."

Brenda heard a muffled sob at the other end of the line.

"It looks as though the perpetrators waited in the field on four-wheelers. When your father stopped the pickup, one of them opened the passenger door and shot him.

"You think my son was with Dad in the pickup at the time?"

"We think your son may have been abducted."

"Tab abducted?" the woman's voice rose and trembled. "For what reason?"

"There were signs of a struggle on the ground near the pickup. He isn't at the farm, and no one we've questioned has seen him. Search teams are out looking for him now, Mrs. Johnson. We'll do everything we can . . ."

"Have you received a ransom note?" the woman interrupted.

"No, we have not."

"I didn't want my son living with Dad." The hesitant voice faded on the final word.

"There was a problem, Mrs. Johnson?"

"That Mexican woman—it's not a good situation."

"Mrs. Johnson, someone also murdered Calli Mendez yesterday, and a second woman named Christina Lopez."

"Oh, my god! How horrible. I didn't care much for that woman, but she surely didn't deserve to die. How did Mother take the news of my dad's death, Detective?"

"Your mother held up pretty well, considering. You'll want to help each other through this, would be my guess."

"This is all so horrible. I need to get up there as soon as I can. Let me give you my cell number. Please call me when you have more information."

Brenda wrote down the number. "Mrs. Johnson, I didn't say anything to your mother about the death of the two women."

"It's good you didn't. I'll break that news to her myself when the time is right."

16

While Brenda Tower, Sheriff Lin Stone, and his team worked to solve multiple murders in Columbia County, Washington, 110 miles to the southeast, the manager at McCormick Lumber Mill wrestled with a different problem—losing money.

"Todd, come to my office," Sam Austin blurted over the intercom. Austin struggled with a financial redline he needed to resolve quickly. While he waited for his yard manager to arrive, he reviewed the production figures and cost runs for the previous month.

"What's up, Sam?" Todd Moore bolted through the door with a clipboard under his arm and a cigarette hanging from the corner of his mouth. He dropped his hardhat on the shelf, poured himself a black coffee, and fell onto a chair next to the boss's desk.

"Todd, we need to talk."

"You look like you missed a night's sleep, Sam," Todd said, momentarily removing his glasses to blow away specks of sawdust.

"Yeah, sleep. Listen, the company is losing money on our one-by-four, No. 2 pine operation. We've got to reduce our operating costs. I'm contemplating a change in practice for shipping low-grade, rough-cut lumber."

"What you got in mind, boss?"

"Stop banding the pallets for this material coming to us from our Cascade mill."

Moore sat up in the chair and snuffed his cigarette. "But Sam, we've always banded that lumber—for safety, you know."

"Yeah, it's what we've always done, I know. But I'm telling you we're losing money banding that low-end pine. We need to continue banding the finished product when it leaves here. The rough-cut, one-by-four stuff we get in from Cascade has to be un-banded before we can plane it. It's costing us a bundle. Boys in the home office are howling."

"What's happened, Sam?"

Austin raised the corner of the spreadsheet on his desk. "The spike in steel prices and the recent labor hike, that's what's happened. It's gotten too damned expensive to continue the banding practice for that cheap lumber."

Moore sipped his hot coffee and stared at Austin over his glasses. "Maybe we should discontinue the line."

"You want to tell a dozen men or more they're out of work?"

"Hell no, I don't."

"I didn't think so. What really counts is that loads are strapped down good when they're in transit."

"Uh-huh. But we both know un-banded lumber can easily *walk* on a trailer."

"It would be different if the loads were coming from a longer distance, say fifty miles or more. Our trucks are on the highway less than thirty minutes from Cascade to McCall."

"Risky business, boss. What happens when a load isn't strapped down as tight as it should be? What do we do then?"

"Easy, Todd. We fire the driver's ass."

"It'd be a little late after he's spilled his load, maybe caused an accident."

Austin got up and went to the window. He peered out at a tractor-trailer leaving the yard. After a minute, he turned back and sat on the edge of his desk closest to Moore. "Here's what I want you to do. Drive down to our Cascade mill and tell Thomas to stop banding the rough-cut one-by-fours. Make sure you tell him why we have to make the change."

"He's not going to like it."

"You think I like it, Todd? It's gotta be done. Forklift operators will be responsible for making sure drivers strap down their loads the way they should before they leave the yard. Tell Thomas his operators are to call him *immediately* if a driver tries to leave without properly strapping down his load. They've been trained—they know what they're supposed to do. We won't tolerate shortcuts for a damn minute. He can call me if he has any questions."

Moore grabbed his clipboard and hardhat. "I'll do it, Sam. I'm not happy about it, but I'll do it."

"I don't expect you to be happy, Todd. I'm protecting jobs here."

17

Deputies Sam Hardesty and John Talbot joined Sheriff Stone Tuesday morning at the Sabin farm. "I just came from the staging area where I briefed Jenkins on the places the team covered last evening," Hardesty informed Stone. "He's working out a plan for today."

"Does he have some good help?" Stone asked.

"He's got three volunteer deputies, plus a handful of people from Elam's Crossing."

"Besides that missing boy, we've got three homicides to deal with," Stone reminded the two.

Talbot chuckled. "And we were going camping in the Blue Mountains this week."

Hardesty kicked aside a small rock and glanced at his partner, "Time we get this behind us, John, we'll all need a few days in the Blues."

These men could use a little joking, Stone thought. Both Talbot and Hardesty lacked experience investigating homicides and tracking killers. Their chances of previous involvement in a murder investigation nearly equaled a fisherman's chance of seeing a grizzly bear floating on an iceberg in the Snake River.

"I want you two to concentrate on the shop and the barn across the way." Stone motioned with his right arm. "Take your time. Be alert to anything that appears strange or out of place. Don't handle anything. Rusty Gates will be here later this morning to examine evidence."

"What about those storage bins?" Hardesty asked.

"Check those, too, Sam. I'll be here at the house if you need me."

The deputies strolled across the central yard to the shop and stepped inside. Hardesty flipped on the lights. They moved cautiously through the center of the building, crammed full of farm machinery and man toys. "Can you believe all these old cars," Hardesty said. "I'd love to have that Pontiac GTO, or the Mustang

GT."

"I'll flip you for the GTO. Hey, these tandem wheel tractors are huge up close," Talbot said.

They passed by extra combine sickles, a spare roller bar, and a grain truck with its engine out on the floor. Talbot pushed open the steel door at the far end of the shop and stepped out into the light. A warm breeze played across his face. "Come out here, Sam," he called over his shoulder. Hardesty followed his partner's voice to the open door.

"The killers may have taken these four-wheelers to the field. Why'd they bother to hide them back here?" Talbot removed his cap and scratched his head.

"They could've had a getaway car stashed back here."

Together, they peered down at the gravel for a short time, but it refused them a clue. Moving from the back of the shop out toward the central yard, they kept their noses to the ground.

"John, recent tire tracks in the dirt. A vehicle did come out this way," Hardesty said.

Behind the shop a second time, they focused again on the gravel. This time Talbot eyed something, and he bent over and rubbed his middle finger on it. He straightened back up and sniffed. "Automatic transmission fluid. Sam, someone parked a car back here."

Reentering the shop, each man took an outside wall for a return trip to the front of the building. Talbot passed by parts bins and tool cabinets below the windows. Hardesty halted in front of a crumpled tarp, about four foot by six foot, concealing something barricading his path. Reaching down, he grabbed a corner of the canvas and flung it back. "Over here, John!" he yelled.

Talbot crossed the building between two tractors and joined his partner.

"Sheriff said to be on the lookout for anything out of place. What do you know about these cylinders?" Hardesty bent down to take a closer look.

"They're core samples taken from the earth, Sam. They're used for testing the metal and mineral content. Someone has done some core drilling."

"Wonder what for?"

Talbot shrugged. "Who knows?"

Hardesty shoved open the door to the shop office, and Talbot moved immediately to a map on the back wall. "Sam, I'll bet these stickpins show where core drilling took place."

Hardesty drew nearer and examined the map. "The heads of the pins are in two colors. Could be the black color tells where drilling is complete and the red-colored pins indicate locations for future drilling. John, this may have something to do with Sabin's murder."

"You could be right. Let's keep going. We need to go through the barn."

Avoiding the heavy double doors at the front of the barn, they headed for a man-sized door on the right side. Hardesty kicked aside tumbleweeds blocking their way and pushed in the door. "Boy, its dark in here. My eyes need a minute to adjust."

Looking around, Talbot said, "This thing is huge. Imagine what it was like when farmers harvested with mules and horses. We've got an old black-and-white photo of my great-granddad standing alongside a big combine pulled by twenty-four draft horses."

"Back then, wheat farmers had big horse barns like this one," Hardesty added.

"I'll look around down here. Sam, why don't you take a look in the hayloft?"

Hardesty nodded and climbed the stairs. Talbot soon heard his partner's feet clomp across the floor overhead. At the rail, Hardesty called down. "Come up here, John, you gotta see this."

Talbot hurried to the stairs, climbed to the floor above, and followed Hardesty to the back. Light from outside outlined the large doors that once had opened to receive winter feed.

~

At the house, Stone stretched on latex gloves and sifted through the papers and books scattered throughout the office. *The burglars must have been frantic to find something of value: a sales contract, a will, bonds, cash, what?* Stone searched for a wall safe or a secret compartment where Sabin kept his valuables.

Shuffling books and papers aside, he surveyed every inch of the floor for an opening to a hidden storage compartment between the floor joists. Nothing.

Frustrated with his progress, Stone opted for a break. Leaving by the front door, he strolled around the house to his left, stopping near the dead dog at the side of the porch. Shaking his head, he mumbled, "The crazy bastard killed everything in sight."

Large locust, maple, and elm trees shaded a lawn starting to yellow from the lack of water. Robins and sparrows fluttered from tree to tree. Although trees were plentiful in the big yard, shrubs and bushes didn't clutter the space around the foundation of the house. Irises and daffodils filled small garden spaces across the front of the porch on both sides of the steps. Three climbing, red rose bushes clung to trellises over the windows on the west side of the house. Stone noticed a stand of tall, thick lilac bushes, almost a miniature forest, some twenty yards from the house on the east side. They blocked his view of the cottage.

Stone scribbled down the license plate number on the car parked in front. Entering the number into the state vehicle registration database revealed the '02 Maxima belonged to Talbert C. Johnson, route one, Elam's Crossing. At the three-stall, open garage, he found a late model Cadillac de Ville, a stretch body Yukon, and a zero-turn riding mower. He searched inside and around the back of the garage.

Back in the office, he plopped into a swivel chair to relax for a minute. What had not been obvious earlier became so as he concentrated on the geometry of the three bookcases. The bottom shelves in two of the three mahogany seven footers extended almost to the floor. The bottom front board on the third case looked to be five inches high. Unfolding himself from the chair, he moved to the odd bookcase. Sliding away some loose papers from the bottom shelf, he uncovered a finger-pull for a cutout. With his index finger in the pull, he lifted the cutout. Below lay a hidden compartment—empty. *Whoever ransacked the room must have found this hiding place.*

Next he made a sweep through the downstairs rooms looking for the weapon the killer used on the women. Climbing the staircase to the second floor, he continued his search. In the bathroom, a bloody thumbprint on the mirror, a band-aid wrapper in the sink, and a soiled washcloth on the floor caught Stone's eye. *Who was in here?* Not Calli Mendez, whose body Brenda had found on blood-soaked sheets the previous afternoon.

When he ripped away the bedding in the front bedroom, Stone heard something clatter onto the floor behind the bed. He grabbed the frame at the bottom and pulled it away from the wall. A cattlemen's pocketknife lay on the hardwood below the window—the largest blade exposed. *Calli must have fought back, driving her assailant to the bathroom. That's good, we'll have blood evidence.* Peering out of the bedroom window, Stone caught sight of Gates' minivan out front. He left the house to go meet him.

~

Deputies Hardesty and Talbot stood together in the back of the loft.

"John, what do you make of this?"

"Must be where some youngsters played, and maybe napped."

"That's what I thought at first," Hardesty said. "But the *Playboy* issues over there aren't exactly kids' reading materials. Could be some horny teens used this barn for shelter last winter." He bent down and, with a pen from his shirt, carefully moved one of the magazines. "This one has a June date."

"Over here's a sack of garbage." Talbot picked up the sack and started to dump the contents onto the floor.

"Don't handle that stuff!" Hardesty yelled out.

"Sam, you 'bout scared the hell out of me. I forgot for a minute, thanks. Judging from the amount of trash, there must have been two people up here."

Hardesty went to where his partner stood and peered into the sack. "That's lipstick on the soda can."

They found nothing else in the barn remotely related to the investigation, and their survey of the storage bins turned up nothing of interest. They strode over to the house where they briefed Stone on the evidence.

"I want you two to get a shovel and bury the dog lying on the other side of the porch. Then I want you to show Gates and me your evidence," Stone said.

During their trip back from the shop with the shovel, Hardesty said, "Yeah right, bury the damn dog. Why do I always get these plum jobs?"

"Patience, Sam. The sheriff's prepping you for an assignment with that classy detective you told me about."

18

Brenda and Stone's deputies assembled at the substation in Elam's Crossing at 2:00 p.m. Once a bank, the small brick building with an oversized oval window looking out on the street housed the mayor's office and town council chambers. Arrangements with the county gave Stone access for police business. On this Tuesday afternoon, he wanted to hear progress made that morning in the case, as well as make new assignments.

They sat around a long table in the large room at the front of the building. Deputy Chet Weber reported first. "We heard Sabin discovered a few years back his son was selling grain on the side and pocketing the money. Sabin fired him and ran him off the place. Maybe the son killed his father."

"Maybe he's a person of interest," Stone said.

"No one we talked with this morning reported seeing anybody suspicious, or anything out of the ordinary, for that matter," Deputy Don Barber said. Barber, Stone's senior deputy, had a short, stocky build and wore his hair below his ears, about six inches longer than his boss liked it.

"All right, then." Stone nodded to Brenda.

"Deputy Carver and I met with Angela Sabin. She said she wasn't happy about what happened between her husband and their son. She seemed adamant Tony wouldn't have anything to do with his father's death."

"Were you able to run down Tony?" Stone asked.

"We did," Carver responded. "He sold the wheat because his father hadn't paid him for months, he told us. An auto accident a few years ago left him with some brain damage."

Stone turned back to Brenda. "What's your take on this Tony, Detective?"

"He appeared quite shaken with the news of his father's death."

"In your opinion, is he a person of interest?"

"Normally, I'd say yes, but the man has an alibi."

"He does? Tell us more."

"Tony's significant other told us he helped her paint a bedroom yesterday morning."

"Could be she's lying for him," Stone said.

Carver interrupted. "She offered to let us question her children about it."

"And we could have inspected the newly painted room," Brenda said, "but we didn't need to because the house smelled like new paint."

"You two are satisfied with the girlfriend's reliability, then?"

"Yes, we are," Carver said.

"Okay," Stone said, and then he glanced down the table at Deputy Hardesty. "What'd you and Talbot find at the farm?"

"We located two four-wheelers behind the shop. There's evidence a car was stashed back there. The killers could've transferred the boy from one of those four-wheelers to a getaway car."

"We found a trash bag with discarded food and drink in the barn," Talbot added. "Playboy magazines were left there. We also identified core samples stacked on the floor in the shop."

"There's a map of the farm we think shows where drilling was done. This drilling might have something to do with our case," Hardesty interjected.

"You could be right." Stone paused. "This morning, I found a pocketknife in the room where Calli Mendez was murdered. Blood and a band-aid wrapper in the upstairs bathroom indicate someone was injured. Gates and I believe Calli stabbed her attacker. We have fingerprints from that bathroom mirror, the basement door, from soda cans, and magazines." Stone ran the back of his hand along his chin. "The search team has been out looking for Tab Johnson on the lower Tucanon River and along the Snake."

"If there's nothing else to report," Hardesty said, "I have a question."

"Sure, go ahead, Sam."

"If the grandson was taken hostage, why haven't his kidnappers contacted the family or the sheriff's office with their ransom demand?"

"I don't have the answer," Stone said, "but we'll hang with our abduction theory till we get something more concrete."

"The killer could be a psycho," Barber said. "Could be the only reason he took the boy was to torture and kill him. There may never be a ransom demand."

Brenda cleared her throat. "Maybe the boy staged the burglary and his own abduction. He may have killed his grandfather, raped and killed the Mendez woman, and then killed the Lopez woman."

Stone arched an eyebrow. "Detective, why would the boy kill his grandfather?"

Brenda leaned forward in her chair and met Stone's gaze. "Could be he has an uncontrollable temper. His grandfather may have told him he couldn't do something, couldn't have something, or couldn't go somewhere—and he snapped. He might be counting on the law to look elsewhere for the killer and for the kidnapper."

"Is there more to your theory, Detective?" Stone asked.

"Let's say down the road Tab mysteriously escapes from his phantom abductors. They are never identified, and he goes free."

Stone leaned back and laced his fingers together behind his head. "You're way outside the box, Detective. We assumed the boy was with his grandfather when the old man was killed. You convinced me someone took the boy from the pickup." Stone brought his hands back to the top of the table. "What if Sabin was killed in another location, placed in his pickup, driven into the field, and left?"

"I'm following you," Hardesty said, glancing around the table at the others.

"I'm piggy-backing on Detective Tower's theory," Stone said. "The boy placed his grandfather's body in the pickup, drove to where he earlier parked a four-wheeler in the field, and after digging some marks into the soil to make it look like there'd been a struggle, he drove away on the machine."

"But Sheriff, we identified *two* sets of four-wheeler tracks near the truck," Brenda reminded Stone.

"Detective, we may have misinterpreted the evidence."

"Forensics from the pickup should give us the lead we're looking for," Talbot said.

"Gates is going over the pickup this afternoon." Stone looked at each deputy in turn.

Weber shook his head, "I don't know, Sheriff, pulling the trigger can be an impersonal thing. But raping and stabbing women to death is pretty damn close up and personal. How could a snot-nosed kid do those things—unless he's a madman?"

"Could be he snapped, went off the rails, so to speak." Stone scratched behind his left ear.

"It's feasible, and he may have had sexual fantasies about Calli," Barber said. "With his grandfather out of the way, he made a run at her. She fought him—he raped her. He got scared she would turn him in, and he killed her."

"Plausible," Stone said. "But why would he kill Christina?"

"Christina might have gone to the house to see Calli," Brenda said. "Tab couldn't risk her finding Calli dead."

"Is it possible the boy hasn't even been here the last couple of days?" Weber asked. "Maybe he went out of town."

"You could be right," Stone said. "Do you have a theory?"

"Let's say the boy was away. Art and Calli were in the truck. The killers shot Sabin, abducted, raped, and killed Calli, and then ransacked the office for money. They killed the second woman when she entered the house to see Calli—like Detective Tower suggested."

"Tab's dating a girl whose father I met yesterday. She'd likely know if he went out of town," Brenda said.

Silence filled the room for several moments, and then Stone said, "This has been a worthwhile discussion. We've got some intriguing theories we can follow. If there's nothing else, Hardesty, you and Talbot spend some time searching the path the pickup took from the farm out through the field. The boy could have been killed out there and dumped. Then I want you two to go through the long ravine behind the barn."

"We're on it," Hardesty said.

"Weber, you and Barber continue canvassing farmers between Pucker Huddle and Elam's Crossing. Find out if anyone out there has seen suspicious-acting strangers in the last day or two." Stone reached into his shirt pocket. "Chet, here's a photo of Tab Johnson. Show it around. Maybe someone has seen him."

"How far south do you want us to go, Sheriff?" Weber asked.

"I'd say to Farley's Corner."

Weber nodded.

"I'll take Detective Tower with me to the Sabin farm. She thinks we should search there again for the boy. We'll meet out there first thing in the morning. We'll exchange information again and coordinate our day."

When the meeting broke up, Hardesty whispered to Talbot, "I could have told you he'd take Detective Tower with him again."

"Why not, he's the boss? I sure as hell would."

Ever since her arrival, Brenda had been too busy, too distracted, too tired, to concentrate on anything but work. But now, suddenly, she noticed Stone in a different way as he stood in front of the large oval window comparing notes with Deputy Weber. Lin is tall with a nice build, and he didn't parade around like a peacock. He's good looking, too, she thought: earnest and caring dark brown eyes, high cheekbones, a square jaw, a straight mouth, and a masculine nose. He keeps his brown hair neatly trimmed—sideburns a little too long to my liking. Brenda decided he had a good sense of humor and could probably laugh plenty when he's not worried about catching a killer.

19

Stone and Brenda intended to search the farm lot again for the missing Johnson boy. Before leaving town following the two o'clock meeting, Stone said, "We could be wasting our time out there. Let's find out if the boy is out of town."

"We should have checked on that yesterday."

Stone frowned. "Oughta, coulda, shoulda—you're right, Detective, but we didn't, did we?"

"The Edwards home is a skip and a jump from here. Suzanna's father is rehabbing a bad back, so he should be home,"

Stone rang the doorbell. Big John Edwards answered his door. "Hello, Mr. Edwards. Sheriff Stone and I would like to speak with you."

Edwards closed one eye and tilted his head "Miss, you were here yesterday, and now you're back with the sheriff. What's this all about?" he nearly shouted.

"Relax, sir, we just need some information. Art Sabin has been killed.

Edwards leaned against the open door. His eyes bugged out as he ran a hand through his hair. "Sabin's dead! Wow, what happened?"

"Someone shot him yesterday," Brenda said.

Edwards glared at her. "Then you knew Art had been killed when you came by here the first time."

Brenda started to answer, but Stone interrupted. "Ms. Tower is a detective with the Portland Police Department. She discovered Sabin's body and has agreed to help with the case."

Edwards shook his head in disbelief.

"Remember, Mr. Edwards, you told me your daughter is seeing Tab Johnson. He's now missing from the farm. We're trying to determine if he might have left town for a few days. Suzanna should know if he's out of town."

"She's babysitting across town. Come in and I'll call her." Brenda and Stone stepped into the living room. Edwards grabbed a cordless phone from an end table and punched in the numbers. When their conversation ended, he told them, "Suzanna doesn't know anything about Tab leaving town. They had planned to go swimming down at the river tonight."

"That's a big help, thanks. Call me if you hear something." Stone offered Edwards his hand. Edwards grabbed Stone's hand and shook it hard. Stone handed him his card, and he and Brenda left.

"I doubt Tab had anything to do with his grandfather's murder," Brenda commented as they drove toward the farm. "Wish now I hadn't mentioned that possibility at the meeting. Perhaps we have it all wrong."

"What do you mean, all wrong?" Stone asked.

"Suppose Tab was never in the pickup. Like you said, maybe Sabin was killed at the farm, put in his pickup, and driven into the field."

Stone glanced over at Brenda. "Know what that means, don't you?"

"Yeah, it means Tab was also likely at the farm Monday morning."

"Was he abducted from there, you think?"

"Who knows?"

"If he wasn't taken, he should still be there, somewhere, right?"

Brenda sighed deeply. "Right. We could use a cadaver dog."

"Maybe," Stone responded, "but I hope we don't need one."

At the Sabin place, they stepped out of the car and moved to the shade of the front yard. "Let's go over what has been searched out here," Brenda suggested.

"Okay, ask away. We can probably eliminate all the buildings."

"Did anyone go through the garage?"

"I did, this morning."

"You went through the sleeping rooms yesterday, right?"

"While you waited for the ambulance."

Brenda motioned across the way. "How about the storage bins?"

"Hardesty and Talbot—this morning."

"We went through the big house and the cottage room by room," Brenda said.

"And I searched the big house again looking for the murder weapon."

"Okay, then." Brenda hesitated, then started across the yard, calling over her shoulder, "Why don't we look out behind the barn?"

Stone doubled over and groaned. "It's a damn weed patch back there, but okay."

He caught stride with Brenda as she hustled to the back corner of the huge structure. Stone grabbed her arm when she stepped into the weeds. "No need for you to get in this mess. I'll meet you on the opposite corner."

Brenda hurried around the barn and waited for Stone to climb out of the weeds. She rolled her eyes when she caught sight of his pants and socks covered with thistles and stickers. Several minutes passed as he removed them and brushed away the dust. "There's nothing back there," he said.

Brenda sneezed three times in rapid succession. "Excuse me—the dust. I watched you coming in this direction."

Stone caught the grin pulling at the corners of her mouth. "You thought me quite amusing, wandering through that thistle patch, huh?"

"I thought you were great," she lied.

They walked back to the farmhouse and went to the kitchen through the side door. "Want a drink of water?" Brenda asked.

"Yeah, sure."

She filled two glasses and handed one to Stone. He gulped his water down and went to the sink for more. "We've been through and around every building here," he said, swallowing from his second glass of water between words.

Brenda stood next to the sink and looked out the window onto the side yard. She turned to face Stone, a question spread across her face, but she said nothing. She flung the side door open and skipped every other porch step as she ran toward the lilacs. Their flowering time had come and gone—no sweet fragrance filled the warm afternoon air. Brenda jogged around to the back of the large, closely spaced bushes, and, squeezing between two, she examined the ground. Hands cupped over her knees, she bent forward for a closer look. Stone wedged in alongside her and peered down.

"Looks like a door to a root cellar."

"Sure does," Stone said as he reached down, grabbed the handle, and tugged hard on the door. Up and over it came, resting on a stop. Crafted from the same wide, rough-sawn lumber as the old barn doors, the heavy door was covered with tin to deny access to field mice, snakes, rain, and the snow. Stone removed his sunglasses and pulled a flashlight from his lower side pocket. Stepping into the dark space, he could feel the cool air from below moving up his pant legs as he descended into the cellar. His eyes gradually adjusted to the darkness. Brenda stood at the opening above, gazing into the dim space. Stone moved his light across the floor at the bottom of the stairs. "There's a body down here!" Stone yelled up. A pause followed, then, "It looks like the boy in that photo I found upstairs. Yes, it's Tab!" He bent down and felt for a pulse. "He's still alive!"

Brenda shivered in response to Stone's words. This was the moment she'd hoped and prayed for. "We've found him—he's alive! Thank God." The promptings she'd experienced the previous day hadn't been in vain. The excitement she felt reminded her of a similar experience—winning the Colorado State Rodeo Barrel-Racing Championship. With clenched fists, her arms shot to the sky, her head flew back, and she did a little victory jig, like an NFL running back in the end zone.

Brenda hurried down the steep, wooden steps, and stood over Tab's body. He lay on his right side in a near-fetal position. Stone handed Brenda his flashlight as he bounded up the steps, opened his cell, and dialed 911.

"Sandra," he told his dispatcher, "get an ambulance ASAP. We've found Tab Johnson at the Sabin farm. We're at the end of

Hidden Valley Lane, three miles east of Elam's Crossing off 261. Tell the driver to run 33-traffic!"

"10-4, Sheriff."

Brenda knelt down next to Tab, speaking softly close to his ear. "Can you hear me?" She waited with anticipation. "Tab, can you hear me?"

Silence.

"If you can hear me, move your finger." She waited.

Stone walked back down the stairs. Brenda repeated, "Move your finger if you can hear me."

"His index finger moved a little," Stone said.

"The ambulance is on its way, Tab, hold on!"

"Brenda. I'm going to the house for a blanket."

"Bring a wet towel, too."

Stone returned quickly. He took his flashlight from Brenda and handed her the blanket. She covered the boy and then held out her hand for the towel. She dabbed it gently across Tab's forehead and along the exposed side of his face.

As Stone watched her, he struggled for a moment to keep his mind on the task at hand.

"I'm heading out to the highway to flag down the ambulance."

"We'll be here," Brenda said, not taking her eyes off the young man at her feet.

Stone climbed the steep, wooden steps from the root cellar. He hurried to his vehicle and drove the dusty lane out through the canyon to the highway, where he turned the Expedition around and parked. While waiting for the ambulance to arrive, he called his deputies to shut down their searches. After delivering his message, Stone noticed a flowered handkerchief on the seat next to him, reminding him of Brenda. It was her dogged determination and inquisitive nature that led them to the cellar and to the boy's discovery. But there was more. His attraction to her had been growing steadily since the previous day.

Before long, he heard the siren and saw the ambulance approaching fast from the east. The driver caught sight of Stone's SUV, turned onto the lane, and followed in his dust to the farmhouse.

Stone stopped at the edge of the lawn, jumped out, and trotted to the ambulance. "There's a boy lying at the bottom of a root cellar near those lilacs." Stone walked alongside the ambulance.

Hearing the approaching vehicle, Brenda climbed out of the cellar. The two EMTs moved past her and entered the cellar. The man with a powerful floodlight on a small stand shone it across the dirt floor, illuminating a pool of blood. They shifted the boy slowly to locate his injuries. Tab's moans floated up from below and reached Brenda's ears. The EMTs located two bullet wounds, one under the boy's right shoulder and another in his right thigh. As they worked, the younger EMT hollered up their findings to the sheriff. After cleaning the wounds and applying compresses, they laid Tab on a stretcher. Again, he moaned. Lifting him up the steep stairs and onto the lawn was a challenge for the two men, even with the sheriff's help topside. An all-conference end on his high school football team the previous fall, Tab Johnson weighed over two hundred pounds.

The two men placed Johnson in the ambulance and secured the stretcher. "He's a strong kid," one of them said, starting an IV. "We're taking him to the emergency room at Walla Walla General."

"His name is Tab Johnson," Stone said.

The driver gave a thumbs-up, and the ambulance tires dug tracks in the grass between the trees, out onto the central yard, and to the lane leading back to the highway.

"Brenda, take my cell. Call the boy's mother and his grandmother. Tell them Tab is on his way to Walla Walla General. Then call John Edwards."

"Roger, Boss."

"I need to call the coroner," Stone said, suppressing a chuckle. *I'm her boss? Wouldn't that be something!*

Stone made the call on his car phone. "Sheriff Stone here, Cliff. What do you have for me?"

"Let's start easy," Cliff Abbot said. "Sabin was shot with a .38 revolver. The weapon used on the younger woman, Christina

Lopez, was not a regular knife blade, Sheriff. She was stabbed with something like a large scissors blade.

"Scissors, you think, huh?"

"Or something similar, I believe. You're looking for a southpaw. The wounds were made from a weapon in the assailant's left hand. It's hard for me to tell about the weapon used on the older woman."

"Getting harder now, I'll bet," Stone said.

"How'd you know, Sheriff? The older woman didn't die from her wounds. Someone strangled her first. The perpetrator carved on her after she expired."

"Anything else?"

"The older woman was raped by two men. I've isolated two semen samples."

"I'll be damned. What about the younger woman?"

"Not raped. But get this. She was about three months pregnant."

Stone snorted and threw his cap on the ground. "It's a miserable son-of-a-bitch who kills a pregnant woman."

"Agreed, Sheriff."

Stone retrieved his cap and slapped it back on his head. "Got photos, Cliff?"

"Plenty."

"I'll stop in tomorrow afternoon."

"Sounds good."

Stone replaced the receiver and moved to the front porch where Brenda perched on a step, talking on the phone with John Edwards. She finished and handed Stone his phone. "Mrs. Johnson broke down when I told her we found Tab alive. She and her husband are leaving tonight for Walla Walla."

"That'll be good."

"Angela Sabin was greatly relieved to hear the news, thanked me several times. Edwards said he'd tell his daughter."

"Come sit with me on the porch," Stone said, pointing to a couple of painted rocking chairs. When Brenda settled into one of them, Stone pulled the second chair closer to her and sat down.

"I appreciate you making those calls. I got an earful from

the coroner."

"What'd he have to say?"

"Calli was raped by two men before she was strangled."

"It wasn't a one-man show out here, then."

"No. Your hunch was right. Abbott told me Christina was pregnant. He believes our perp is a left hander."

"So the bastard took *four* lives?" Brenda's jaw hardened and her eyes turned a shade darker.

"You got it. By the way, what made you decide to stick your head in the lilacs?"

"I can't tell you, Lin. I just felt the need to go in there. Hard to image a person lying injured in a root cellar all that time—in the dirt and the dark."

"Yeah, I know." Stone grimaced.

"Tab's disappearance reminded me of my own experience. Remember, I told you I was abducted?"

"I do. Want to tell me about it?" Stone waited with raised eyebrows.

She stopped rocking. "I was fourteen at the time and alone in a pickup in my dad's field. My kidnapper didn't molest me, nor did he harm me. The moron took me to an abandoned farmhouse and talked me half to death—for hours. I'll never forget the crazy look on his face, and his drool when he spoke. He finally drove off and left me tied to an old iron cookstove in that rat-infested shack. I was filthy, hungry, cold, tired, and scared out of my mind when a distant neighbor in the search party located me."

Tears welled up in Brenda's eyes and slid onto her cheeks. She quickly brushed them away. "Sorry."

Stone reached over and put an arm on her shoulder. "It's okay, Brenda. You've been through a hell of a lot the last two days. Your experience helps me understand your determination."

"I'm totally thrilled we located Tab Johnson—alive. I grieve for the innocent women who were murdered. I'm reminded of how fortunate I was. That's why I couldn't give up searching, Lin. The volunteer in my case refused to quit searching until she investigated the old Meldrum place where she found me."

As they drove toward Elam's Crossing, Stone looked at Brenda, glanced away, then back again. "Now that we've found the boy, my guess is you'll want to get back to Portland."

Brenda heard a hint of melancholy in his voice. "What I want to do is catch the psycho who murdered these people." She looked over at him. "Do you care if I stay a while longer?"

"I'd like that, Brenda. You give us new thinking—a different perspective and a fresh set of eyes."

"Is that your best reason for my being here?"

"Reason enough, don't you think? We'd have never found the boy alive on our own." Eyes softening, he added, "I've gotten used to you being around, Brenda, and that's been nice, as well."

Brenda blushed. "Good answer, Sheriff. I'll stay for a few more days."

Stone smiled. He didn't take his eyes off the road, but he reached across the seat and cupped his hand over Brenda's. A few minutes later, they arrived at Aunt Annie's. "Do you want me to drop you at Huber's for supper?"

"No, I need the walk."

"I'll pick you up here in the morning, then. I'll call you later when I have something specific about young Johnson."

"I'd appreciate that. Until later, then."

20

Ken Gear and Ramiro Sanchez stepped out of Sanchez's black Impala and lit up cigarettes. Joey Valentine reluctantly climbed out and leaned against the car, chewing on a stalk of wheat. The three had come to a vacant field at the south edge of Elam's Crossing late Tuesday night to talk in private. It was their first day of harvest; they were tired and irritable after twelve hours in the field. Gear and Valentine were both so mad about what had happened Monday morning, they wanted to stomp a mud hole in the middle of Sanchez.

Suddenly, the three were distracted by the lights of an approaching vehicle. "Who the hell's that?" Gear asked, scratching his head

"Stand back, man!" Sanchez yelled. As he backed away, a pickup came up alongside his car and stopped.

Valentine turned to Sanchez. "Who told that son-of-a-bitch where we'd be?" he muttered, kicking the dirt hard with his boot.

"Beats me, man."

Carlos Mendoza slid out of his truck and slammed the door hard. He hurled an empty beer can at Sanchez's feet and shot him an evil eye. Sensing trouble, Valentine and Gear backed away. Mendoza growled, "Ramiro, you lied to me. You told me there would be ten grand in the house. I end up with three hundred bucks. Shit, that's chicken feed, you hear me? It's nothing." He slammed the side of Sanchez's sedan with the palm of his hand.

Sanchez threw up his arms. "How was I to know, man? There should have been a lot more money in that office."

Mendoza tried to grab Sanchez's shirt, but Sanchez quickly retreated. Mendoza shook his finger in his face. "You lied to me, you fucker. The whole thing was a waste of my time."

"Last year, man, I saw a huge stack of hundreds on his desk."

It was Gear's turn. He stepped forward. "Ramiro, you said

it would be just the three of us. You lied again!" Gesturing to Carlos, he added, "Why'd you cut this one in?"

Gear didn't give Sanchez time to answer. Turning to Mendoza he cried, "You hurt us bad, hurt us all real bad! Our asses are in a sling because of you."

"The Mexican woman and that gringo kid barged into the house. Shit, I had to stop them."

Valentine was also furious. "It was supposed to be a simple job Carlos, but no, you had to come along and screw up everything."

"What's the big fuckin' deal?" Mendoza asked.

"We've all got blood on our hands for what you did—*that's* the big fucking deal. Know what it means?" Valentine screamed back.

Mendoza stepped closer to Valentine, his eyes blazing "No, you tell me, little man."

"It means we'll be hunted down like wild dogs. Why'd you have to kill those people?"

With uncharacteristic boldness, Valentine held Mendoza's stare and jutted his chin up close to Mendoza's face. "You're one crazy son-of-a-bitch. You know that, don't you?"

Mendoza clenched his fists. "Don't you ever say that again, you sorry little prick. We didn't need no damn witnesses blabbing their faces off." His spittle sprayed Valentine's face.

"But, man, you raped Calli," Sanchez butted in. "She was one fine woman—one of our people."

Mendoza's sneer turned to a ghastly grin. "Balling that sexy Mex broad was all right, you know."

Sanchez yelled at him, "But you killed her, man!"

"The bitch knifed me. She boiled my blood—I had to choke her."

"And you knifed the other woman, too!" Gear said.

Mendoza swung around to face Gear. "She shouldn't have busted in on us. What difference does it make? She was an ugly bitch."

"Are you kidding, Carlos? We're all in one hell of a mess here because of what you did," Gear said.

"You shot that gringo kid, too. He didn't see anything," Valentine added.

"He saw our cars, didn't he, you little piss-ant?"

"You shot him, but what if he ain't dead? He'll finger us, sure as hell," said Gear.

"Believe me, he's dead. I put three slugs in him. We dumped him in the cellar. If he wasn't dead, he's damn sure dead by now." Perspiration dripped from Mendoza's forehead. He wiped it away with a hand and stomped the ground several times.

Valentine's hands went to his ears. "I can't sleep! I keep hearing that woman's screams."

"You're a sorry little candy-ass," Mendoza mocked.

"We can't hang around anymore. We gotta cut out of here," Gear urged.

"I agree with Ken," Valentine said. "If we stay here, we'll be picked up for sure."

"But if we pull out now, old man Wattenburger will wonder what's up," Sanchez reasoned. "He could squeal to the sheriff."

"Ramiro's right. Nobody's got nothin' on us. We just gotta stay cool till it blows over," Mendoza said, wiping the sweat from his brow onto his shirtsleeve.

"Yeah, we gotta stick together. It's the only way, man," Sanchez said.

"Bull—shit! Why should we stick together?" Valentine shook his head. "Harvest will be over here in a few weeks. We'll all be going off to other places, anyway."

Mendoza grabbed Valentine by the front of his tee. "Look, you little bastard. I want you here where I can keep an eye on you. If you all scatter, it'll be too easy for one of you monkeys to chatter to the law." He shoved Valentine backwards.

"Who said anything about the law?" Valentine countered, as he stumbled and regained his balance.

"We'll beat this thing if we keep our mouths shut and stay cool." Mendoza pulled his knife from its sheath. "We'll take an oath of silence—no one talks about this." He made a cut on the underside of his wrist. Blood surfaced. He held out his arm. Sanchez appeared ready to follow Mendez's lead. Gear and

Valentine looked at each other, shaking their heads.

"What the hell is this?" Gear said. "Carlos did the murders and now he's telling us what we have to do."

Sanchez tried to reason with his fellow workers. "If any one of us talks, we're all had, you know that. This will be a token to remind each of us to keep silent."

"I don't like being told what to do," Valentine said, but then he noticed the way Mendoza gripped the hilt of his knife. Valentine remembered Mendoza also carried a small gun, the one he used on the gringo kid. He worried should he or one of the other two refuse to take the oath, the crazy Mendoza could come down on all of them.

"I'll kill any man who snitches about what happened," Mendoza bellowed. He stared at the others, eyes crazed with hate.

When Gear saw Valentine step forward to join Sanchez, he followed. Each made a small slit on his wrist with the knife. Valentine's hands shook. Crossing wrists, the four of them mingled their blood. Each repeated, "I'll stay, and I'll keep silent about what happened."

Mendoza broke away first, stepped into his pickup, and sped off. Moments later, the others climbed into the black sedan and Sanchez drove away.

"How'd Mendoza know we were here? Ramiro, did you tell that bastard?" Valentine asked.

"No, man, I haven't seen him since yesterday morning."

"He must be stalking us," Gear said, pounding the top of the seat in front of him

"I didn't know Carlos would go ape-shit like he did, man," Sanchez said.

"Once he saw Calli, the horny bastard couldn't keep his hands off her." Valentine wiped the perspiration from his face.

"We should've stopped him the moment he grabbed her," Gear said. "Things would have been different."

"He's crazy as a loon. He loves killing—it's his recreation," Valentine said.

"What can we do, man?" Sanchez's hands gripped the steering wheel harder. "We can't turn him in. The law would be after us as soon as they questioned him."

"We're hanging out as long as he's running free," Gear said. "What if he goes to drinking and comes after one of us?"

Valentine stiffened. "We may have to kill him," he said, staring out the window into the dark. He knew not one of them was a killer, not yet at least. But in their defense against this insane man, it might become necessary.

Sanchez shot Valentine a startled look. "Let's sleep on it. We'll talk tomorrow."

Silent, Valentine continued to stare out the window.

21

The phone rang in Brenda's room late Tuesday evening.

"Hello, Brenda."

"Hi, Lin. What's up?"

"I wanted to let you know that Tab Johnson is out of the operating room. The doctor removed two .22 slugs: one from his leg and another from under his shoulder."

"Great news! Thanks for letting me know. When do you think we'll be able to talk with him?"

"I couldn't get an answer from the nurse. I'm going to see Dr. Hastings tomorrow sometime."

"The sooner we can talk with him, the better." Brenda heard Stone sigh.

"I should have taken you to dinner tonight. You must have thought I was pretty rude."

"You weren't rude at all. It's not your job to entertain me."

"Well, okay. I'll change the subject. I'm still amazed you gave up a vacation to stay and help out."

"I could tell you could use some assistance."

"Boy, and how."

"I kind of threw myself at your feet. You could have turned down my offer."

"Yeah, but your price was right. Besides, I knew my deputies could learn some things from you."

"And what about you, Lin, what could you learn from me—anything?"

"To trust a good female detective, maybe even trust a woman again."

Stone thought about how she made him feel when they were together and how attractive he found her. But he couldn't bring himself to say those things. *Get a grip, man, the woman's here for four or five days at most, and then she'll be gone. Don't make a fool of yourself.*

"It sounds to me like you haven't gotten over your experience with your ex-wife."

"I'm working on it. I could use a little shrink therapy."

"Couldn't we all?" Brenda glanced at the clock. 11:00 p.m. Interesting, she thought, that Stone would call so late.

"I'll let you go, Brenda. See you in the morning."

Disappointed with how he so abruptly ended their conversation, she merely said, "Okay then, in the morning," and hung up the phone. Brenda placed her book on the side table and turned out the light. She woke once in the night from a bad dream, feeling oddly restless and lonely.

22

Brenda was sitting on the front porch Wednesday morning when Stone pulled up. She padded over to the Expedition and settled into the passenger seat.

"Good morning, Brenda. Sleep okay?"

"Yes, eventually. How about you?"

"Oh, so-so. I'm a light sleeper when I've got worries," Stone replied as he maneuvered his vehicle toward the main highway and Sabin's farm.

"The weatherman says it's going to be a little cooler today."

Brenda, deep in thought, completely missed Stone's comment about the weather. "You know, women are sexually assaulted all the time, but few of them are brutally murdered and mutilated."

Stone glanced across the seat at her. "You're into it early this morning, Detective."

"I'm thinking we're facing a madman—someone seriously deranged," Brenda said.

"I think we've pretty well established that."

"Remember me telling you Sabin treated his Mexican workers poorly? Could be this sicko is also full of hate and revenge because of what went on there."

"One of the perps may have worked at the farm!" Stone said, as he turned onto Hidden Valley Lane.

"A former field hand would have known about Sabin's treatment of Mexicans. He might also have known whether the man kept large sums of money in the house."

Stone squinted into the early morning sun's blinding rays. He reached up and pulled down his sun visor before responding. "We know at least two men broke into the house and raped the Mendez woman. Could be they were former harvest workers. We need a good lead or two about the killer."

"Those leads will come, Lin, maybe even today."

They pulled up to the farmhouse and stopped. Detective Tower joined four deputies on the front steps. Stone opened the morning briefing.

"Deputy Carver is questioning people this morning in Elam's Crossing." He glanced in the direction of the lilacs. "Detective Tower and I found Tab Johnson barely alive in an abandoned root cellar over there late yesterday. The theory that the boy killed his grandfather, staged his own abduction, and murdered the two women seems highly improbable now, knowing what we know."

"The kid doing all the killing never set right with me," Hardesty whispered to Talbot and the others.

Talbot nodded, but Weber and Barber didn't react.

"What do you men have to report from late yesterday?" Stone asked.

Hardesty spoke first. "John and I drove the ATVs through the field, following the pickup tracks, looking for Johnson's body. We also scoured the long ravine behind the barn. We stumbled across the bones of an old range cow, but that was about all."

"No reports of suspicious strangers," Barber noted. "People are frightened over these killings—worried about their own safety. One woman told us her husband stayed up in a chair all night with his shotgun. Sheriff, I believe the guys who did these killings are in Denver or Las Vegas by now. There's no reason for them to hang around here."

"You could be right, Don. Maybe they were drifters passing through. We have to keep investigating, though, and continuing to be on the lookout until we're certain they're no longer here . . ."

"Wait a minute! An Elam's Crossing man was once the foreman out here," Brenda broke in. "He told me Sabin paid his Mexican workers a lower wage than he did the Anglos. He also loaded extra work on them, work for which they were not paid."

"The burglary and the killings could have been a vengeful payback," Barber said.

"I don't believe those who did the house murders killed

Sabin." Hardesty shifted his position on the steps and frowned in concentration. "There's a different feel about his murder. I think something quite different led to his death."

Stone leaned forward. "Go on—tell us what you're getting at."

"I've done some checking. Uranium oxide sold for eight to ten dollars a pound for many years. But now it's selling for eighty-five dollars a pound, down from a hundred thirteen dollars back in April. Could be the core samples we found in the shop contain uranium. Greed does funny things to people."

"Interesting theory, Sam. We'll follow up." Stone looked around at the others. "Anything else?"

"We've been looking at these murders as though they're related," Talbot said. "Maybe they're not related at all—like Sam suggested."

Stone nodded. "Gates may have some data to help us make that determination."

Weber wasn't convinced. "Could be a lone gunman did it all: killed Sabin, burglarized the place, killed the women, and shot the boy."

"Chet, the coroner's report will show two men raped Calli Mendez," Stone said.

"So two men did it all, then," Weber concluded.

"Let's not forget Tony Sabin," Hardesty said. "He was disowned by his old man a few years back. Carver told us Tony had an accident that left him brain damaged. Maybe he's the killer."

"But Tony has an alibi," Brenda reminded them.

"Oh yeah, I forgot about that." Hardesty looked down and shook his head.

"Is there anything else?" Stone waited for a few moments. "Assignments: Sam, you and John go through the shop office here. Find out what you can about core drilling on the farm. See when it was carried out. Find out who did the drilling and call them. See if any core samples were sent out to be tested and if the results are in."

"Understood," Hardesty said.

"Don, you and Chet set up a checkpoint at a busy

intersection in Elam's Crossing. Ask people if they've seen any suspicious-acting strangers, or anything unusual."

Barber nodded. "We'll get right on it, Sheriff."

"Detective Tower and I need to talk with Johnson's surgeon. We'll visit the coroner, and we'll talk with our criminalist."

As Hardesty walked away from the meeting, he shot a backwards glance at Stone, then muttered to his partner, "Looks like the sheriff has teamed himself once again with that hot detective."

Talbot rolled his shoulder. "Hey, the man's consistent."

23

The drive to Walla Walla gave Brenda time to enjoy the scenery in the Palouse countryside. Rolling wheat fields interspersed with ravines choked with cottonwoods and small streambeds made up the view along the first part of the hour-long drive. From the highest elevations, she could see a colorful patchwork of agriculture for miles ahead.

"Pea fields covered thousands of acres here after World War II," Stone said, taking his eyes from the road briefly to follow her line of vision. "Dayton operated the largest pea cannery in the country in the '50s. Remember, I told you my father worked here in the pea harvests when he was in high school."

"Yes, I remember. That's interesting."

They passed through Dayton and then Waitsburg, a farming community of twelve hundred people. Stone turned south toward the village of Dixie, not more than twenty miles from the Blue Mountain breaks. Brenda leaned back in her seat, relaxed. "What a refreshing change from the brick, mortar, and asphalt of the city."

"I never get tired of this drive."

In another fifteen minutes they entered the flatlands. "Is it true the state offered the Walla Walla city fathers their choice of either the state university or the state penitentiary, and they chose the gates and guns?"

"That's the story." Stone pointed to her side of the road. "Look at all the onion fields. Famous Walla Walla Onions, you know. It won't be long before all this will be gone. Agricultural land here is all going into grapevines."

"Table wine, I suppose."

"High quality, too—some of the country's best, they say."

At Walla Walla General, Stone spoke with the head nurse at the ICU desk. "Tab's a strong kid; he's making a good recovery," the nurse reported. "He'll be transferred to our step-down unit tomorrow."

"Has Dr. Hastings seen him this morning?"

"The doctor was here less than thirty minutes ago, so I think he's still in the building. I can have him paged if you like."

The doctor arrived shortly, and he, Brenda, and Stone sat in comfortable armchairs in the consultation room. A slightly built, dark-skinned man, Hastings looked much younger than his fifty-five years. He had a full head of sandy hair, young-looking skin, bright blue eyes, and a friendly smile.

"The bullets I removed from the Johnson boy were .22 hollow points. If they had been solid point 40-grain rounds, they would likely have exited his body. He has a good flesh wound up here," Hastings placed his index finger on his torso. "The leg wound is somewhat problematic, but he should heal quickly. You can retrieve the rounds at the nurses' station."

Stone cleared his throat, eager to get the doctor's approval to talk with the boy, but Brenda jumped ahead of him with a question of her own. "Was the shooter up close when he fired, or was he some distance away?"

"I found no evidence of gunpowder stippling or tattooing, so the shooter wasn't up close. My guess is he was maybe ten to fifteen feet away—and to the rear. If he'd been closer, the wounds would have been more pronounced." Hastings looked down briefly and then fixed his eyes back on Brenda. "More torn flesh, so to speak."

"He could have been running, or perhaps he was shielding someone." Brenda said.

"That's hard to say, miss."

Brenda glanced over at Stone as she sank further into the plush upholstery of her chair.

"Young Johnson may have seen who killed his grandfather. It's important I talk with him as *soon* as possible," Stone pleaded.

"I understand your urgency, but he's weak and heavily sedated now. He won't be any use to you today, Sheriff. Come back tomorrow afternoon. He'll be able to talk then, at least for a little while."

"Doctor, just so you know, the boy's parents will be in town today. They'll want to see him, and they'll likely want to talk with you as well."

"They may have to come to my office, but it's not far from here."

"Thank you for your time," the sheriff said. They all stood, and both Brenda and Stone shook hands with the doctor.

Stone picked up the bullets at the nurses' station as he and Brenda left the hospital.

24

Deputies Weber and Barber stopped cars at the Tucanon Street exit off 261. People they talked with that morning expressed shock at hearing about the murders, yet no one could give them a lead on suspicious characters or unusual circumstances. About 11:00 a.m., Deputy Barber questioned a woman in a green sedan while her little boy fidgeted in the back seat.

"My daughter told me something last night that may interest you. Emily was with friends down at the Snake River when a stranger tried to crash their party."

Barber removed his sunglasses and listened attentively.

"He was a Mexican fellow, hair in a ponytail, Emily said. When the kids ignored him, he swore at them in Spanish and left."

Barber pulled a notepad from his shirt pocket. "May I have your name and address, ma'am?"

"I'm Melody Robbins." She recited her address and phone number while Barber jotted down the information.

"My partner and I would like to speak with your daughter as soon as we can."

"She'll be home at noon today. Come by then if you want."

"Mommy! Mommy! When can we go to the toy store?" The little boy's voice rose higher and higher, shrilled with impatience.

"We'll stop in then, Mrs. Robbins, and thank you."

The woman nodded, and, before driving off, she reached back and smacked her boy on the leg. "Don't interrupt like that! How many times have I told you?"

A rotund, gray-haired man in overalls working on an old truck in front of a vacant gas station, motioned to the deputies as they passed by. Weber swung the Jeep Liberty around and stopped near the truck.

The man shuffled to the passenger window. "My neighbor tells me you've been asking questions about suspicious goings on."

"Sir, you heard right. We're investigating the Sabin

murders," Barber told him.

"I might have something." The man wiped grease from his hands with a rag.

"Okay, go ahead."

"Late last night I saw vehicle lights in the field across from my place."

"Is that unusual?" Weber asked, shading his eyes from the sun.

"Damn sure is! Nothing goes on in that old vacant field, even at night."

"Maybe it was teenagers horsing around?" Barber suggested.

"Not likely." The man fingered the whiskers on his chin. "It's not a spot where the kids hang out, not since that woman committed suicide out there some years back. I saw a pickup bounce out from there last night. A dark sedan followed a few minutes later."

"Can you show us the spot?"

The deputies followed the old Studebaker pickup to a field at the edge of town. They got out and examined tire tracks in the dirt at the edge of the field. "There's no visible tread on one of the tires on the driver's side," Barber noted.

"That wider track is likely from the pickup," the old man said.

Led by the tire tracks, the three men walked into the field to where the tracks ended. Weber spotted something reflecting light in the weeds. "A single beer can—not what you'd call a party."

"Like I told you fellows, this place is not a hangout for local kids."

Barber mopped his brow and glanced at his watch. "We need to be going."

The men walked back to their vehicles.

"Give us your name and your phone number, sir, in case we need to contact you again," Weber said.

Barber wrote down the information: *Clyde Simons, 434-7813*.

"Thanks for your help, mister," Weber said, shaking the

man's hand.

"I'm pleased to be of help anytime, officers.

~

Following a quick lunch at Huber's, Barber and Weber approached the Robbins' front porch a little after noon. Weber rang the doorbell. Shortly, they heard little feet inside scurrying toward them just before the door flew open.

"Is your mother home?" Barber asked the boy who had whined in the back seat of the sedan earlier that morning. Melody Robbins promptly appeared with a dishtowel in her hands and led them to a sitting room just off the entryway.

"Come in and have a seat. I'll get Emily." The woman disappeared through the doorway toward the back of the house.

Barber and Weber remained standing, waiting for Mrs. Robbins and her daughter to appear.

"This is Emily, our oldest," beamed Mrs. Robbins. The deputies introduced themselves and they all sat down. Weber pulled out his notepad.

Emily had bright blue eyes and blond, curly hair framing a tanned, near-flawless complexion. Her figure, showcased in an undersized tee shirt and last-year's cutoff jeans, caught the deputies' eyes.

"Emily is a reporter on her high school newspaper," her mother announced with a broad smile. "She's also on the debate team."

"Your mother told us you had an experience with a stranger last evening, Emily," Barber said. "Can you tell us about it?"

"Sure, I can. We were at a bonfire down by the river. This weird guy came over and tried to start up a conversation with us. None of us had ever seen him before. We tried to ignore him— it was awkward, you know."

"What do you think he wanted?" Barber asked.

"He was trying to crash the party, I guess. He wanted in, but he wasn't one of us, and we didn't want him hanging around."

"Was he trying to pick up one of the girls?"

Emily rubbed her nose. "If he was, it wasn't obvious, at

least not to me."

"Can you describe him for us?"

"He was a Mexican, or Hispanic at least—had that accent. He was older, maybe thirty, with long, straight hair in a ponytail."

"How tall?"

"I'd say he was medium height. Real husky, though."

"Do you remember what he was wearing?"

"I do. He had on a brown Old Navy tee shirt, blue jeans, and boots. Oh, and a gold chain."

"Did he have any tattoos, scars—other distinguishing features?"

Emily wrinkled her nose and lowered her eyelids. "He had a large, jagged scar on his upper arm. I remember that."

"Did he threaten anyone—show aggressive behavior in any way?"

"Not really. But he carried a big knife on his belt, and he acted real nervous, or maybe more agitated than nervous. He swore at us in Spanish because we wouldn't answer his questions."

"Then what did he do?"

"He ran to his pickup and drove off, squealing his tires."

"Was anyone waiting for him in the pickup?"

Emily's hand lightly cradled her chin. "I don't think so."

"Can you describe the pickup he drove?"

"It was a light gray Ford—all one color. It had a matching gray topper over the bed."

"Do you think this guy's a harvest worker?"

"Well, he dressed like one."

"Now, think carefully, Emily. Did he give you any clue that he's living in this area?"

Emily frowned, glanced at her mother, then up at the ceiling, then down at the floor, all the while twisting strands of hair around her finger. "He asked about Palouse Falls. But we didn't answer him."

Barber nudged Weber. "Any questions for Emily?"

"What did the boys say about this man after he left?"

"A couple of the boys said he spooked them. That's one of the reasons I told Mom about him when I got home."

"You did the right thing. Call 911 if you see this man again or if you spot his pickup," Weber said.

"Okay, I will."

"Emily's a good eyewitness. She's given us a description we can use," Weber told her mother.

The deputies stood and thanked Emily for her cooperation. As they walked out to the car, Weber glowered. "It's back to the roadblock grind."

Barber called Stone during their short drive. "Sheriff, we talked with a girl in Elam's Crossing who gave us some dope on a stranger she saw down on the Snake last night."

"Go ahead, tell me more, Don."

Barber briefed the sheriff on everything the girl had told them.

"Nice work, you two."

"There's something else, Sheriff. Let me fill you in on what we heard from an old mechanic up here this morning," Barber continued.

25

Cliff Abbott, the County Coroner, was a small, bony man in his mid-fifties sporting curly, mud-colored hair spiced with gray, untrimmed eyebrows, and an ugly burn scar on his right arm. After Stone introduced Brenda, the three walked to a stainless-steel counter on the left side of his examination room. Abbott laid out photos of the bodies of Art Sabin and Christina Lopez. "Like I told you, Sheriff, I took plenty."

Stone lifted one of the Sabin photos for a closer look. "This wound in the back suggests one of the bullets hit bone and took a quick exit."

Brenda moved in closer for a better view.

"You're right, Sheriff. The bullet fired higher up into the chest, glanced off a rib, tore through part of the spinal column, and exited."

"What about his other wounds?" Stone asked.

"Two others." Abbott lifted another Sabin photo. "You can see the entry wound here, lower down on his chest. The bullet passed through soft tissue, punctured his lower lung, and exited on the left side of the body."

"And this one?" Stone asked, indicating a third photo.

"The shooter also fired a bullet into the victim's neck, from above. Likely the first shot, it ripped through vital organs and lodged in the left hip." Abbott dug into his pants' pocket and dropped the bullet in Stone's open hand.

Brenda studied a photo of Christina Lopez. "This poor woman must have been stabbed a dozen times."

"Actually fourteen," Abbott said.

"What kind of blade was used?" Stone asked.

"At first I thought the weapon might have been the larger half of a big pair of separated scissors." Abbott held up a pair of common scissors, the kind elementary school teachers keep tucked away in their desks. "I've changed my mind about the scissors," he said, laying them back on the counter.

"What's your best guess now about the weapon?" Stone asked.

Abbott rubbed his chin, slowly shaking his head. "I think it was some kind of modified bayonet. It was a long, straight blade, that much is certain. Wielded with force, it would produce the massive kinds of wounds you see in the photo."

"Still think our killer was a left hander?" Stone persisted.

"Most definitely." Abbott took up another photo. "This is the torso of the Lopez woman. Notice the angles and the locations of the thrusts. They are almost exclusively on the right side of her body, some moving toward the middle." Abbott moved his pen along the major stab wounds. He then grabbed a close-up photo of the woman's head and upper shoulders. "The slashes to the neck are on the right side. If the killer was standing opposite her, those wounds wouldn't likely be inflicted by a right hander."

"Show us photos of the Mendez woman," Stone said.

Abbot pushed the photos of Sabin and Lopez aside and spread out those of Calli Mendez. "Note the variations in the wounds in this photo compared to those we saw in the photos of the Lopez woman."

Stone nodded.

"As I told you on the phone, Sheriff, the killer strangled her before he carved on her. These are not deep thrust or slash wounds. They were caused by gouging, twisting motions."

Stone slammed the side of his fist on top of the stainless steel counter. "I want to get the psycho bastard who did this!" He paced the floor. Abbott and Brenda leaned against the counter, silent and waiting.

Stone took a deep breath. "Sorry about the outburst."

Abbott waved off Stone's apology. Brenda realized just how sensitive Stone could be. She liked it.

"Has Angela Sabin's funeral director called about her husband's body?" Stone asked.

"His body left here this morning. So did the body of the Mendez woman. Attorney Everett Schuster is taking care of the costs and arrangements for her graveside service and burial."

"We're still trying to locate Lopez's family. Call me when your report is complete. Thanks for your time, Cliff."

As Stone and Brenda walked to the vehicle, he admitted, "I have a hard time looking at photos of murder victims, especially of women and children."

Brenda placed her hand on his arm. "It's a nasty part of our business."

Just then Stone's cell phone rang. He motioned Brenda to a shaded area on the side lawn.

"Sheriff, Hardesty here. We found some core drilling paperwork in the shop office. Talbot called Childers Drilling in Spokane and talked with the man in charge of the drilling on Sabin's property."

"Good, good—go on." Stone's voice rose with excitement.

"This Childers fellow, named Bennion, said Sabin told him he was negotiating with a Spokane-based mining company. Bennion thought it was Sun-Bright Mining. Sabin intended to do exploratory digging on his property if the tests showed positive."

"Have the tests been completed?"

"Sabin arranged for Bennion's crew to drop off some core samples at EG&S Engineering. Bennion didn't know whether the test results were in. Sabin wanted another outfit to test additional samples. He had Bennion's men store some core samples in his shop, the ones we uncovered yesterday"

"Anything else, Sam?"

"The core drilling took place in a twenty-acre area about two miles east of the farmhouse. We found a lath marked with a red ribbon and a reference number next to each hole."

"Sam, get a hold of someone at EG&S. Find out if their analysis is complete and ask for the results. Then I want the two of you to learn as much as you can about uranium mining in Washington, including public sentiment about it."

Stone turned to Brenda, filling her in on the other side of the call. "We may have an answer soon on the core sample results."

"Maybe Sabin was murdered over a mining deal," Brenda mused.

26

Two television vans were parked in the courthouse lot, accompanied by what Stone referred to as "the tabloid press." Brenda surveyed the scene and turned to Stone. "I wondered how long this would take."

"Just what we need," Stone growled. Once outside his cruiser, he pulled Brenda aside and handed her his cell phone. "I'll deal with these reporters. You call Rusty Gates. His number is in my contact list. Find out what he has for us."

"I'll do it," Brenda said, already looking for a spot out of the heat. She found a bench under a tree on the courthouse lawn, away from all the commotion. She chose the far end of the bench, smoothed the front of her beige slacks, and dialed.

"Hello, Mr. Gates?"

"Yes, this is Rusty. You have the sheriff's phone, miss, but for doggone sure you're not Lin Stone. Who do I have the pleasure of speaking to?"

"This is Detective Tower. I'm working with Sheriff Stone on the Sabin murders. He asked me to call you for a rundown."

"Grab a pen, Detective."

Brenda pulled a small notepad and pen from the front pocket of her slacks. "I'm ready when you are, Mr. Gates."

"First thing, call me Rusty. And now to business. Those four-wheelers behind the shop: batteries are dead in both of them, their fuel tanks are nearly dry, and the tire pressures are down. Four-wheelers may have been in the field Monday morning, Detective, but it wasn't those two."

"I got it, Rusty."

"Next, the blood in the upstairs bathroom doesn't match the Mendez woman's blood. Stone found a pocketknife in the bedroom where she was murdered. We believe she stabbed her assailant."

"That confirms our original thinking." Brenda heard paper rattling in the background.

"I have fingerprints from the medicine cabinet mirror upstairs and from a marble figurine I found in the upstairs bedroom. The prints on the marble *don't* match the prints on the mirror. The prints on the mirror *do* match the bloody prints on the basement door."

"Your evidence shows two men were in the room with the Mendez woman. Rusty, the coroner confirmed for us she was raped by two men."

"So, we're good there?" Gates said.

"Yeah, we're good."

"There's more. I made a casting of a tire track in front of the Sabin house. Tread was almost worn smooth."

"Good, anything else?"

"Yep. Fingerprints on the soda cans and the magazines in the barn *are not* consistent with the fingerprints in the house."

"That's interesting. Something else was going on there."

"You know what barn lofts are to teenage boys, Detective?" There was a pause. "Places they take girls when they want to get a little *bolder*."

"A little bolder? I don't get your meaning."

"You know, a little b-o-u-l-d-e-r, when there's no rock canyon nearby."

"Oh, I get it!" Brenda laughed. "You might have something there."

"I dusted Sabin's pickup for prints. Someone wiped the cab down pretty good. My vacuum didn't pick up any meaningful microfibers, either. Most importantly, there should have been bullet fragments in the cab. There weren't. Tell Stone Art Sabin was shot somewhere else, loaded into his pickup, and driven into the field."

"Rusty, you've confirmed the sheriff's theory."

"Have you found the weapons?" Gates asked.

"No, we haven't. We only have bullets removed from the victims. The coroner believes the weapon used on the two women was some sort of sharpened-down bayonet."

"I'd trust Abbott's judgment until something tells you different."

"Okay, Rusty, thanks. I'll relay this information to the sheriff."

"Say, Detective, when will I get to meet you?"

"I'll have the sheriff get back to you on that. Goodbye, Rusty." Brenda flipped the phone shut and finished her last note. *Gates is a flirt.*

When Brenda entered the courthouse, she found reporters crowded around the sheriff in the small lobby outside his office.

"We were standing in the kitchen when the detective darted out of the house, running for the lilacs." Stone glanced in her direction. "Here she is now, Detective Brenda Tower, the woman who discovered the hidden cellar where we found the boy."

A woman reporter from the Walla Walla ABC affiliate stepped toward Brenda. "We understand you left your vacation to help Sheriff Stone with his murder case. Do you believe the three murders were committed by the same person?"

Motioning to Stone, Brenda answered. "Please direct your questions to the sheriff." She folded her arms across her chest and stepped back.

"Detective, we know you discovered Art Sabin's body, and that you and the sheriff found the two dead women in his home," the reporter persisted. "Surely, you have an opinion about who perpetrated these crimes."

"I assure you, ma'am, my opinion is of no importance."

"Off the record, Detective?" a Tri-City Herald reporter queried.

Brenda glared at the man. "Mister, there are *no* questions off the record as far as I'm concerned." Brenda cut a beeline for the dispatcher's office on the opposite side of the curtained glass.

A Spokane CNN affiliate reporter charged, "Sheriff, the public has the right . . ."

Stone cut him off. "I'm aware of what the public has the right to know. Listen, one of my deputies will escort any of you who want to go out to the Sabin property. You're welcome to take all the exterior shots you want. No cameras will be allowed in the house."

"But Sheriff, we have . . ."

"Sir, that's the way it's going to be. I'll issue a news release when we have something specific to report on a suspect. Thank you for coming this morning." Stone nodded briskly and slapped his cap back on his head—he was going back to work. The reporters reluctantly left the building, shaking their heads and grousing to each other. The Walla Walla Union Bulletin reporter left her card on Stone's windshield, hoping he would alert her first to any breaking news.

Joining Brenda in the dispatcher's office, Stone remarked, "I'm not about to let this become a reporters' feeding frenzy. They'd camp here if I let them—they'd hound me to death."

"They're just doing their job," Brenda said, handing Stone his cell.

Stone turned abruptly and eyeballed her. "Yes, and we're just doing ours, Detective."

"No argument from me, Sheriff." Brenda threw up her arms.

Stone arranged for a deputy to escort the reporters to the Sabin farm. When his cell phone rang, he turned to the window to take the call. He listened intently, tossing in an occasional "mm-hmm" and "got it." A few moments later, Stone snapped the phone shut. "That was Deputy Carver. Melba Townsend at Huber's Café told him a husky, Mexican-looking guy in a ponytail was in her place last night. He carried a large knife on his belt, his shirt had a blood spot, and he acted agitated. Drove a gray pickup, she said."

"Lin, a guy in a gray pickup stopped along the highway Monday where Sabin was killed. He stared at me through binoculars for the longest time. I caught him spying on me later that same day in Elam's Crossing. He sped away before I could get a good look at him."

Stone raised an eyebrow. "Why didn't you mention this before?"

"It didn't seem important at the time. I thought he was some guy wandering around with nothing to do."

The wheels began turning in Stone's head like the start-up

of a carnival Ferris wheel. "Deputy Barber reported a conversation with a teenager who described a husky Mexican with a long ponytail at the Snake River last night. He carried a knife and drove a gray pickup. Counting you, three witnesses have seen this same stranger."

"Hmmm, I wonder if that pickup's running on a bald front tire. Gates has a casting of a large, near-bald tire from the Sabin place."

"Barber and Weber were shown a bald truck tire track this morning. The witness reported seeing two vehicles parked in a vacant field across from his place last night. One of them was a light-colored pickup."

"Remember what I said to you this morning about acquiring clues?"

"Indeed, I do." Stone smiled. "We have enough now to start a hunt for the suspect. I need to speak to my dispatcher." They approached the dispatcher's desk. " Pamela, call my day-time deputies and tell them to knock-off for a few hours. Have them meet me at 6:00 p.m. at the sheriff's substation in Elam's Crossing. I want them in street clothes, but carrying their weapons and radios. They'll be on the lookout for a suspect in the Sabin murders. Make sure they get the message straight."

"10-4, Sheriff."

"We may get lucky tonight." Turning to Brenda, Stone added, "Right now we need to go see Angela Sabin."

27

Angela Sabin was sitting at a picnic table under a canopy with her daughter and son-in-law when Brenda and Stone arrived at the city park. Before leaving the car, Stone spoke. "Mrs. Sabin balked when I invited her to my office. This is a good neutral place, I suppose."

"Why should she care where she meets you?"

"She's probably one of those who's spooked by law enforcement. A lot of people are nervous about going to a sheriff's office."

They left the car, walking through ankle-deep grass to where the three were waiting. Stone tipped his cap. "Good afternoon folks. I'm Sheriff Stone and this is Detective Tower."

Mrs. Sabin's faint smile acknowledged Brenda from their Tuesday morning meeting. "This is my daughter, Kathy Johnson, and her husband, Ron. They've been on the road all night."

"Pleased to meet you," Stone said. No one made a move to shake hands. Stone and Brenda remained standing.

"Sheriff, I want to know why my grandson is at Walla Walla General? He should have been taken to Saint Mary's."

The scowl on her face and the tone of her voice conveyed a deep annoyance. Stone took in a long breath. "When we found your grandson late yesterday, he was barely alive. The ambulance took him to General because it has the best Emergency Room and ICU."

"I told you I didn't want Tab taken to General."

"You may have told someone, Mrs. Sabin, but it wasn't me. You know, where an ambulance takes an injured person for treatment is not the sheriff's call."

Brenda felt the hot summer air thicken between the two of them. "Doctor Hastings told us a few hours ago that Tab is recovering well. He expects him to be moved out of the ICU tomorrow." Brenda turned to Mrs. Johnson. "Have you been to the hospital yet?"

"Yes, we saw Tab. I was told he will recover." Her voice trailed off and she slumped on the bench. Ron Johnson put his arm around his wife and drew her closer.

"Mrs. Sabin, the coroner has released your husband's body to your funeral director," Stone said.

"Yes, yes, I know," Angela answered impatiently. She ran her hand along the top of the table, raised it suddenly, and slapped the surface. "What's being done to catch my husband's killer, that's what I want to know?"

The furrows deepened in Stone's forehead. "My deputies are combing the north end of the county, talking with people and gathering evidence. We're pursuing a suspect we believe killed the two women."

"I don't want to hear a damn thing about any women!" Mrs. Sabin screeched. "I want to know when you're going to arrest the man who murdered my husband!"

Searching for something to say that could calm her, Stone responded, "Tab may have been an eyewitness to your husband's murder."

"So, you're just waiting around to talk with him, I suppose?"

Kathy Johnson placed her hand on her mother's arm. "They found my son, mother. I think they're doing what they can to find Father's killer."

"Looks to me like you need some help, Sheriff," Mrs. Sabin went on. "Your people aren't homicide experts, are they?"

Stone's patience had worn thin. He glared at this presumptuous woman. *My men and I are working hard to solve these murders, and this woman is treating us like we're the enemy.* "I worked homicide for years in St. Louis. Ms. Tower is an experienced detective who has solved numerous homicides in Portland. We're competent investigators. My entire department is working this case."

"Then why don't I have some answers?" Angela Sabin shouted back, despair spreading across her face. "I want my husband's killer found."

Stone sucked air in between his teeth. "So do we ma'am, but evidence related to your husband's death is close to nonexistent." He counted on his fingers as he held her gaze. "One, we have no witnesses; two, we have no weapon; three, no fingerprints; four, no micro-fibers. We have a bullet taken from his body, and that's about it."

"Sheriff, was Art's murder related in any way to the deaths of the two women and to my son's shooting?" Ron Johnson asked.

Stone cleared his throat and turned to Johnson. "At first, we thought the murders were related because they took place at the farm on the same day. Now, we're not so sure. My men found core drillings in the shop yesterday that were taken on the property. We learned today Mr. Sabin intended to explore for uranium ore." Stone turned to Mrs. Sabin. "Did your husband say anything to you about mining on your land?"

"No, he did not."

"Someone could have found out your husband intended to do business with a mining firm. That may have led to his death."

"That's preposterous! Art was a farmer."

"Did your husband say anything to you about selling or leasing some of your land?"

"Never."

"We're trying to find out if the tests on the core samples have been completed. We'll know the results before too long."

"Sheriff, I want you to keep me informed of your progress. Please." Mrs. Sabin spoke more softly now.

"We certainly will, ma'am. One last question: Is Everett Schuster the family attorney?"

"Yes, he is."

Stone tipped his cap. "If there is nothing else, we'll be on our way." Stone and Brenda turned and walked back across the grass to the Expedition. Once they were out of earshot, Stone exhaled hard. "Wasn't that a bowl of cherries?"

"Lin, you were dealing with an angry, frightened, woman. Her life has been torn apart. Don't take it to heart."

"I wanted you along. When Mrs. Sabin refused to meet in

my office, I could tell she wanted a bite out of my hiney."

Brenda slowed her pace and looked behind Stone. "Well, your hiney looks fine to me," she reported, grinning.

Stone slowed and quickly peeked behind Brenda. "Your hiney looks fine to me, too."

They laughed, and Stone blushed a little at this new intimacy between them. He realized he liked it and even felt comfortable with this woman.

"Speaking of a bite," Brenda said, "it's after 2:30, and I'm starved."

"The Wagon Wheel Café here in Dayton has great cheese burgers and potato salad."

"That'll work."

"By the way, do you want to work tonight?"

"Sure, I'm game."

"Good, I'll include you in the plan."

Following lunch in Dayton, Stone dropped Brenda back at the B&B. She could use a little rest before the evening assignment. "No need to pick me up, Lin, I'll walk to the substation. It's not far from here."

Stone drove to the substation and sank into a chair in the mayor's office. He needed time alone to get his head around the case and to formulate a surveillance plan for the evening. When he finished with his case facts list, he jotted down another list: questions he needed the answers to. One thing he was certain of— Huber's was the only café in Elam's Crossing. His gut instinct told him the suspect would return there for supper, and that's where he would be waiting for him.

28

Field dust and wheat chaff covered Joey Valentine's once-white tee shirt and no-name baseball cap. Already dog-tired on his second day of harvest, he still had two hours before quitting time. Pulling away from the eighteen-wheeler at the edge of the field where he had unloaded, he traveled back along the gravel road for a quarter mile before turning his tractor and bank-out wagon into the field and up the hillside to take on another load from the combine.

Valentine spied Mendoza's pickup off to the side of the road facing his direction. His eyes caught Mendoza's movements as the large man stepped out of his pickup and leaned against it, arms folded across his chest, waiting for the tractor's arrival. Valentine's first instinct, to ignore Mendoza and drive on, would mean trouble for certain. He stopped his tractor in front of the pickup. Mendoza hopped up on the step and grabbed the steering wheel.

Valentine took a deep breath. "Carlos, what are you doing out here?"

"I'm keeping my eye on you, Joey boy," Mendoza sneered.

"Eye on me? Why?"

"To make sure you don't turn chicken shit on me." Mendoza pulled the blade from its sheath and stuck the sharp point to the side of Valentine's neck.

Valentine flinched, but he breathed slowly, in and out, saying nothing.

"I won't stand for no double-cross from you, Joey boy. Know what I mean?"

"Yeah sure, I know what you mean."

Mendoza twisted his menacing face and growled, "You stay cool now, you hear me, butt- face?"

Valentine felt the point of the blade push harder against his neck, and he struggled to remain motionless. "Carlos, why are you threatening me like this? I took the oath didn't I, and I'm here, aren't I?" Scared spitless, Valentine realized Mendoza had been stalking him, threatening him now with a knife. He slowly raised his hand and pushed Mendoza's knife arm away from his neck.

"Don't turn chicken shit on me, or you'll be sorry, you little prick."

Valentine removed his cap and slapped it on his knee. Dust and wheat chaff fell about. He held the man's stare, but anything more could have ignited Mendoza.

"I'll be watching you, *gilipollas.*"

"I gotta be going, Carlos, I can't be late at the combine." Valentine repositioned his cap on his head.

"Don't forget what I told you, Joey boy." Mendoza snorted as he spit on Joey's boot. He returned his blade to its sheath and lowered himself to the ground.

Valentine knew too well what Mendoza was capable of doing. He'd witnessed the maniac's ruthless slaughter of the Mexican woman at the farmhouse, and later he'd heard from Ramiro how Mendoza shot the gringo kid. Mendoza could snap even now and tear out after him—for no reason. Valentine had suggested to Sanchez and Gear they might have to kill Mendoza. He'd tell them how Mendoza threatened him and push the idea of killing this crazy one in self-defense.

His hands shook on the steering wheel and a vein in his neck throbbed. His throat made a dry, clicking noise when he tried to swallow. Valentine guided his tractor and wagon up the incline in the direction of the combine. He'd called Mendoza a crazy son-of-a-bitch to his face the previous night. He wished now he hadn't said that, even though he knew it was true.

29

Brenda met with Sheriff Stone and several of his deputies at six o'clock Wednesday evening when Stone laid out his plan. "We're on the lookout for the man who I believe committed the Sabin murders. An eyewitness saw the suspect last night down by the Snake River, and later Mrs. Townsend reported him in Huber's Café. They describe him as a husky Mexican with a long ponytail. He carries a large blade on his belt and drives a gray Ford pickup with a shell on the back."

"How is he linked to the Sabin murders, Sheriff?" Carver asked.

"The coroner believes the killer used a bayonet-like blade on Christina Lopez. We believe Calli Mendez stabbed her attacker. We have the knife she used. The blood in the bathroom upstairs is his. Melba Townsend reported the suspect had a bloodstain on his shirt."

"Good evidence," Carver concluded, as he leaned back in his chair.

Stone cleared his throat and glanced around the room at the members of his team. "Here's the game plan. We'll take up positions here in town where we can spot the suspect if he comes in tonight. I want Ned to stay with his car in case we get into a chase. I'll stay with the command center. If you spot the suspect, radio me with his location. He'll be armed and dangerous. *Do not* confront him alone. Any questions about that?"

"Where do you want us stationed?" Hardesty asked.

"I have a hunch he'll be back here tonight for supper. He'll go to Huber's. There, he'll be restricted in his movements. We can take him down without too much trouble: no footrace, no car chase, and no gunplay."

"Only one door in and out of there, except through the kitchen," Carver said.

"That's correct." Stone nodded. "Hardesty, I want you and Detective Tower in the café. The two of you have a long and enjoyable meal together."

"We'll be undercover, like in the movies," Hardesty cracked.

"You'll be ready to assist in the man's arrest—like in the movies," Stone added, throwing Hardesty a stern glance.

Hardesty wondered why Stone finally decided to partner him with the doll face from the city. He'd had a fantasy about making time with Brenda. This could be his opening, he thought. He'd thank Stone later.

"Some of you will be on foot tonight," Stone explained. "Talbot, you take North Main. Weber, you take the south end of Main. Barber, you hang out on First and McNeil. Ned, I want you to patrol Tucanon and Front Streets in the cruiser. I'm going to be tucked back in the alley off Baxter. Get the jeeps out of sight. Hold your positions till ten o'clock."

"What if he comes into town but doesn't go to Huber's?" Weber asked.

"Radio the command center as soon as you spot him. Ned and I may have to chase him down. Ned, be alert for a message from me."

"Okay, Sheriff."

"We've got faster vehicles. If he turns rabbit, we'll run him down—ram him if we have to. We can't let him slip away."

"What if he's on foot, Sheriff?" Talbot asked.

"Again, radio the command center. I don't want anyone playing Lone Ranger on the street with this guy. We've got the manpower. We'll take him down together."

Everyone on the team was in position by 6:30. More than two hours passed without a sign of their suspect. About 8:50, Weber spotted the gray pickup as it passed him heading north on Main Street. He radioed Stone, who then alerted Talbot at the other end of the street. Weber and Talbot ran the short distance to Huber's, converging on the pickup within moments of the driver entering the café.

Stone pulled up at almost the same time, wedging in the suspect's pickup with his Expedition. He got out and signaled to Weber. "Cover the kitchen around the corner. Talbot, you cover the front." Stone followed the walkway to the entrance and peered in through the bottom corner of the nearest window. His plants were the only two customers in the place.

Hardesty and Brenda watched the suspect as he approached the table in the corner near them and took a seat. The waitress sauntered up with a menu. Oblivious to her presence in the room, Stone burst through the entrance with his weapon drawn.

"Stay where you are, mister," he shouted.

The man spun out of his chair in a flash and grabbed the waitress around the neck with his right arm. His left hand pressed a large blade against her throat. She screamed and went limp.

"Drop your gun, lawman, and move aside, or this one gets it," the man yelled. He struggled toward the door, half dragging the waitress with him.

"Okay, take it easy. I'm putting down my weapon." Stone laid his revolver on the floor, put his hands up to show his palms, and stepped back from the exit. The cook stuck his head out the kitchen door but quickly retreated.

Back in her booth, Brenda carefully and silently un-holstered the baby Glock from her right ankle, rose, and took quick aim. Two shots rang out. The suspect winced and cried out, letting go of the waitress. He slumped to the floor, clenching his right leg and groaning with pain. Weber and Talbot heard the shots and rushed in, guns drawn.

Stone pounced on the man while Hardesty cuffed him. The waitress screamed and staggered back into the kitchen. The suspect blurted out a string of profanity in Spanish as Talbot righted an overturned chair. Hardesty and Stone lifted the man onto the seat with considerable difficulty. During the movement, Brenda caught a glimpse of his belly from the side, plastered with a large bandage.

Stone picked up the knife, also taking the man's wallet and his truck keys.

"What's your name, mister?" Stone asked

"Fuck you!"

Teeth clenched and jaw set, Stone repeated, "I asked you

your name, wise guy,"

"You go to hell."

"You smartass!" Stone raised a fist but kept it cocked in the air between them.

"Get screwed, pig."

Hardesty interrupted. "Let me take this joker to lockup. We can transport him to the Dayton hospital tomorrow sometime."

It didn't matter that there was no lockup in Elam's Crossing; Hardesty's suggestion brought the man around.

"Carlos Mendoza."

Brenda stepped forward, hands on her hips, and scowled down at him. "Carlos Mendoza," she repeated in a disgusted tone, her upper lip curled and eyes shooting sparks. Thinking about the people Mendoza might have killed and how he threatened to kill the waitress moments earlier, she hissed, "You bastard. I ought to kick your sorry ass around the block for what you've done."

"Who's this gringa bitch?" Mendoza snapped.

"Just the woman who put you on the floor, sucker."

"Get her away from me!"

The cook, along with the waitress, came forward with large towels and a pair of scissors. He cut the injured man's jeans away, wrapped the two wounds on his right leg with the towels, and tied them off with smaller dishtowels. "They appear to be flesh wounds," the former Vietnam medic told Stone. He turned to Brenda. "You're quite a shot, ma'am."

She raised her leg onto a chair and holstered her weapon. "Thanks."

"Sam, you and John get this man to the hospital," Stone said.

With Weber's help, Hardesty and Talbot loaded Mendoza into the back of the Jeep Liberty and sped away.

"Who fired the shots?" Barber yelled, pushing through the front door and breathing hard following his run from McNeill Street.

Before Stone could answer, the waitress pointed to Brenda. "She shot that fool. Someone had to, or he would've killed me."

"She's right," Stone said, giving Brenda the once-over.

"Detective Tower shot his leg out from under him."

"He'll bleed some, and he'll be in pain all right, but he'll stand trial," Brenda said.

Barber slapped his thigh. "Detective, I figured you for window dressing here tonight. Man, did I get that wrong!"

Brenda grinned at him.

"I knew you'd be some help, Detective, but I didn't count on you stopping the guy," Stone added.

"Protect and serve," Brenda answered, smiling widely.

"I got that." Stone nodded as he flipped open his cell. "Ned, we've got our man suit-cased."

"What's his name, Sheriff?"

"Carlos Mendoza. He's hospital bound."

"Hospital, huh? Break his arm, did you?"

"No. Detective Tower shot him."

"Better sign her up, Sheriff. Look, I'm going on home if we're finished here."

"Go home, Ned, and thanks. We've had an exceptional night."

Stone pocketed his phone and turned to Weber. "Chet, you and Don take charge of the prisoner tonight."

"I saw that coming," Barber confessed.

Stone cracked a smile. "Work out a schedule between the two of you. I'll arrange for your reliefs in the morning. Both of you take tomorrow off as a recovery day."

"Good trade, Sheriff," Weber commented over his shoulder, as the two men left the café for a night of hospital guard duty.

Stone adjusted his cap and looked over at Townsend. "I apologize for the roughhousing here tonight. I could see through the window that Detective Tower and Deputy Hardesty were your only dinner guests. I figured we could corner the guy in here and arrest him without any fuss."

"Things don't always go as planned," Townsend said.

Noticing the nametag on the waitress's blouse, Stone asked, "Are you hurt, Carline?"

The young, slender brunette shook her head. "I'm okay,

now."

"I'm sorry for what happened to you." Stone turned again to Townsend. "We knew Mendoza had been in here last night. I figured he might show up again. I hoped we could take him without gunplay. Once he grabbed Carline, someone had to stop him."

"I understand, Sheriff. We're glad that one's off our streets."

Stone looked at his watch and then over at Brenda. "It's been a long day. Want a lift to your B&B?"

"That'd be nice."

Stone had a word with Barber before he and Brenda walked out into the night air. Stopping at Mendoza's pickup, he bent down with his flashlight and examined the left front tire. "My guess is Rusty's casting will be a match." He checked to make sure the doors were locked. "I'll have a car hauler here in the morning to pick up this rig."

30

Brenda and Stone walked to the corner past the post office and entered the alley behind the old boarded-up drugstore. Moonlight played across the brick walls and illuminated their way. Stone opened his door, removed his gun belt, and laid it on the floor in front of the driver's seat. They both climbed into the Expedition. While starting the engine, he glanced over at Brenda. She stared back at him with searching eyes, teeth clenched on her lower lip. He'd never seen this look on her before. Brenda's hand slid across the seat between them and lightly touched his right forearm. Despite the warm summer night, Stone shivered.

"Lin, I don't want you to take me home yet."

He hesitated, afraid he'd misinterpreted her words. After all, it was past 10:00 p.m. They'd had a long day, and he still faced twenty miles of winding road before he could shed his uniform and lay his head down.

"Where would you like me to take you, if not back to your bed and breakfast?"

"Anywhere with you—it doesn't matter. I just don't want be alone now." She sat quietly listening to the sound of the engine, waiting for his answer, her fingers still resting lightly on his arm.

"It's quiet and peaceful down by the Snake River," Stone finally said.

"Let's go there."

Winding through the north end of town, Stone nosed the car onto the highway. Brenda removed the baseball cap and barrettes holding her hair and let it tumble onto her shoulders. She tossed her head from side to side, running her fingers through the thick, dark strands.

"Turn the air down, would you?" Brenda opened the passenger window and breathed in fresh, cool air. The breeze blew across the side of her face, teasing her hair, which caught Stone's eye. Her silhouette held his gaze for a long moment, and he felt the strain of the day begin to dissipate.

The copper-streaked sky now surrendered to various hues of dark gray and charcoal black. A three-quarter moon streamed its brightness onto the hillside, on Brenda's side of the car, in stark contrast to the shadowy blackness on Stone's side. He drove through the winding ravine, leaving the highway at the entrance to the picnic grounds. Pulling into the parking area, he drove as close to the river as he could and parked.

Turning to her, he asked, "Is this okay?"

"It's perfect, Lin."

They were alone, not another car in sight. Brenda opened her door and stepped silently from the vehicle, walking through the tall grass toward a concrete picnic table. Climbing up, she perched on the top and placed her feet on the bench below. Stone sat next to her.

In the distance they heard the warning of a train whistle. The growl of an approaching marine diesel caught Stone's ear. "Keep your eyes on the water. I think there's a barge coming."

The moon's reflection on the water confirmed Stone's assumption. They watched the barge pass and listened to the water gently lap the shoreline in its wake.

"Hear the crickets?" Stone asked

Brenda nodded. "I do. It's so peaceful down here," Brenda said.

"I'm amazed how you took Mendoza down tonight."

"Thanks for the compliment."

"I'm certain Hardesty would have handled it differently."

"How so?"

"Mendoza would be lying in the morgue."

"I had the advantage in there. Mendoza wasn't expecting a dinner guest to be carrying."

She slipped her arm under Stone's and reached for his hand "I don't want to talk about work, Lin. Will you tell me more about yourself?"

He cleared his throat and swallowed hard. "All right, I'll tell you more if you'll tell me more about you."

Brenda snuggled the side of her face against his shoulder. Stone fingered his chin with his free hand, wondering what he should tell her; what would she want to know about him? "Let's see. I'm buying a home on the west side of Dayton," he said finally. "My place needs painting pretty bad on the inside, and I can't seem to find the time. I drive a Ford Taurus. I'm in the middle of restoring a '68 Ford pickup."

"One of my high school boyfriends drove a late sixties Ford pickup."

"Today, those models are very collectable. I do a little fishing on my days off. I hate yard work. It's good exercise though, and I need to keep the place presentable. Once in a while I'll drive to the Tri-Cities, or to Walla Walla, for a nice dinner and sometimes a movie."

"Do you date?" Brenda asked, hesitantly.

Stone threw his head back and laughed. It was the first time she'd heard him laugh out loud. "Am I being interrogated here, Ms. Prosecutor?" He leaned closer, looking for an answer in her eyes. "I dated a woman in Dayton for a few months. We were getting along great, I thought, but then out of the blue she ran off to Alaska with a bush pilot."

"She flew away, so to speak. Then what?"

"Word got around I was available. You wouldn't believe some of the predicaments I got myself into."

"Pretty rough, huh?"

Brenda felt his muscles tense against her arm. "You can say that again. Women called the office wanting me to retrieve their cat from a neighbor's tree or have a man-to-man with their teenage son."

"That's it, nothing more?"

"One night a woman called my cell, claimed someone was trying to break in. She met me at the door, cool as a cucumber, in only her bra and panties."

Brenda snickered. "A little eager, was she?"

"I beat it out of there, fast. It's too easy to get a reputation in a small town, so I stopped dating local women."

"So, the women you date now are in the Tri-Cities, I suppose."

"Some fine single women there, for sure. To be honest,

though, I haven't run across one yet who keeps me awake at night." He shifted his position on the table. "Okay, your turn. Tell me something about yourself."

"I live in Lake Oswego, south of Portland. I drive a Nissan Maxima coupe. The Oregon beaches are where I like to relax, or on the Columbia River—to windsurf. I've climbed most of the way up Mt. Hood, and all the way to the top of Mt. Adams. I play tennis, and I like to watch a good football game on TV."

"Wow! You're an active woman."

"I suppose. I also love to shop. Both my sisters have kids, and I'm forever buying them things for their birthdays and for Christmas. I'm told I'm a decent cook. I hate housework with a passion, but I hate filth and clutter more, so I do it."

Stone shuffled his feet back and forth on the concrete bench. "I'll bet Steve had some strong competition for your companionship."

Brenda's heart beat a little faster. "Sure, I have some single men friends. I don't have a lover, if that's what you're hinting at." She paused to listen for a response, but nothing came. "The men I'm around these days aren't the kinds who keep me awake at night, either."

"Been in love though, I'll bet."

"I was in love once with a Delta pilot—not too long ago, either. He asked me to move in with him, and I came close to doing so."

"What stopped you?"

"I found out he was married."

"Ouch!"

"He was leading a double life. Since then, I haven't allowed myself to get emotionally close to another man."

Stone let go of Brenda's hand and put his arm around her shoulders, drawing her closer. "I know how it feels to be hurt by someone you love. When Lena left me in St. Louis, I almost killed myself with booze and self-pity. You're a good woman, Brenda. I'm going to miss you when you leave." He kissed her softly on the cheek.

"I wondered if there was more you wanted to say to me last

night when you called."

Stone sat up straight and drew in a deep breath. "There was more, Brenda. I wanted to tell you how lovely I think you are, and how I feel when you're with me." He ran his fingers through her hair, placed a lock behind her ear. He gently turned her face toward his and kissed her on the lips.

They ended the kiss and watched the Snake River move, slowly and quietly, moonlight shimmering on the surface. Not far away a coyote howled. Brenda and Stone stepped down from the table and faced each other, a slight breeze ruffling their hair. Stone took her in his arms, pressing her close to him. Their eyes met and then closed as he kissed her, long and deep. Brenda kissed him back, and he felt a stirring deep inside. "I've wanted to kiss you. I've thought about it ever since dinner Monday," he whispered.

He touched her face with his fingertips and held her close at the waist with his other arm. It had been a long time since he'd felt the warmth of a shapely woman's body close to him.

Brenda breathed in Stone's earthy scent. Brushing her hand across his cheek, she kissed him again.

"If I could, I'd take a few days off. We'd go up into the Blue Mountains and hide out."

"Maybe sometime we should do that," she answered, slipping her arm under his.

Stone hoped this meant what he wanted it to mean. They walked back to the car, arm-in-arm.

Stone could think of nothing but his time with Brenda during their drive back to Elam's Crossing. She seemed eager to take their short friendship to another level; she had kissed him back, held him close. He had wanted more of her, but it wasn't the time or the place. Besides, I'm a small-time sheriff in a backwater county, far from the glitter and excitement of the big city, Stone thought. Brenda is a professional woman: well educated, highly skilled, and on a good career track. *What would she want with a man like me?*

Back at the bed and breakfast, he walked her to the steps, holding her hand.

"See you tomorrow, Brenda," he said, gently touching her

cheek before returning to the car.

Brenda sat on the front porch thinking about her day. It had been a long and eventful one, filled with meetings, travel, more meetings, and then the drama—stopping Carlos Mendoza. She remembered the tantrum she threw Monday in front of Stone at the farmhouse and the vow she made to catch the killer. Surprisingly, she had already realized that promise. And then her day had ended in the arms of the county sheriff. Lin might be afraid of a lasting relationship, she thought. *Perhaps he's worried he might start something with me he can't finish?* She didn't want him to humor her, knowing she'd be gone in a few days. *Whatever the future holds, tonight I felt genuinely cared for.* Brenda entered Aunt Annie's and climbed the stairs to her room, sure that spending the previous hour alone with Stone had been good for her—and hopefully good for him.

31

While Sheriff Stone scratched out assignments Thursday morning for his deputies, eighty miles northeast of Dayton a weathered-looking man with shaggy gray hair and pale blue-gray eyes padded along US 95 heading north toward Coeur d'Alene. An old-fashioned canvas backpack hung from Brad Summers' stooped shoulders, along with a sleeping bag that formed an inverted "U" over the pack. The bag had served him well through the many nights he'd already been on the road, as had his old winter coat.

Summers knew driving his Buick on this trip was out of the question. Fear of having cataracts removed had not made him delay the eye surgery, but his reluctance to shell out the money had. Besides, hadn't his doctor advised him to lose thirty pounds, and what better way for the sixty-eight-year-old widower to shed weight? Although Summers could easily log sixteen to twenty miles a day, he felt no urge to be in any particular place at any given time—not anymore.

Margaret Giles has lived alone since losing her husband to prostate cancer in April. When she heard her brother, Bradley, was about to launch an odyssey trek across northern Idaho, she insisted he come visit her. Summers figured he'd be on his sister's front step sometime Sunday evening.

After nearly a month hiking through northern Idaho, Summers knew too well the pedestrian hazards associated with trekking the highways. Because of their awe-inspiring size and their bent-for-hell speed, logging trucks presented the most dangerous hazard for a man on foot. When Summers heard one coming, he headed for the shoulder and waited for the big rig to pass by. But eighteen-wheelers were not his only concern. The previous evening, two wild dogs followed him unseen into a rest stop. At the last minute he heard noises behind him, and turning, he spotted the large mongrels running hard toward him, growling, the hair on the backs of their necks bristling. Summers bolted for the nearest port-a-potty, jumped in, and pushed the door shut against their noses. He guessed the smell of the hard salami in his backpack had attracted the hungry pursuers.

The desperate animals hurled themselves against the door, rocking the whole structure. It seemed to Summers as though it went on for hours. Finally, he heard the crack of a gunshot fill the air along with quickly fading yelps.

"Hey buddy, you can come out now," a gruff voice had shouted out to him.

Summers cautiously inched out of his humble sanctuary to meet face-on with a trucker in a black vest, jeans, and field boots, gripping a large revolver at his side. "Thanks for running off those dogs, mister. But how'd you know someone was in there?"

The man chuckled. "They were fooling around so close to the door. And that's not a place dogs normally would be crowded up to." The trucker raised his gun hand. "I squeezed off a round from this bear gun and they skedaddled. Hey, are you afoot?"

"Sure am. I'm kind of like old Willy Nelson, you know, 'on the road again.'"

"I gotta be in Spokane tonight. You want a lift?"

"No, I'll stay with these." Summers raised a leg and hit his walking shoe with his hand.

"Thanks just the same."

"You sure?"

"Yeah, I think those dogs are gone for good."

~

By 9:30 Thursday morning, Summers had shrugged out of his long-sleeved shirt. He wore a bright blue tee, dungarees, and well-worn New Balance walking shoes. The sky overhead showed clear, and the scent of pine perfumed the air. Sounds of an occasional great horned owl hooted from inside the forest, reminding him he was never completely alone. Rapidly moving water flowed over the rocks in the nearby stream, playing a tune reminiscent of one he remembered from his boyhood days alongside the west fork of the Priest River.

Summers had just passed Moscow, Idaho, a place he

remembered with great fondness. It was where he'd studied and met Helen, the woman he'd loved for nearly fifty years. Remembrances of her drifted in and out of his mind. Losing her had caused him terrible pain, plaguing him now for months. The director at the state mental institution assured him his wife had been a model patient. Why, then, was her frail body discovered hanging from a third-story hallway window? What drove her to take her own life? Summers strained for an answer that wouldn't come.

As he tramped along the side of the highway, he fell to daydreaming about his early days and his life with Helen. Surprising as it had been to young Summers, he won the senior science project contest at his high school in 1954. At the state competition in Boise the next year, he was named Idaho's most promising future scientist. Also surprising was how he had attracted Helen's attention while in their junior year at the University of Idaho. They met at a homecoming bonfire rally sponsored by her sorority. Back then, he would have gladly staked silver dollars on her being the prettiest girl on campus.

The daughter of Montana cattle money, Helen Jacobsen had enrolled at the university in the footsteps of her older sister. In addition to earning her degree in English Literature-Education, Helen longed to fall in love with the man of her dreams, marry, and move as far away as possible from the dirty cattle ranch and the cold winters near Missoula. In keeping with Brad's promise to Helen, they married in June, 1959, following their graduations.

A logging truck roared by, blasting its air horn. Summers jumped off the road. The noise drove up his adrenalin, and he felt his heart rate quicken. "Damn that was close! I've got to pay better attention."

32

Determined to interrogate Carlos Mendoza, Stone had arranged for Brenda to work with Deputy Carver Thursday morning. They were to meet with a geologist friend of Carver's to learn something about uranium mining that might be helpful to the case. Carver told Brenda to expect him around 9:30, but it was still early, and he was far from ready to leave his bed.

Evelyn Carver ran the nail of her index finger along her husband's chin-line—her customary green light for intimacy. "Stay with me for a while longer," she whispered next to his ear. Pleased to comply with Evelyn's invitation, Carver stayed put.

He had travelled all the way to Colfax to find Evelyn Lund, the daughter of one of Whitman County's oldest and most prominent pioneer families. The tall Scandinavian blonde was well educated, talented, and Hollywood beautiful. Her parents never understood how she ended up in Elam's Crossing, married to a deputy sheriff. To Ned, Evelyn was more woman than he ever dreamed of having. She had given him two beautiful children and kept their home as spotless as a realtor's open house—every day. And he liked the fact she didn't run to Spokane or to the Tri-Cities to spend money on a regular basis, the way some women did.

Ned took full advantage of this private time with Evelyn while the kids watched reruns of Sesame Street. One of the things he treasured most about her was her lovemaking. She could put a grin on his face that would embarrass a Baptist preacher. The neighbor kids in the yard next door heard Carver singing in the shower and later saw him skip along the walkway to his cruiser.

People in Elam's Crossing admired Ned Carver for his easy manner with their children. Far more teen drivers than the law allowed came home with a warning ticket rather than the more serious speeding ticket they deserved. He routinely picked up younger kids who wandered too far from home and chauffeured them back to their parents. Some kids, it was said, were more familiar with the back seat of his cruiser than they were with the back seat of their family sedan. Early in his career, Carver had pulled a sixteen-year-old girl from a burning pickup that rolled on its side and caught on fire after clipping a county dump truck. And townspeople still talked about his rescue of little Jimmy Short from the Tucanon River when an eroded bank gave way, dumping the four-year-old into the spring floodwaters. Jimmy's grandfather sent Carver a check for two thousand dollars for saving the boy's life. The check found its way into the bank account of the local chapter of St. Vincent de Paul.

~

Brenda had time to kill before meeting Carver and decided to go for a walk along Main Street. A bright sun, almost no breeze, and few clouds overhead promised a warm day. She passed by hollyhocks in full bloom across the street from her bed and breakfast. Sunflowers in a side yard had stretched to their full height. Brenda could make out seeds in the pancake-sized flowers, but they had not yet filled out. A gray and white cat scampered across her path, followed by a shorthaired terrier in hot pursuit. The air carried the leftover scent of a skunk. From a distance, she spotted a car hauler loading Mendoza's pickup. Drawing closer, she noticed several gawking people on the street.

"What's so interesting?" she asked a plump, older man in a straw hat, his hands clutching the bib of his overalls.

He glanced at her and grinned. "Mrs. Townsend was telling us about the shooting in her place last night. Some Mexican grabbed a waitress at knife point and got himself shot up." He pointed to the car hauler. "When this rig pulled up to haul away the man's pickup, we naturally wandered out to watch. The driver just now removed a gun from inside the pickup."

"Thanks," Brenda called over her shoulder. She hurried to where the driver stood, strapping down his haul. He reminded Brenda of a one-time heavyweight boxer who'd stayed in the ring too long a few too many times. "Sir, you'll make sure the gun gets to the sheriff's office, won't you?"

He eyeballed her while still holding tight to the tie-down. "This ain't my first rodeo, lady. What business is it of yours, anyhow?"

"I'm working on a murder case with Sheriff Stone. I'd like to see the gun, if you don't mind?"

The driver scowled at her and muttered something under his breath. "Got some identification?" he asked.

Brenda showed him her badge. He grunted and secured his tie-down. She followed him to his cab where he lifted the weapon off the seat with a small screwdriver he carefully placed in the barrel. She examined the piece as he held it out away from her face.

"A .22, just what I expected. Thanks." She smiled.

The driver scowled at her and returned the pistol to the seat of his cab. Brenda walked away, intending to cross the street and continue her stroll. A few bystanders crowded around her, curious about her exchange with the driver,

"You're a stranger here, aren't you miss?" a man asked.

"Yes, I'm from Portland. I'm helping the sheriff with the Sabin murder case."

"What can you tell us about Art Sabin's grandson?" a woman asked.

"I don't mind telling you anything about the case that Sheriff Stone has previously released to the press. He and I located Tab Johnson late Tuesday afternoon in an abandoned root cellar on the Sabin farm. He is recovering at Walla Walla General."

"The boy must have been injured," the woman said.

"He'd been shot."

"It must have been you who stopped that Mexican here last night." the woman said. "Melba told us the guy was getting away with her waitress when a female detective shot him."

Brenda nodded. A grin appeared at one corner of her mouth.

"Is he the murderer?"

"Sheriff Stone is interrogating the man this morning."

"Detective," a man standing beside her asked, "was Art Sabin's no-account son involved in his death?"

Brenda glared at the man and walked away without a word.

Business seemed brisk at Varner's tackle shop judging by the number of vehicles parked out front. Stone had told Brenda that anglers came to fish this portion of the Snake River from spring until fall, hoping to reel in perch, walleye, Chinook, catfish, and more. Several men were standing around the bed of a knobby-tired Dodge 4 X 4, looking inside. Brenda's curiosity wouldn't let her pass without taking a peek. She moved close enough to glance into the bed and immediately jumped back, nearly losing her balance. It took her a moment to catch her breath. She stayed quiet, too embarrassed to reveal ignorance about what she'd just seen.

"That thing must be nine feet long," she heard a man say.

Another man added, "In Great-Granddad's day, they used to pull them out of the Clearwater with a team of horses."

"I see you're still in town," Brenda heard a voice exclaim from across the truck bed. It was Art Sabin's friend, Squeaky—the man she'd met at Varner's Monday afternoon.

"Guess your story on Art Sabin has taken quite a turn since we last talked?"

Brenda walked around to where he stood and quietly asked, "Can I speak with you privately, Squeaky?"

"Sure, why not. Let's grab that bench." The two walked to the canopy overhanging Varner's and sat down.

"What's that monstrous-looking thing in the pickup?" she asked, with a look of bewilderment on her face.

Squeaky laughed. "It's a sturgeon—isn't it something?"

"Something is right. It nearly scared the wits out of me! Squeaky, I'm a little embarrassed about Monday. I knew Art Sabin had been killed when we talked, because I discovered his body. I'm a detective with the Portland Police Department. I was trying to gather information that might help the sheriff."

"Aw shucks, I didn't mind talkin' to you about Art. I'd like nothin' better now than for you and the sheriff to catch his murderer."

"Do you have any idea who might have wanted to kill your friend?"

Squeaky removed his straw hat and scratched his head. "No, I can't think of no one who hated him that bad."

"What if I told you he was planning to lease some of his

land to a uranium mining company?"

"That'd stir up a hornet's nest here, for sure. I can't believe he'd do somethin' like that."

"Why do you say that?"

"This ain't mining country, Detective—this is wheat country—some of the best. Whitman County, northeast of here, produces more wheat than any other county in the U.S. Most people around here would fight a mining company tryin' to come in here, especially a uranium mine."

"Wouldn't it bring jobs and tax revenues for the county—for Elam's Crossing?"

"Agreed, and there was a time when people here needed somethin' like that to help the economy, to keep 'em here. People are here today because they're suited to the way things are. We're country folk, but we ain't stupid. All the health risks and potential damage to the ecology make that kind of mining pretty unacceptable."

"Let me ask the question in a different way. Who would want to put a stop to uranium mining bad enough to kill your friend?"

"Are you thinking someone acted alone?"

"We don't know what to think at this point," Brenda said.

"It might have been a conspiracy, you know. Could be some fellers knew what Art was up to and put a contract out on him. It might have been a professional job, you know."

Brenda wrote the sheriff's name and cell number on a card and handed it to Squeaky. "If something comes to mind, be sure to call that number. I've got to catch my ride in a few minutes."

"Okay, I'll get in touch. Take care."

"You take care as well."

33

Brenda waited at Aunt Annie's for Carver's arrival. When he pulled in the side yard, she crossed the lawn and slid into the cruiser beside him.

"You must have had quite a night," Carver said as he glanced over at her.

Almost certain Carver was referring to Mendoza's apprehension and not to her private time with Stone, she said, "It wasn't much, Ned."

"I know better. Hardesty called me with the details. Sheriff must have been impressed."

"He was happy that I didn't kill his suspect."

Carver arched his neck and peered through the windshield into the sky. "Weatherman says it will be a warm one today. Farmers love this country. Rain comes in the spring when the wheat needs it. Summers are very warm and dry—what the wheat needs."

"Ned, it's too warm in here," Brenda noted.

Carver adjusted the air conditioning. "Think this Mendoza is our killer?"

"I believe he's responsible for the house murders, at least."

"Quite a buzz among some deputies yesterday about Art Sabin's mining scheme. I told the sheriff about a geologist friend I know. He wants the two of us meet with him this morning."

"That should be interesting."

"Chauncey West was an engineer on the Little Goose Dam—also a good friend of my dad's back in the day. It's a ways out to his place. You'll see some country."

"That's good, Ned. I'm a country girl."

Carver drove for twenty minutes through the coves and ravines along narrow paved roads leading in a westerly direction out of Elam's Crossing. The cruiser eventually left the asphalt, starting its climb up the south side of a long, low hill. To call the narrow lane to West's front door a road would be insulting to the other 850 miles of paved and graveled roads in the county. It was a rutty, dirt affair that looked more like a cannonball-torn lane in a Civil War battlefield than a road to anywhere. By the time they arrived, Carver was surprised he hadn't broken a shock.

West heard the car laboring up the incline and walked outside to greet his visitors. "It's good to see you, son. Are Evelyn and the little ones doing okay?" he inquired, as they exited the cruiser.

"They're all fine, my friend. She wanted you to have some of her famous brownies." Ned reached in the back seat and handed a plate to West.

West pealed back the tinfoil and popped a walnut-laden brownie into his mouth. "Man, this is good. I haven't had a treat like this in a spell. Be sure to thank her for me."

"I will, Chauncey. I want you to meet Detective Brenda Tower."

Brenda smiled and extended her hand.

"Pleased to meet you, Detective," West said, shaking her hand. "May I call you Brenda?"

"Yes, of course."

"Detective Tower is lending us a hand with the Sabin murder case."

"I knew Art Sabin some in the old days. What an awful tragedy." West made the sign of the cross in the air.

"We came to talk with you about something related to the case."

West gestured with a sweep of his hand. "Sure, let's go inside."

The house had been built in the side of the hill. The roof, back wall, and side walls were below ground level. Constructed of river rock and concrete, it was, West told them, believed to be one of the oldest inhabited houses in the county. Inside, cool air swept Brenda's face and arms.

"Take the rocker, Brenda. Ned and I will sit in these straight backs."

Brenda rocked slowly in an old grandma-sized rocker. While the men talked, her gaze wandered about the inside of the house. A Ben Franklin wood-burning stove squatted, idle, in the corner of the living area. Brenda thought the primitive blanket chest and the rocker looked old enough to have accompanied Narcissus Whitman, the first white woman to cross the country in a covered wagon, in 1836. The low, straight-back chairs had lost their finish long ago. West pumped water to an old wooden dry-sink in the house. From the healthy look of the geraniums she'd seen at the front door, Brenda guessed his dirty sink water ended up there. A blanket separated his bedroom in the back from the living area. An old yellow, set-back cupboard in the open kitchen area caught Brenda's eye, and a wind-up, Ansonia shelf clock on the bookcase across from her appeared to still keep good time. These furnishings would be perfect in a *Country Sampler* magazine, Brenda thought.

"Art Sabin may have been planning to put a mine on his property," Brenda heard Carver saying.

West, a wiry old timer who spent too much time in the sun, shook his near-bald head. "You're joshing me, right?"

"Nope. Core samples from his place were sent off for testing."

"This is serious."

"Yeah, it appears to be. Sabin told the drillers he hoped to find uranium. He intended to do a deal with a mining firm if the tests came back positive," Carver said.

West rubbed his peeling scalp with his right palm. "What a crazy thing, a uranium mine in Columbia County." He thought for a moment. "The demand for uranium oxide is strong right now—price is sky high. It's understandable why someone would want to get in the business. It's hard to imagine such a thing around here, though."

Brenda rocked gently back and forth in the old chair. "Maybe Sabin had a partner. Could be that partner got greedy and decided to cut him out."

"You said the mine would be on Sabin's property? Unless the partner has legal ownership to his land, taking Sabin's life wouldn't do him much good."

"If an heir were to inherit the farm, eliminating Sabin would be a more likely scenario," Brenda said.

"You're right, Detective. But you know, uranium mining is a heavily regulated industry. Chances for a successful startup are nearly as slim as teaching a goat to ride a bicycle."

Brenda threw her head back and laughed.

"Tell us what you know," Carver said.

"Open-pit mining and tunneling for uranium aren't used much anymore in this country. Today, uranium oxide is retrieved by what the industry calls *in-situ leaching*, or solution mining. Ore is recovered by flooding the area underground and pumping the solution to the surface. This is a safer process: much less surface disturbance, and there are no waste rock or mill tailings to deal with.

"Interesting. Go on," Carver urged.

"The federal government imposes strict regulations on all sites and installations where radionuclide materials are present. The mining company would be required to prepare a detailed environmental impact assessment and also produce an in-depth management plan. Both of these documents have to be preapproved by the Nuclear Regulatory Commission. Acquiring a radioactive materials license can be brutal—extremely time consuming and expensive."

"That kind of stuff is on the news from time to time," Carver said.

"Yup. Construction and operation of uranium processing sites are monitored by NRC inspectors, as are the nuclear-fired electrical generation plants. The Environmental Protection Agency also imposes clean air and clean water standards. The production costs are staggering. When the price for uranium oxide is low, say less than thirty dollars, production goes dead-cold."

"There would be plenty of opposition from the public, too, I bet." Carver said.

"Since the Three Mile Island accident in '79, the American public is sensitive about all things nuclear. The NRC would hold numerous public hearings before any decision was made to proceed."

"Look at all the trouble in recent years over the radioactivity found in the water at the Midnight Mine Site. And weren't there also heavy metals and acid found at that site?" Carver asked.

"And that place hasn't operated for twenty-five years. The Washington State Department of Health has been in a constant battle with the mine owners over site cleanup," West said.

"Sabin may have been killed to put a halt to his mining plans," Brenda said.

"More probable." West nodded.

Brenda stopped rocking. "Ready for a hardball question, Chauncey?"

"Fire away."

"With that motive in mind, can you think of someone who might have killed Art Sabin?"

"Detective, you're asking me to finger someone without any supporting evidence." West turned to Carver. "Ned, ask yourself, who stands to lose the most if a mining operation were to come to this end of the county?"

Brenda glanced over at her partner.

Carver cocked an eyebrow as he thought. "That would probably be Ken Wilber, the largest landowner up here."

"Next question is who's been the most vocal opponent of nuclear power?"

Again, Carver pondered this for a moment. "Pete Nogota."

West continued. "Ask yourself, too, who in the Sabin family would benefit the most from Sabin's permanent absence?"

"Probably the grandson, Tab Johnson," Brenda answered. "He's lying in a hospital bed recovering from gunshot wounds."

"Was he with Art when he was killed?"

"No, Detective Tower and the sheriff found the boy in a root cellar near the house," Carver said.

West's shoulders fell as he shook his head, "Horrible goings on—what's this world coming to?"

"That's the question law enforcement everywhere is grappling with," Brenda answered.

"This has been a help, my friend. You've given us plenty to chew on," Carver said.

"Then, it's been worthwhile."

"Yes, it has." Carver glanced at his watch. "We need to be going."

He and Brenda stood up and moved toward the door.

"Chauncy, stop by the house next time you're in town."

"I might do, son. It was sure good to see you, Ned; you too, Detective."

West waved to them as they pulled away from his front door.

Partway down the long incline to the highway, Ned turned to Brenda. "Evelyn is expecting us for lunch."

"How nice, Ned. I'd like to meet your better half."

"Better half, you got that right."

34

A typical small-town, acute-care hospital built in the 1960s, Dayton General carried twenty-five beds for both adults and children. Inside, Stone spotted one of his volunteer deputies sitting guard in the hallway outside Room 7 and headed his way.

"How's your prisoner doing, Hammer?" he asked.

"He's good. I keep an eye on him through the open door."

Stone's cell rang. "Excuse me." He stepped back.

Another volunteer deputy's gravelly voice hit Stone's ear. "Sheriff, I came across something unusual you might be interested to know."

"Go ahead, Neil."

"I found some biker leather gear in the back of that gray pickup. The pants and jacket are real small—like for a woman."

"Interesting—is that it, Neil?"

"What would that Mendoza guy be doing with an expensive set of women's leathers?"

"We'll have to find out. Thanks for the call." Stone closed his cell and walked into his prisoner's room.

Mendoza lay in a raised position watching *The View* on TV. His eyes never left the screen as Stone stood waiting, arms crossed. Reaching for the remote, Stone clicked off the TV and examined the prisoner's arm restraints.

Mendoza pulled away and hissed, "What do you want?"

"For one thing, mister, one of my deputies will be in here in a little while to take your fingerprints."

"The hell he will! He ain't printin' me. You got no right." Mendoza jerked hard on his restraints, and his eyes bugged out as he scowled at Stone.

"I have every right to print you. You were arrested for pulling a knife on a woman. If you give me any shit over it, we'll do it the hard way."

"You came at me with a gun. What was I supposed to do?"

"You were supposed to stay calm and do what I told you. Instead, you pulled a knife, said you'd kill the waitress if I didn't back down. What were you afraid of?"

"I ain't afraid of nothin' or nobody. I want a lawyer."

"You'll get a lawyer when I say you can have a lawyer, not a minute sooner."

"I'm done talkin' here." Mendoza turned away, jerking hard again at his restraints.

Stone opened his cell and rang the office. "Pamela, put the INS Agent on the line." He waited for a moment. "Agent Milam, Sheriff Stone here." Stone's voice boomed in the small room. "Didn't you tell me this morning Carlos Mendoza is in the country illegally?" Mendoza rolled his eyes in the brief silence that followed. Stone continued. "He is, huh. Is the INS prepared to take custody of him and expedite his return to Mexico?" At this, Mendoza's jaw tightened. "You can? Good. I'll have him ready. You want him by noon, you say? You have a flight out of Pasco at three?"

"What the fuck you pulling here?" Mendoza blurted. "You ain't sending me back to no Mexico."

"Hold on a minute, Agent Milam." Stone turned to Mendoza. "You better get your ass straightened around, if you know what's good for you."

Mendoza squirmed. "Bullshit," he yelled, spittle shooting from his mouth.

"Mister, the authorities in Mexico will know what to do with you."

Mendoza continued to yank uselessly at his restraints. Stone waited, arms folded across his chest, the phone open in his right hand.

"Okay, okay, print me, what the hell do I care? So, I made a mistake last night. I'll spend time in your jail, but I ain't going back to Mexico."

Stone lifted the cell back to his ear. "Agent Milam, my prisoner has decided to cooperate. If he fails to comply in any way during the next hour, he's yours."

The make-believe call over, Stone told Mendoza, "You behave yourself, and we won't need the INS. Mess with me again, mister, and you're gone."

"Okay, now leave me alone. I want to watch my show."

"Later. I need to ask you a few questions."

The furrows deepened in the prisoner's forehead and his eyes darkened, but Mendoza nodded. "All right, go ahead."

"What are you doing in my county?"

Mendoza wiped his mouth on the shoulder of his hospital gown. "I'm on vacation."

"Where have you been staying?"

He shrugged. "No place special. A day here, a day there."

Stone removed his cap and laid it on the table. "Are you traveling alone?" he asked.

"Yes."

"Where'd you come from?"

"Bakersfield, California."

"Washington's a big state. Why'd you decide to come here?"

"See one of my relatives."

A nurse came into the room, carrying a pill cup and a glass of water. "Time for your pain medication, Mr. Mendoza."

Carlos held his head back and opened his mouth. She placed two pills on his tongue, brought the water to his lips, and watched as the restrained man swallowed the medicine and water.

When the nurse left, Stone continued. "What's your relative's name?"

"Ramiro Sanchez—he's a cousin of mine."

"What does Mr. Sanchez do here?"

"Works in the wheat harvest."

"Do you know where?"

"Not far from Elam's Crossing."

"Is that the best you can do?" Stone's gaze remained hard.

"The farm is about five miles south of town, but I've never been out there."

"You didn't come here to work?"

"Nah, I got money. I worked plenty hard for years down

below."

"Then why were you at the Sabin farm Monday morning?"

Mendoza sent Stone a blank stare. "Sabin? I don't know nobody named Sabin."

"Well, your pickup was seen going into his lane. Someone else driving it, maybe?"

"Oh, that. I went there to help Ramiro get his clothes."

"Clothes at the Sabin farm? How so?"

"He worked there last year and left some things in the bunkhouse."

"Your cousin left things that he wanted at the farm, is that correct?"

"Yeah, that's what he told us."

Stone paused. "Told us," he repeated. "Who's 'us'—you and who else?"

After hesitating for a moment, Mendoza pushed the words through tightened lips. "Ramiro works with a couple of guys who also went along."

"What are their names?" Stone asked, shifting his weight from one foot to the other.

"I never seen them before—don't know their names."

Stone thought for a moment. "Who drove the other car that morning?"

Pleased the sheriff had not pressed him for the names of the other two men, Mendoza loosened up. "Ramiro drove."

"What make of car does he drive?"

"An Impala."

"And the year?"

"An '89, he told me."

"Are you sure it's an Impala and not a Malibu or a Corsica?" Stone probed.

"Sure I'm sure. Guys in California love those '89 Impalas. Ramiro's is loaded."

"What color is it?"

"Dark blue. No, it's black."

Stone hoisted his gun belt off his hip. "Why didn't you all go in his car?

"I don't ride no more. I been rolled over twice and banged up other times—bad drivers."

"Why'd Ramiro want you three with him that morning?"

"He thought the old man might not hand over his stuff. Ramiro wanted us along so he wouldn't try no funny stuff."

"Did Mr. Sabin give him a hard time?"

"We never saw the man. A Mexican woman at the door said he was gone."

"Ramiro got his things back okay, then?"

"Yeah, the woman brought out a large bag and handed it to him."

"What was her name?"

Mendoza wrinkled his nose as he tried to remember. "Ramiro called her Calli."

"Did you see a white boy when you were there?"

"Nope."

"Did you see anyone else at the farm?"

"Nope."

A deputy with a fingerprinting kit entered the room. Stone watched while he printed Mendoza. When the process was complete and the deputy had left, Stone continued his questioning. "Did you see a man in a red pickup that morning?"

"Not me. I left ahead of the others. They might have seen him."

"We found a set of women's biker leathers in your pickup."

"What the hell you doin' in my truck?"

"It's been impounded. We're required to inventory it, for your protection. I'm interested in why you would have women's leather gear. Was a woman traveling with you from California?"

"I don't pick up hitchhikers."

"You didn't answer my question."

"Someone must have left them there by mistake."

"I asked you if a woman was with you."

Mendoza's eyes bulged and he frowned. He threw his head back, shaking it from side to side. "I told you already, I came alone."

"I'm going to give you a little time to think about that

question. Now behave yourself in here."

Mendoza turned his head away and said nothing.

Stone picked up the remote, clicked on the TV, and left the room. "Stay safe, Hammer," Stone told his deputy. "Remember, only hospital staff is allowed in the room—no exceptions."

35

The postmistress reported to a customer Thursday morning, "News of the shooting last night is spreading through the county like a hillside blaze in a Santa Ana Wind."

The grain elevator operator where the Wattenburger grain trucks unloaded passed along the information to drivers when they came in to dump their loads. While Sanchez's bank-out wagon augered its load into the grain truck, the driver told him, "Some Mexican guy was shot in town last night."

"A Mexican, shot?" Sanchez repeated.

"Yeah, they said some bitch with a gun and a badge took him down. He's been arrested."

"What's his name, man?"

"It's Mendez . . . umm, Mendoza, something like that. You know him?"

"Nah, I don't know nobody up here with that name," Sanchez said, shifting his gaze away from the driver. He walked to his tractor on spongy legs and climbed into the seat with some difficulty. *Carlos shot and arrested. Man, we're in trouble. I need to tell Ken and Joey what's happened. We gotta blow this place.* He could see Valentine's tractor up ahead when he re-entered the field. Sanchez drove to where Valentine was parked, set the brakes, and cut the engine. He jumped down from his tractor and scaled the side of Valentine's tractor.

"What's up, Ramiro?"

"Carlos was shot last night in town. He's been arrested, man."

"Shit! We gotta get away from here. Carlos won't keep quiet. He'll give us up."

"I know, man. You let Ken know as soon as you see him. I'll do the same."

The horn blew on the combine, indicating Valentine's

wagon was full and needed to move. Sanchez jumped back so Valentine could pull his tractor away.

"You and Ken meet me at the car," Ramiro said. "We'll have to stop and grab our stuff at the trailer."

"Okay—see ya in a few minutes." Valentine pulled away, heading off the hill.

Sanchez hurried to his car and waited for Gear and Valentine to arrive. He checked his watch and focused his gaze along the hillside. They were both out of breath by the time they reached the car at 11:15.

"Jump in, man, we're out of here!" Sanchez yelled.

Gear grabbed the seat behind Valentine, and the car sped away. Sanchez drove fast along the dusty, gravel road. Two miles farther he forked right. The road meandered along the floor of the narrow ravine toward the junction with 261, northwest of Elam's Crossing.

Back at their single-wide trailer, the men gathered up their belongings and threw them into the trunk of the car.

~

Stone knew Mendoza had lied to him about Monday morning at Sabin's farm. But if the information about Sanchez was accurate, his time with the prisoner could have been worthwhile. There would be plenty of time to interrogate him further. Outside the hospital, Stone opened his cell and keyed in his dispatcher. "Pamela, I want you to contact my on-duty deputies. Tell them to cover Highways 12 and 32. They're looking for a black, '89 four-door Impala with California plates. The driver is Ramiro Sanchez. He's a suspect in the Sabin murders—approach with caution. I'll call Deputy Carver myself."

"Right away, Sheriff."

Stone looked at his watch. It was 11:45 a.m.

~

Carver and Brenda had barely pulled into the driveway to have lunch with his wife when his car phone rang.

"Ned, I have a hunch whoever was with Carlos Mendoza at the Sabin farm has heard by now he's been arrested."

"You're probably right, Sheriff."

"According to Mendoza, one of the men with him was a man named Ramiro Sanchez."

"Okay."

"Sanchez drives a black, '89 four-door Impala with California plates. He's working in the harvest somewhere around Elam's Crossing."

"Got it."

"Is Detective Tower with you?"

"Yeah, she is."

"I want the two of you to hightail it out to 261 going east. Hole up along there someplace and keep your eyes peeled for his vehicle. Call for help if you spot it. The dispatcher will inform the other on-duty deputies to be on the lookout."

"10-4, Sheriff." Carver slammed the side of his fist against the door panel. "Silly-ass assignment," he muttered, glancing at Brenda. "I've got some dope on one of the men who was with Mendoza at the Sabin farm."

"That's a break. Do we have a name?"

"Ramiro Sanchez. He's working in the harvest somewhere around here."

"What does the sheriff want us to do?"

"We're to hole up on 261 East and keep a lookout for a black '89 Impala."

"Doesn't sound like that's what you had in mind, Ned." Brenda's eyes twinkled.

"It's not." Carver heaved a sigh. "Look, the Snake River is the county line. A man on the run would head for the nearest line, wouldn't you think?"

"I'd say so."

Carver brushed his hand across his lower face and paused. "Can you handle a shotgun?"

"Daddy taught me to hunt pheasants when I was twelve," Brenda answered reassuringly.

Carver opened the trunk of his cruiser and brought out a twelve-gauge pump. Brenda held out her hand for the weapon, racked it back, checked the breach, and racked it forward. She clicked on the safety and looked up at Carver with a smile. From the driveway, Carver opened his cell phone. "Honey, I'm sorry. We've got no time for lunch now; we're going hunting."

His wife's voice pleaded in his ear, "But Ned, I've fixed something special. Why can't you take a few minutes?"

"High priority, Evelyn, and the clock is our enemy. I'll tell you all about it later. Bye."

"You be careful," he heard her say as he snapped his cell shut.

Ignoring the sheriff's specific instructions, Carver headed in the opposite direction out of Elam's Crossing—toward the Snake River. He was used to working by himself and didn't mind facing difficult challenges alone, but today it was different. He could be facing an armed and dangerous man, maybe more than one. He was pleased to have Detective Tower at his side.

They stopped at the entrance to the bridge over the Tucanon River. There was no traffic on the highway. Carver swung his cruiser around to block the way in front of the bridge. He stepped out, unlatched the carbine mounted on the safety cage, and grasped it. Brenda climbed out of the cruiser with the shotgun in hand.

~

At their trailer, Sanchez, Gear, and Valentine piled back into the Impala and headed to 261. At the stop, Sanchez hesitated for a moment. When it looked to Gear as though he might turn right, he leaned forward from the back seat and shouted, "Ramiro, go left—get us the hell out of the county, quick! Head toward Othello. No one will be looking for us up there."

"Yeah, go left." Valentine seconded the decision with a sweep of his arm.

Ramiro jerked the wheel to the left. In a few minutes they would be over the Snake River and into Adams County.

~

Ned thought about taking a defensive position behind the cruiser. He knew that made some sense, using the vehicle for protection, but it could give Sanchez an advantage. "I think the man will stop when he sees my weapon. He won't risk being shot," Carver said over his shoulder to Brenda. "You can join me if you like, Detective, or you can be my back-up."

"Your back-up! The hell with that." Brenda moved forward alongside her partner.

The two stood together with the butts of their guns resting on their hips. Carver adjusted his cap and glanced at his partner. "If the driver decides to plow through us, stand to the side and shoot out the tires."

~

"Step on it Ramiro, we need to get some miles behind us," Gear urged. He knew the rebuilt engine, now minus the emission control equipment, could make this vehicle fly. Ramiro pushed hard on the gas pedal and the car hit eighty in a matter of seconds. He held the wheel steady with both hands. The Impala roared along the ravine, its exhaust system bellowing hard.

~

From their position on the bridge, Carver and Brenda heard a car approaching fast. Facing that direction, they brandished the weapons in the air above their heads. Brenda spotted the sun's reflection off the approaching car's grill. At a distance of six hundred yards, they assumed a firing stance, held their positions, and waited.

~

"Aw, shit, the cops!" Sanchez shouted. "They've got guns on us!"

"Pull up hard!" Valentine yelled, clutching the edge of the dashboard. Gear braced himself against the front seat as Ramiro hit the power brakes, putting the car into a skid and bringing it to a stop, angled across the lane in front of the two lawmen.

"How would they know we're on the run?" Valentine asked.

"They don't, man," Sanchez snapped back, pounding the top of the steering wheel with his open hand. "Keep your mouths shut. Stay cool, both of you. We were goin' a little too fast, that's all."

"They're after us for something more than that," Gear snorted.

"I told you guys to keep quiet. Don't say nothin', man. Let me do the talkin'."

Carver moved to the driver's side of the car, his carbine trained on the open front window. Brenda stepped to the passenger side, her shotgun at window height.

"Are you Ramiro Sanchez?" Carver growled.

"Yes, sir."

"Mr. Sanchez, cut the engine and drop the car keys out here on the road."

Sanchez did as he was told. "Sir, I have my license here in my wallet." His right hand went for his back pocket.

Carver stepped forward, pointing his carbine directly at Sanchez. "Get out and put your hands on top of the car. You other two men stay put, you hear me?"

"We'ain't goin' no place," Gear assured Carver.

Valentine felt warm urine trickling down his leg inside his jeans.

Carver called across the car to Brenda, "Keep an eye on these two while I get this one settled."

"You got it," she said, focusing most of her attention on the small-built man in the passenger's seat.

"Officer, I was driving a little fast, but you don't need no gun on me, man," Sanchez said.

"I didn't ask you to talk, mister. I told you to get your ass out of that damn car. Now move it!"

Ramiro slid out from behind the wheel.

"Put your hands up over the car and spread your feet." Carver patted down Sanchez, cuffed him, walked him to the cruiser, and placed him in the back seat. He walked back to the driver's side of the car, retrieved Ramiro's keys from the asphalt, and strode over next to Brenda with his weapon at the ready. Brenda moved to the back door.

"You, in the front, step out here. Put your hands on top of the car and spread your feet. You, in the back seat, stay still," Carver ordered.

Valentine obeyed. Carver frisked and cuffed him and walked him in the direction of the cruiser. Gear watched Brenda as her eyes momentarily followed Carver. At that instant, he flung his door open and lunged toward her. Catching movement out of the corner of her eye, Brenda deftly stepped to the side. Gear stumbled and nearly fell, quickly correcting himself. He pivoted in a crouch and bolted back along the road toward a thicket.

Brenda raised the barrel of the twelve-gauge and pulled the trigger. Gear halted and looked back, shaking his head. He hadn't counted on an out-of-uniform female taking a shot at him.

With the shotgun still at her shoulder, Brenda hollered to Gear, "Get back here, you—you peckerwood!"

"I'm coming, I'm coming," Gear answered, walking toward her.

"Put your hands over your head and keep right on moving." She gestured with her chin.

"Shit, you didn't have to shoot," Gear groused, his heart pounding hard as he raised his arms overhead.

"You're damn lucky I wasn't aiming at you."

Within minutes, Brenda and Carver had three handcuffed suspects sitting together behind the cage. After Carver re-latched the carbine, he moved the cruiser off the highway to a nearby turnout. Cars on both sides had been lining up, waiting for the road to clear.

Carver gave the Impala keys to Brenda in exchange for her shotgun. She moved the Impala to the turnout and locked it up. As traffic resumed, she walked toward Carver, who was stowing the shotgun in the trunk. "Were you expecting there'd be three of them?" Her voice shook a little as they leaned against the cruiser.

"I didn't know what to expect," Carver said, touching her shoulder lightly. "You did great, Detective. We've got 'em suit-cased slick as a whistle."

"It wasn't all that slick, Ned. I could've lost the last one."

Carver's eyes locked on Brenda's. "You didn't let it happen, though, did you?"

"This could've gone down a whole lot differently. What if the driver had refused to stop? What if they'd had guns and were willing to use them?"

"That's why we brought the insurance—the carbine and your cannon."

Brenda swallowed hard and shuddered. "It's over now, thank God."

"Ride shotgun with me to the courthouse?"

She smiled slightly, grateful for Carver's understanding, and climbed into the car. Brenda stared absently out the side window. "I've had more excitement these four days than anyone on vacation should ever experience. These arrests could have easily gone south." She turned toward Carver, pointed a thumb over her shoulder, and whispered "These guys could have been armed killers. We were very fortunate." She leaned back in the seat and closed her eyes. *This is not the vacation I'd planned.*

36

Stone's cell phone rang in the middle of lunch at The Long Branch in Dayton. "Hello, Sheriff. Carver here. We've got something for you."

"Hold on, just a minute." Stone rose from his table and walked out the side door. "Go ahead, Ned."

"We've got three cuffed men in the back of my cruiser. They're out of a black '89 Impala driven by a Mr. Ramiro Sanchez."

Surprised at what he was hearing, Stone stammered, "Out—outstanding, Ned! Where . . . where'd you apprehend them?"

"About two miles northwest of Elam's Crossing on 261, in front of the Tucanon Bridge."

"Do you need help?"

"Negative, Sheriff. We're on our way in."

"I'll meet you at the courthouse."

Knowing Carver wouldn't arrive for another twenty minutes, Stone finished his burrito, paid the bill, and drove to the courthouse. Carver drove up within minutes. Stone strolled over to the cruiser, eyeing the men behind the cage as Carver and Brenda slid out. He shot Carver a wide smile. "You suit-cased these jaybirds just like that," he said, snapping his fingers."

"Right time, right place, Sheriff."

"You said it. Did you make formal arrests?"

"Didn't take the time; we had the highway blocked."

Carver opened the back door on the driver's side. Stone took hold of the nearest man's arm. "Step out of the car."

Sanchez stumbled out and Carver shut the door. Brenda studied the suspect. Mid-twenties, Hispanic, medium build, a sullen expression on his face. He wore a soiled shirt, well-worn jeans, and dusty boots.

"What's your name, mister?" Stone asked.

"Ramiro Sanchez. Sheriff, I know I was speeding a little. I won't do it again."

"No, I don't think you will. You're under arrest on suspicion of burglary and murder. You've been transported here to the county jail where you'll be booked and placed in a cell."

"I don't know what you're talkin' about, Sheriff. You pickin' on me 'cause I'm Mexican, maybe?"

Valentine nudged Gear. "The sheriff just told Ramiro he's being arrested on suspicion of murder," he said under his breath.

Gear pounded his knee with his handcuffed fists. "Shit, we had nothing to do with those murders," he whispered back. "This is crazy. I'm not going to prison for murder—not me."

"I told you we were dead meat because of that crazy-ass Carlos. I'm not going to prison for murder, either," Valentine hissed.

"You and me gotta stick together. It was Ramiro who took the money from the office, right? And Carlos killed the two women and the kid."

"I'm with you, Ken. We were there, but we didn't steal the money. We didn't touch the women, or the kid," Valentine repeated, wiping away the perspiration on his forehead with the back of his hand.

"That damn Ramiro wants us to keep quiet. All that's going to do is make us look guilty. Screw that, Joey. We gotta tell them what we know, right?" The two men stared at each other, exchanging slight nods.

Brenda stayed with the cruiser while Stone and Carver escorted Sanchez into the cellblock. When they returned, Carver opened the back door.

"Get out of the vehicle, mister," Stone ordered.

Gear stumbled out and stood up next to Stone, who held him by the arm.

This is the one who tried to run, Brenda reminded herself. He's got a guilty look about him.

"What's your name, mister?" Stone asked.

"Ken Gear."

"Mr. Gear, you're under arrest on suspicion of burglary and murder. You'll go into the courthouse and be booked, and you'll be detained here in my jail."

Gear hung his head, silent. Momentarily, the same routine took place with Valentine. This one looks like he could still be in high school, Brenda thought, shaking her head. How'd he let himself get mixed up in those horrific murders?

Stone placed the men in separate cells.

"I gotta talk to you, Sheriff," Valentine blurted when Stone closed his cell door.

"I can't talk now. I'll get back to you, maybe later today."

Ramiro slouched on the bed in his cell, face in his hands. He had worried that something like this would happen if Carlos was picked up. *He musta given my name to the law. I can't be blamed for what he did. I gotta take care of number one.*

Stone, Carver, and Tower met for a few minutes in the sheriff's office. Stone looked at Carver, a grin tugging at the corners of his mouth. "Ned, you didn't follow orders. Lucky for us you didn't. If you'd followed my instructions, you would have missed those birds altogether. How'd the two of you take them without a ruckus?"

"We waved a carbine and a shotgun at Sanchez as he drove toward us. He must've known we'd fire on his car if he screwed up. When you see how cherry that black Impala is, you'll understand why he hit the brakes. He didn't want his baby hurt."

"I had a runner, Sheriff. The tall skinny one tried to jump me. When he ran, I fired the twelve-gauge. His fleeing instinct died when that cannon blustered." Brenda blushed as she recounted the scene.

Stone laughed out loud. "When the 'cannon blustered,' hey?"

"Detective Tower was real good help, Sheriff."

"You told me last night I should hire her." Turning to Brenda, Stone asked, "Did Ned say the two of you were going bird hunting?"

"No, he didn't, Sheriff, but he didn't give me much time to think about what we *were* going to do, either."

"If we'd done too much thinking, we would've missed them," Carver said.

"Here are the keys to the black Impala." Brenda set the ring on Stone's desk.

Stone placed his hand on Carver's shoulder and looked his deputy squarely in the eyes. "You're one hell-of-a lawman, Ned."

"Don't know about that," Carver said.

"*The Bulletin* police reporter will want to do a story on the capture of these men. And I don't want to hear you were too busy to talk with her." Stone glanced at his watch. "It's nearly two o'clock. Did you two get lunch?"

"We were just pulling into my driveway for lunch with Evelyn when you called."

"Go eat," Stone said, handing Carver his credit card. "Bring Detective Tower back here afterwards. Ned, I want you to help me interrogate one or two of these prisoners later. Can you meet me back here about six?"

Ned wondered if Stone had found out he was not on the job first thing that morning. Was that why he was asking him to work tonight? *Hell, I worked till ten last night.* "Sure, I'll be here."

Stone turned to Brenda. "Mind working over a couple of hours this evening?"

"Just try sending me home."

Stone laughed at his gung-ho volunteer detective. "Want to go with me to question the Johnson boy when you finish lunch?"

"Sure."

Stone handed Sanchez's car keys to his dispatcher, instructing her to call Mike's Towing to pick up the black Impala.

37

The receptionist at Walla Walla General typed in the requested name and browsed her computer screen for the room number. "Talbert Johnson is in 218." She turned and pointed. "Take the elevator to the second floor. The room will be on your right."

Brenda and Stone approached Tab Johnson's door at the moment an RN exited. She cocked an eye at Stone and, checking her watch, announced, "Visiting hours are over."

"Nurse, I need to speak with the young man in this room," Stone said.

"You'll have to get permission from the director if you insist on seeing him after visiting hours."

Stone stood straighter and let out a sigh. "Believe me, Nurse—Pettibone," the sheriff said, squinting at her ID tag, "you don't want me to speak with Victor Washburn about this."

"Well!" the RN said. Bristling, she wheeled around and strutted away in military fashion.

Hand over her mouth, Brenda snickered. "Lin, you're so smooth."

Stone blushed. "I have no patience with people like her. The name *Petti*bone says it all."

Brenda pushed open the door to Johnson's room. They found him lying in bed with the head cranked up as high as it could go. "I'm trying to find out the Dodgers' standing in the National League West," he said as he clicked off the remote. "Mother told me to expect you, Sheriff." He thrust out his right hand toward Stone and they shook. "I heard it was you who found me."

Stone motioned to Brenda. "Tab, this is Detective Tower. She stumbled onto the cellar where you were found."

Johnson's face lit up. "Many thanks, Detective . . . for

saving my life."

"You're welcome." Brenda turned to Stone. "Tab looks a whale of a lot better now than he did two days ago, wouldn't you say, Sheriff."

"Yes, he does."

"Will you two have a seat?" Johnson asked.

Brenda settled into a plastic-cushioned, steel-framed chair near the bed.

"I'll just stand," Stone said. "Been sitting too much lately."

"How can I help, Sheriff?"

"We're here to ask you some questions about Monday morning."

"Sure, I'll tell you what I know."

"First, what you have been told about your grandfather?"

"My mother said he was killed; she told me someone shot

h . . . ." Johnson's voice trailed off. He didn't say anything for several moments. Swallowing hard, he fought to hold back tears.

Brenda left her chair, poured water from a plastic pitcher into a glass on his bedside tray, and handed it to him.

"Thank you." He raised the glass to his lips and drank.

"Take your time; we're not in any hurry." Stone brushed back his hair with a sweep of his fingers.

Johnson wiped his eyes quickly with the edge of the bed sheet.

"When did you last see your grandfather?" Stone asked.

"It was Monday morning after breakfast. We were rebuilding an International engine in the shop. He handed me a list of parts he wanted from NAPA in Dayton."

"What time was that?"

"Around 7:30, I think."

"So you drove to Dayton at that time?"

"I did."

"What time did you return?"

"Around 9:00, maybe a little later."

"Did you return to the shop?"

"No. Grandpa's pickup wasn't there, so I pulled in at the

house." The young man's voice trembled a little.

"What did you think when his pickup was gone?"

"That he'd probably gone to check on the wheat. He does it every day this time of year."

"Were there cars near the house when you drove in?"

"Yeah, there were."

"Can you describe them?"

"Sure. One looked to be an almost-new Ford pickup. The other one was an older, black sedan, a late 80s maybe."

"Who did you think the vehicles belonged to?" Stone tilted his head, eyeing Johnson carefully.

"Harvest workers checking in early. I went into the house, walked through the living room, and then just as I entered the dining room, someone hit me alongside the head with something hard— everything went black."

"You didn't see anyone?"

"No. I must have fallen to the floor. When I came to, I went into the kitchen for some water. Then I heard a noise at the front door."

"Go on."

Johnson leaned his upper body forward in the bed. "I ran out the side door into the yard. Someone was chasing me. There were gunshots, and I was hit, and I went down. I played dead."

"Did you see who fired the shots?"

"No. But I do remember someone saying, 'Let's drop him in the cellar.'"

Stone shifted his weight from one leg to the other. "Did you recognize the voice?"

Johnson cupped his hand under his chin. "It was a man's voice, a Mexican accent. I remember that much."

"Do you remember the names of the Mexican workers from last year?"

Tab's eyes closed for a moment and his forehead creased in concentration. "There was Calli's nephew, Antonio; there was Juan; and—yeah, Ramiro."

Stone cleared his throat. "What can you tell me about each of those fellows?"

"Juan was a respectful guy—went to church." Johnson scratched his head. "Antonio loved Calli. I don't think he'd do anything bad. Ramiro was kind of distant—seemed to carry a chip on his shoulder about something."

"Did your mother say anything to you about Calli Mendez and Christina Lopez?" Stone asked.

"No, I haven't heard a thing. Are they both okay?"

"They were also killed on Monday."

Color drained from the boy's face. He pulled the sheet up over his face, and Brenda could hear muffled sobs. Moments later, he lowered the sheet. "That's horrible!" His eyes met Brenda's. "Calli was an outstanding woman, so good to everyone. We all loved her."

"What do you know about Christina Lopez?" Stone asked.

"She was Calli's niece, Antonio's sister. I overheard Calli tell Grandpa one night that Christina was pregnant. Her boyfriend was giving her a hard time about having the baby. Grandpa told Calli that Christina could live in the cottage and cook for the harvest crew. She could stay and have the baby here next winter. Calli liked the idea." Johnson sighed deeply. "Why would anyone want to kill those women?"

Stone shook his head. "We don't know. What can you tell me about your grandfather exploring for uranium ore on the farm?"

"Well, a drilling rig showed up about three weeks ago. Grandpa didn't want to talk much about it with me."

"Can you think of anyone who would want to harm your grandfather?"

"No, I can't."

Turning to Brenda, Stone asked, "Do you have questions for Mr. Johnson?"

"Just a couple." Brenda stood up and moved closer to the bed where she'd have a better view of Johnson's face. "Help me understand something, Tab. Why did you take a girl up into the barn loft? You could have used the little house or one of the sleeping rooms."

Johnson's face blushed tomato red. With a sharp intake of

breath, he closed his eyes and lowered his head. Brenda waited for a time, and then continued. "We're trying to solve some serious crimes that took place at your grandfather's farm. The mess left in the loft is a mystery to us. The crime lab will have answers, but it would help a lot if you could be honest about this."

Johnson fidgeted in the bed and then asked haltingly, "You won't—tell my parents will you?"

"Not unless it has something to do with the case."

"Nothing to do with your case, believe me." He shook his head.

"What then?"

"Sheila came over one day last week when Grandpa and Calli were gone to Spokane. I knew no one would look for us in the loft."

"Who's Sheila?"

"Sheila Wattenburger. Her dad's a wheat farmer."

"Okay," Brenda said, nodding at him encouragingly. "Don't worry. I remember what it's like to be a teenager. Tell me about the four-wheelers that were recently in the wheat field."

"Grandpa doesn't allow vehicles of any kind on seeded ground."

"If your grandfather forbids it, why did you and your friends take them into the field?"

"Well," Tab started. He rubbed the knuckles of his right hand against his chin. "Well, I didn't want to. I told them I could get into trouble."

"Must have been pretty important, huh?" Brenda sought his gaze, and the boy finally met her eyes directly.

He blew out a long, resigned breath. "Okay, one night Cory brought his dad's pickup and a trailer with a couple of four-wheelers. He had two Dayton girls with him. We doubled up on the four-wheelers and drove out behind the hill together."

"So you'd be out of sight?" Brenda asked.

"Yeah, out of sight."

"Tell me about a scuffle that took place out there that night."

"What? There was no scuffle between me and Betty. Could

be that Cory and his girl scuffled some."

Brenda glanced at Stone, her eyebrows arched. Stone realized her questioning had effortlessly cleared up two nagging physical-evidence quandaries that were muddying up his case.

"Other questions, Detective?"

Stone appeared somewhat dumbfounded, she thought. "No, I'm good."

"If you think of anything else, Tab, I want you to call me." Stone handed the young man his card.

"I will, Sheriff. I'll do anything to help catch the killer."

On their way to the parking lot, Stone needled Brenda about Johnson's tom-catting. "I've already heard about three girls Tab's been romping around with." He counted on his fingers. "Let's see, there was the Edwards girl in Elam's Crossing, now Sheila the farmer's daughter, and also Betty, a Dayton girl. What are you going to find next?"

"Come off of it, Lin. I'll bet you dollars to donuts you had some rolls in the hay when you were a teen."

Stone dodged her gamble. Maintaining a straight face, he said, "It's incredible how easily you delved into those matters. I'm going to be way more careful how I answer your questions from now on."

Brenda punched him lightly on the arm. "Look, my intuition told me Tab had a girl in the barn. Remember the *Playboy* magazines and the lipstick on the soda can? His involvement in the wheat with the four-wheelers was just an educated guess."

"Educated guess or not, you cleared up the mystery of the boot prints and four-wheeler tire tracks."

"If you remember, Lin, it was my raving on about the boy being abducted that sparked your interest in my helping you."

Stone winked at her. "Yes, and what we thought was evidence of an abduction turned out to be some horny kids with the means, motive, and opportunity."

She laughed. Brenda never had learned how to wink, and she didn't think this was the time for practice.

38

Stone's car phone rang while on the road to Dayton following their visit with Tab Johnson. Stone reached down and lifted the receiver.

"Sheriff, Everett Schuster is available to meet with you," he heard his dispatcher say.

"Paula. Tell him we'll be at his office in about fifteen minutes." Stone hung up and glanced over at Brenda. "We've got an appointment with Sabin's attorney."

"That should be an interesting meeting."

"Feel free to ask him questions."

A fine old Queen Anne Victorian on South Fourth in Dayton doubled as Schuster's personal residence and law office. Brenda studied the structure from the curb. "I adore the patterned wood shingles on the second story. Lin, look at the balcony off the large bay window on the second floor and the cantilevered tower on the right corner. Wow, what a place!"

"It's just an old house," Stone said.

"Don't you love those big white columns in front?"

Stone rolled his eyes. "You're not on a house tour, Detective."

"Oh, I know," Brenda said. She felt a tiny stab of disappointment she couldn't quite pinpoint.

They walked up the wooden steps onto the porch, where Brenda remarked on the stained glass window in the front door. "What a beautiful wheat-land scene—there's a rising sun in the background!"

Stone shook his head as he rang the doorbell. "You women."

She kicked him gently on the ankle, and Stone caught a glimpse of her glaring at him. They heard heavy footsteps approaching, and the door swung inward. Everett Schuster's face wore the smile of a mass tort lawyer who'd just won a two-hundred-million-dollar settlement from a hapless pharmaceutical giant. A heavy-built man in his late sixties with a full head of thick, gray hair combed straight back, Schuster looked the part of a hardworking, small-town lawyer. Wide-strap suspenders wrinkled a fawn-colored dress shirt, encumbering his stooped shoulders.

"Please come in—I've been waiting for you." He stretched out his hand and shook hands with Stone. "It's nice to see you, Sheriff, outside of the courtroom."

"Mr. Schuster, I appreciate you taking the time to speak with us. This is Detective Tower. She's helping me with the Sabin case."

Brenda smiled.

"I'm pleased to meet you, Detective."

"I'm pleased to meet you, sir."

"I know you're the Sabins' lawyer," Stone began. "We'd like to ask you some questions related to our case."

"Of course. Let's go into the office."

What must have once been a magnificent parlor now served as the office for the most powerful attorney in the county. "I could have taken an office up on Main Street. Working here has allowed me to be close to Joanne. She's battling MS."

"I'm so sorry to hear that. You have a beautiful place here," Brenda commented.

"Thank you, we're quite comfortable. I had a lift installed on the staircase so Joanne can move between the floors without much trouble. But you two didn't come here to talk about the house. Please sit down."

The three folded themselves into burgundy-colored leather chairs. Stone leaned forward, rubbing his palms together. "I'm looking to shed some light on Art Sabin's murder. First, is ownership of the farm in both Art's and Angela's names?"

"It is. They've been separated for many years, but they're still legally married."

"Was there a will?"

"Art wanted the grandson, Tab Johnson, to take over operation of the farm and become its legal owner when he turns twenty-one. We talked recently about preparing the paperwork to have on hand. The boy's still young, so Art wasn't in much of a hurry."

"What's your impression of the Johnson boy?"

"The kid's cursed with an overabundance of testosterone. His Casanova reputation spilled over into our family last summer when our daughter refused to let the granddaughter date him."

"We've recently learned a little about his romantic capers," Stone said. "Can you tell us anything else about the boy's character?"

"Only what Art has told me. The boy is apparently one hell of a worker. He also gets on well with harvest workers, as well as people who go there to visit."

"Can you tell us the beneficiary of Sabin's life insurance policies?"

"Art didn't believe in life insurance. He owns the farm and all the equipment free and clear. There's a substantial savings account, and a separate account at the bank takes care of the farm's operating expenses. He believed Angela would do fine without life insurance."

"What about Sabin's son? Does Tony figure into an inheritance?"

"Art didn't want to break up the farm in any way. A few years back, he sold off several of his toys.

"Toys?"

"You know, a houseboat, a plane, a motor home, a large condo in Reno. With the proceeds, he bought commercial bonds in Tony's name. I oversee the portfolio."

"What are we talking about?"

"The face value is in the neighborhood of a million five. This asset will be transferred to Tony next July."

Brenda scooted forward in her chair. "Did Art make any provisions for his daughter, Kathy?"

Schuster's voice quieted. "Detective, Art didn't feel the same about his daughter as he did about his son. He and Kathy didn't get along in the least, he said, because she constantly hounded him about Calli. You may have noticed Art has several rare automobiles stored in his shop. He planned to turn the titles for those vehicles over to Kathy, but nothing was ever put in writing. They'll be Angela's property now."

"The farm going to the grandson, a sizable inheritance going to the son—it seems to me Angela could feel left out. She's also been humiliated by Art's philandering over the years. Maybe she engineered her husband's death," Stone said.

Schuster frowned at Stone. "Sheriff, I've known Angela for forty years. She hasn't had a storybook marriage, for sure. She left the farm because of health problems. Art always provided handsomely for her. He came to town to see her regularly—they had time together over the years. Angela would have had plenty to live on after ownership of the farm transferred to Tab Johnson. Art assured me of that." Schuster cleared his throat. "I'd be surprised if your evidence points to Angela."

"Sir, the hell of it is, the evidence in Art Sabin's case doesn't point anywhere yet. Would you say Angela is a greedy, vengeful woman?"

"No, Sheriff, I would not. To the contrary, I believe her to be a fine, upstanding lady, incapable of murdering her husband."

"What do you know about Art's plan to mine uranium on his property?" Stone asked.

"I strongly advised him against it."

"There's uranium on his land. We know that much."

Schuster hung his head, raised it, and eyed Stone. "Did someone kill him to squash a mining deal?"

"It's crossed my mind. Did he confide in you about any trouble he may have been having with anyone?"

"Never."

"Can you think of anyone who might have wanted to do the man harm?"

"I don't know of a soul who wanted to hurt him." The lawyer shook his head sadly.

"No more questions from me." Stone turned to Brenda. "Do you have any questions, Detective?"

"I have just one. Why do you think Calli Mendez stayed all those years with Mr. Sabin?"

"Good question, Detective. She was an extremely attractive woman in her early thirties when Art met her. As I remember, she moved into the house with him after cooking one summer for the harvest crew. Art provided Calli the financial stability she longed for." Schuster placed his hand over his mouth and sneezed. "Excuse me. Darned allergies. Art cherished the woman — treated her like a queen. He never gave a tinker's damn what people thought of their arrangement." Schuster sat silent for a moment and then added, "They were a strange couple, those two: an adopted orphan boy who became a well-to-do wheat farmer and a poor Mexican girl from the wrong side of the tracks who grew up beautiful, with a heart of gold and an infectious smile. Those who knew her loved the woman."

"We've heard that before. Thank you for your explanation," Brenda said.

Stone and Brenda stood as Schuster rose from his chair.

"Thank you for your time." Stone shook hands with the attorney again. "You've helped us clarify a few things. Call my cell if anything else comes to mind."

"You can count on it, Sheriff. Let me show you out."

39

Joey Valentine's eagerness to spill his guts earlier in the day galvanized Stone's determination to go ahead with the interrogation that evening, in spite of his fatigue. He met with Carver and Brenda in his office at 6:00 p.m. "Detective, I want you to take the lead with Valentine. Ned, you do the follow-up questioning. I'm going to sit in the back and take some notes."

When Valentine was read his rights, he only reacted to "the right to remain silent" and "anything you say can be used in court."

"I don't intend to remain silent," he told the deputy who read him his rights. "What I have to say will only help me. I've heard too many stories of innocent people being jailed, dragged into court on murder charges, and sentenced to prison for years, sometimes for life."

The deputy only nodded. He ushered Valentine into the interrogation room and marched him to his seat. An old oak table and four mismatched oak chairs furnished the small, windowless room with its cucumber green walls and brown floor tiles. Tower and Carver took seats across from Valentine. Ashen, he looked scared to death—probably his first brush with the law, Brenda thought. She began her questioning.

"How old are you, Mr. Valentine?"

He leaned forward in his chair. "Twenty-one."

"Where are you from?"

His hands lay still in his lap. "Sunnyside, Washington."

"What are you doing here?"

"I work in the wheat harvest."

"Who do you work for?"

"Clyde Wattenburger."

Brenda slid a pencil back and forth between her fingers. "Does Mr. Wattenburger have a daughter named Sheila?"

Valentine's eyes narrowed. His hands fumbled for the top

of the table. "Yeah, he does." Believe me, I've never touched her."

"No one said you did, Mr. Valentine. What is your relationship with Mr. Gear and Mr. Sanchez?"

"We work together. Live together, too."

"Where?"

"We rent a place in Elam's Crossing."

"What's the address?"

"301 Pataha Street."

Brenda laid the pencil carefully on the table and eagle-eyed Valentine. "Why was Sanchez speeding today when we stopped you guys?"

"We heard Carlos Mendoza had been arrested."

"What does his arrest have to do with you three?"

His fingers tapped nervously on the table. "We figured he'd . . . he'd rat us out."

"Rat you out? About what?"

"About what happened at the farm."

Brenda leaned her arm over the back of her chair. "What did happen at the farm?"

Valentine sighed heavily. "Ramiro told Ken and me this farmer he worked for last year had lots of money. He said the old man had cheated his people on their wages for years, and we had a right to take some of the money back."

"What time did you arrive at the farm?"

"Some before 8:00 a.m., I think."

"You went there to steal from the man, then?"

"Ramiro told us it would be easy. We'd get in, grab the money quick, and get out."

"But it wasn't so easy, was it? Mr. Sabin must have put up a fight?"

Valentine nervously bounced the ball of his right foot. "We never saw him. Trouble started because Ramiro invited his crazy cousin to come along."

"But the burglary should have gone easier with an extra man." Brenda leaned closer over the table.

"Carlos went ape when he laid eyes on the woman. He forced her upstairs and said he raped her. Told us later he killed her when she knifed him. It was Carlos who killed the other woman, and the kid, too." Valentine's breathing had become ragged, and perspiration beaded his top lip and forehead.

Stone brought out the blade he'd confiscated from Mendoza. "Is this the weapon Carlos used to kill the woman downstairs?"

Valentine wiped his brow with his hand. "Sure looks like it, all right."

Brenda scooted her chair a little closer to the table. "What do you know about this Carlos Mendoza?"

"Never saw him before Monday."

"Did you go upstairs that morning?"

"No."

"So you didn't see Calli Mendez's naked, bloody body on the bed?"

"None of the rest of us went upstairs. Why was she all bloody?"

"Someone carved on her."

Valentine gritted his teeth and cringed. "I told you Mendoza was crazy."

"Why didn't you stop him when he attacked the woman downstairs?"

"We heard the woman come in and walk through the living room. Carlos jumped her right off." Valentine breathed harder. "It all happened so fast. He was on her like a wild animal—lunging, stabbing, slicing. I knew he'd knife me if I tried to stop him." He wiped his brow again with a shaky hand. "He scared the hell out of me, you know."

"Did you find money in the house? Did you take any money?"

"Ramiro told Ken and me there'd be maybe ten grand. We only got about twelve hundred."

Brenda leaned back suddenly, her eyes widening. "So, for all that, you came away with three-hundred dollars, is that about right?"

Valentine tented his elbows on the table and cradled his head. Looking down, he tried to talk, but his words were garbled.

"Take your time." Carver motioned to him, "Here, have a drink of water."

Valentine drank deeply and then started again. "I let Ramiro talk me into going there with him."

"When did Mendoza shoot Mr. Sabin?"

Valentine's voice rose. "I told you, we never saw the man. We left right after Carlos shot the kid."

"Tell me about that," Brenda said.

"After Carlos killed the woman downstairs, a dog started running around the front yard, barking like mad. Carlos ran to his pickup and grabbed a pistol. It took him three tries to hit the dog."

"Do you think the boy saw any of you in the house?"

"I don't think so. Carlos clubbed him on the side of the head as soon as he entered the dining room. The blow knocked him out."

"When he came to, he could have spotted you outside. Is that why Mendoza shot him?"

"Yeah, I suppose. I felt awful. I was sick to my stomach, and I was mad as hell at Ramiro for inviting Carlos. He ruined everything."

Brenda turned to Carver. "Do you have questions, Deputy?"

"I do." Carver stared at Valentine. "Are you a hundred percent sure Mendoza was the only man who went upstairs?"

"I swear it, sir. We were plenty busy trying to find the money. Carlos had blood on him when he came down. He told us the woman stabbed him. He had to kill her, he said."

"You said Mendoza attacked the woman downstairs with that knife." Carver jabbed an index finger toward the weapon on the table in front of them.

Valentine nodded.

"No one else punched her, slammed her against the wall, or did anything to harm her?"

"No one. Carlos did it all in a few seconds."

"Why did you hang around after what had happened?"

Valentine whispered. "I wanted to leave."

"Speak up."

"Carlos was afraid one of us would squeal. He threatened to kill us if we didn't promise him we'd keep quiet and we wouldn't run."

"Anything else you'd like to tell us?"

"I didn't have anything to do with the murders. And it was Ramiro who found the money."

Having no more questions, Carver and Brenda looked over at Stone.

Stone stood and came forward. "Mr. Valentine, you'll be our guest here for a while." He turned to Carver. "Take Mr. Valentine back to his cell and meet us in my office."

He motioned to Brenda to accompany him, and they waited for Carver to join them.

"Valentine spilled his guts in there," Stone said when they were all together again. "Do you two think he gave us the straight dope, or did he spin us a yarn?"

"I think he told the truth," Carver said.

Brenda nodded. "I agree. He got sucked into a crazy burglary scheme that went awfully wrong."

"I'd like to interrogate Ken Gear while Valentine's statements are fresh. Okay?"

"I'm game," Carver said.

"Whenever you're ready," Brenda added.

"I'll take the lead this time. Ned, you ask the follow- up questions. Detective, feel free to question Gear when we've finished."

40

A deputy accompanied Ken Gear into the interrogation room and led him to a chair. Gear wore a faded blue county-issue jumpsuit that hung loosely on his narrow body, accentuating long puny arms. Stone and Carver took seats at the table across from him. Brenda stood in the corner. Gear glared squarely into the eyes of his interrogators.

"I'm Sheriff Stone. This is Deputy Ned Carver, the man who arrested you earlier today."

Gear barely nodded and remained silent.

"Were you read your rights, Mr. Gear?"

"Yeah."

"How old are you?" Stone asked.

"I'm twenty-three."

"Are you an American citizen?"

Gear sat back in the chair, a grin spreading across his face. "Yes sir, I was born in Arizona."

"Ever been in trouble with the law?"

"I got two speeding tickets years ago, no crimes."

"You share a place with Joey Valentine and Ramiro Sanchez?"

"Yeah, we rent a single-wide trailer with another man."

"What were you doing at the Sabin farm Monday morning?"

Gear leaned forward, arms propped against the table. "I went there with Ramiro and Joey. We planned to take some cash from the place."

"You mean you planned to steal the farmer's money, don't you?"

"Yeah, okay. Ramiro told Joey and me that the guy kept a lot of cash in the house and we could get to it without much trouble."

Stone shot Gear a steely eye. "When did you decide to murder Art Sabin?"

"Murder him, are you kidding? We never saw the man. None of us did."

"Who raped and strangled the woman upstairs?"

Gear glanced back and forth between Stone and Carver. "Wasn't me, Sheriff."

"Was it Valentine or Sanchez?" Stone demanded.

"It wasn't them either. We were all busy hunting for the money."

Stone rested one arm on the table and studied Gear. "Then who was it?"

Gear folded his arms across his chest. "Carlos did all the stuff."

"You mean to tell me he killed both of the women *and* Mr. Sabin?"

Gear's jaw tightened and he gave Stone a defiant glare. "I told you already, we didn't see Sabin. Carlos killed the two women and the kid."

"Tell me how he killed the boy."

"He shot him in the back when they were running through the yard."

"How did the boy end up in the root cellar?"

"Carlos and Ramiro dragged him there and threw him in. Me and Joey were in the car. We didn't see them do it—Ramiro told us later."

"We found the boy. He's recovering in the hospital."

"Carlos killed two people, then." Gear said.

"No, three. You were right the first time. The woman he killed downstairs was pregnant. Who helped Mendoza do the murders?"

"Helped him? Hell, nobody helped him, Sheriff! He was alone upstairs when he raped the woman. He told us he strangled her because she stabbed him. He knifed the second woman when she came into the house and startled us."

Stone uncovered the modified bayonet on the table. "Is this what he used?"

"Yeah, that's it."

"Have you been involved in other burglaries in my

196

county?"

"No. I was clean till Monday morning."

Stone pushed his chair back from the table. "I'm through with this man for now."

Carver took up the questioning. "Why did Sanchez ask Mendoza to come along on Monday?"

Gear shrugged. "I don't know. Sure wish I did. That crazy bastard screwed everything up."

"Did you know him?"

"I'd never seen Carlos before. He turned out to be one scary son-of-a-bitch."

"Why didn't anyone go upstairs to check on the woman?" Carver asked.

"Ramiro headed to the back of the kitchen for the stairs, but Carlos stopped him. We knew he had a weapon. I don't mind saying I was scared to death of him."

"He was carrying the .22?"

"No, he got that later." Gear pointed to the knife on the table. "That big blade, that's what I'm talking about. I could tell he wasn't afraid to use it. And he did use it later, on the woman downstairs."

"Who told you what to do once you got into the house?"

"Ramiro had worked for Sabin. He'd been in the house, claimed he knew where the money was kept. He told Joey and me to go through the office. We stayed busy for a while."

"Did Mendoza take directions from Ramiro?" Carver leaned closer.

"Hell, no. He grabbed the woman right off and took her upstairs. We saw blood on his shirt when he came back down. From then on, he stood around complaining about his knife wound."

"Why didn't you leave right when you found out Carlos had killed the woman he raped?"

"I don't know. Wish now we had. I had no way of knowing there would be more killing."

"Were you guys planning to rob other farmers in the area?"

"No. We went along with Ramiro because he said the old

197

man had cheated Mexican workers out of lots of money over the years. We were taking some of it back—evening out the score."

Carver sat back in his chair. "Anything else you want to say?"

Gear ran his hand along his jaw and stared off into the corner of the room. "I'm sorry for what happened. Ramiro, Joey, and me never planned to hurt nobody."

41

Gear assumed the questioning was over, at least for the day. He pushed his chair back and stood up, expecting to return to his cell. Brenda strode to the end of the table closest to him.

"Sit down, Mr. Gear, we're not finished here," she demanded.

Gear fell back into the chair. Brenda leaned close and glared at him—her face within inches of his. "You thought Calli Mendez was a pretty fine-looking woman, didn't you?"

He held Brenda's stare, but his voice remained quiet. "I guess so; sure, she was okay."

Carver chanced a sideways glace at Stone, who had his eyes on Brenda.

Brenda stepped back, pacing the room a few steps, never taking her eyes off Gear. "You were thinking how nice it would be to have sex with her, isn't that right, Mr. Gear?"

"Are you kidding me? The woman was old enough to be my mother."

"But that didn't matter, did it, Mr. Gear?" Brenda smiled. "She was a sexy woman, wasn't she?" Brenda walked behind him and leaned over the back of his chair, her mouth close to his ear. "Beautiful body, long shapely legs." She moved around in front of him again and perched on the table. "Don't tell me you didn't want to have sex with her—it insults my intelligence."

Gear fidgeted nervously, his face red with embarrassment. He turned away, confused as to where this might lead. "Carlos told us he killed her. Hellfire, miss, I'd never have sex with a dead woman."

Brenda slid off the table and stood facing Gear. "But she wasn't dead when you raped her, was she?" she shouted. "When Carlos came down, you sneaked up the stairs. You found her on the bed, and you raped her, didn't you?"

"No, you're wrong!" Gear's voice soared and he tried to still his shaking hands.

"You knew she was stuck up there, didn't you? If Carlos could have her, why not you, right, Mr. Gear? You tried to take her, but she resisted, didn't she?"

Stone sat up straighter in his chair, astonishment sweeping across his face.

"No, not so!" Gear cried out, gripping the edge of the table with both hands.

"You grabbed the marble figurine on the bedside stand and clubbed her with it, didn't you?"

"No, no, you're all wrong. Why are you saying this stuff?" Gear pounded the table with his fist and thrust his chin forward. "You can't prove it."

"We got your prints from the marble," Brenda said, her voice quieter now. There were prints all right, but she and Stone didn't know yet who they belonged to. Nevertheless, she decided to play her best card.

Brenda stood back and folded her arms across her chest. "The blow to her head only stunned her. You're the one who tore the clothes from her body. You were mean and ugly with her, and you hurt her, didn't you?"

"It wasn't like that at all. I didn't do that stuff!"

"Mendoza had already raped Calli Mendez. If that had been the end of it, she would be alive today. But no, you went to the room with more on your mind than dipping your wick, didn't you? You wanted to humiliate her. You were brutal with her, frightened her. She'd have done anything to stop the abuse."

"How do you know what happened? You weren't there!" Gear shouted.

"Then Mendoza decided he wanted another go with Calli, didn't he? He climbed the staircase a second time. Calli was ready, though, and she stabbed him when he tried to pin her to the bed. That's when the trouble really started."

"You got it all wrong! It wasn't like that at all."

"My guess is she hurt him pretty bad. It sent him into a rage. That's when he strangled her. Later, he carved on her body.

Did you know that, Mr. Gear?"

"I *didn't* know that," Gear said more quietly now, shaking his head.

"Carlos Mendoza killed her all right, but the murder took place after you maliciously raped her."

Gear said nothing.

"Deputy Carver, bring Sanchez in here," Brenda directed. "He'll tell us whether this man went upstairs."

Carver stood.

"Okay, okay, don't bring Ramiro in here. So I did her. But I didn't kill her."

"No, you're not a murderer, Mr. Gear. You're a pathetic, sadistic, little rapist. You were more than happy to have seconds with Calli because, frankly, you couldn't handle her any other way, isn't that right?"

Quiet now, Gear looked down at his hands. Brenda's eyes were shooting sparks. Perspiration trickled down the sides of her face.

"Sheriff, I'm finished with this sorry rapist. Get him out of here."

"Deputy Carver, take Mr. Gear back to his cell."

"I'm so pissed at that little coward," Brenda spat, after Gear and Carver had left the room.

Stone noticed her hands shaking. "I can tell. You got pretty worked up."

She used a handkerchief to dab away the perspiration. "Lin, I want you to drive me home tonight."

They stood in silence for a moment, looking into each other's eyes, before he smiled and touched her cheek. "I wouldn't have it any other way, Detective," he said softly.

Stone phoned Rusty Gates while they waited for Carver.

"Rusty, can you meet me at Sabin's place in the morning?"

"I can be there about half past nine."

"Good, and be sure to bring your luminal spray bottle so we can detect traces of blood. I want to check my theory about where Art Sabin was killed."

"All right, Sheriff, in the morning."

Stone hung up the phone just as Carver entered the office with a big grin on his face. "Detective, how did you know to go after Gear for raping the Mendez woman?"

"We knew from the coroner two men had raped her. I eliminated Valentine. He's still a virgin, don't you think?"

"Probably so."

"I knew Ramiro worked for Sabin last year. He knew Calli some, at least—a Mexican like him. His raping her didn't feel right to me."

"Remember Gear said Sanchez had gone to the stairway at the back of the house to check on Calli, and that Mendoza stopped him?" Brenda said.

"Yeah, I do."

"I guessed Gear had been back there himself. That's how he knew where the stairs were. Once I accused him of wanting Calli, he couldn't hide his guilt from me. I could read him like a book. It was in his eyes, his mannerisms, his responses to my questions."

Carver turned to Stone. "I think you ought to hire her, boss."

"She's good, all right. But I hate to think we'd need a full-time detective. Valentine lied to us about Gear's involvement with Calli." Stone rubbed his face with the palm of his hand and sighed. "It's been a long day, Ned. In the morning, I want you to visit the Wattenburgers. Tell them that three of their harvest workers are with us at the Dayton Hilton. Gather up anything of theirs they may have left at the farm. Go to their residence, too, and suitcase whatever they left behind."

"What was the address again?" Carver asked.

Stone flipped through his notes from the Valentine interrogation. "301 Pataha."

"Want me to take Detective Tower home?"

"We've got another stop tonight—I'll run her home."

After Deputy Carver left the office, Brenda said, "Lin, I hope the stop we have to make has something to do with dinner."

"There's a little Italian place here in town I think you'll like."

42

On the way to Elam's Crossing following their late evening meal, Stone asked Brenda, "Have you given any thought to when you want to return to Portland?"

She rolled her tongue against the inside of her cheek. "How about right after Labor Day, Sheriff, would that suit you?"

"Labor Day! What in the world would I do with you for six more weeks?"

"If you have to ask, Mr. Stone, you're not the man worth losing my job over." Brenda stretched across the seat and knuckled him in the ribs.

He flinched and smiled playfully in her direction. "There would be an arrest warrant out on me for kidnapping long before the arrival of Labor Day. Seriously, when do you want to go home? I can put you on a train, a bus, a plane, or I could have one of my deputies drive you. What do you prefer?"

"You're not getting off that easy. I insist you chauffeur me yourself," Brenda chirped.

Stone touched her hand. "I'd be proud to do it if that's your wish. What day do you want to leave?"

"I need to be back to work on Monday."

"Then we'll go Sunday if that suits you."

"Sunday it is then," Brenda said.

"We were fortunate to capture Mendoza and stop the other three before they vanished from the county."

"We were very lucky. You must be living right."

Stone's eyes left the road as he looked over at his passenger. "You've been terrific, Brenda."

She tilted her head to one side. "I'm glad I could help. These four days have really been something." She swept a hand through her long, brunette hair. "Luck could shadow us yet. We might nab Sabin's killer before I have to leave."

"We have no suspects—nothing to go on."

"Maybe we can find the weapon."

"Come with me to the farm in the morning? I'm meeting Gates at 9:30. Could be we'll discover some new evidence, maybe even locate the .38."

"Would you mind picking me up?"

"Of course not."

Stone negotiated the hard left turn off Highway 12 onto 261, pulled off the road, and stopped. Without saying anything, he stepped out of the car, trotted around to the passenger side, and opened her door. "Come out here for a moment."

Brenda looked quizzically at him as she slid out of the Expedition.

Stone moved close to her, taking her by the hand. "Look at the stars with me for a moment. They're unusually bright tonight."

Brenda gazed up into the sky. "Do you have a little story about the stars you'd like to share with me?"

"I want a star to wish upon, one that can aid me in keeping you here for a while."

Brenda pulled her hand away. "Isn't this something? I offered to stay till Labor Day, but you made fun of that. Now you want to fudge a few days out of me."

Stone stroked Brenda's hair. "A little while longer, that's all I'm asking."

She reached for his hand. "I'm kidding. I'd like nothing more than to spend a few days away from work with you, but I can't. I have to be back on the job Monday."

"I guess all I can do is dream." Stone took her elbow and held the car door for her, closing it securely as she buckled her seat belt. He padded back around to the driver's side and stepped in.

After returning to the highway, Stone eased off the accelerator and leaned back in the bucket seat. "Do you think someday you could consider being with a man like me—someday, I mean?"

Following a pause, Brenda asked, "Is there something about this man like you that would cause a woman like me to avoid him?"

"I don't know, really. This man doesn't have a checkered past. He's been skittish, though, about any serious involvement since—well, for a long time, anyway. A woman like you is maybe the first female this man has been comfortable around."

"Anything wrong with that?"

"He's not as educated as she is, and he's not cosmopolitan in the least. A friend has told him over and over that he has the personality of a tree stump. This woman like you would probably think he's pretty boring."

Brenda laughed. "Don't you think she'd like him for who he is, this man like you? She'd be drawn to a man who knows where he's going and is confident in his own abilities. He's smart, and she probably thinks he's handsome."

Stone's head jerked in her direction. "She does? You do?" His attention to driving faltered, and the tires on the passenger side drifted off the asphalt. The car bounced along the side of the road. He yanked the wheel hard to the left and returned to pavement.

Brenda chuckled, first at what Stone had said, and then at his driving. "Someday, I could see myself with a man like you." She trailed her fingertips across his cheek. "Why do you ask?"

"Your being here these past few days really got me to thinking—thinking too much I suspect—about you."

"It's your turn now, big guy. Could you see yourself with a woman like me, someday I mean?"

"Of course I could. I like the way you handle yourself. You're not a needy woman. You make me feel good when we're together, and you're attractive. No, that's not right—I think you're gorgeous. And I love how you kiss me." Stone chuckled a little self-consciously. "What else is there?"

"You're sweet, Lin. I wish time wasn't running away from us. What am I going to do with you, anyway?"

They entered the darkened village. Stone turned off Tucanon Street and parked the car. He looked longingly at Brenda in the dim light. She undid her seatbelt, slid sideways in the seat, and angled her upper body toward him. Running a hand up his left side, she clutched his shoulder. Stone encircled her shoulders with one arm while pressing his other hand firmly on her lower back. Brenda reached behind Stone's neck and pulled him closer. His lips grazed her cheek and then met hers in a long, searching kiss.

When their mouths finally parted, Stone breathed heavily. "What a way to end my day." His fingers trailed up her back and through her hair while he looked into her eyes. "You're wonderful. I want this to last, Brenda. Do you understand what I'm saying?"

"Yes, I think I do." They kissed again, hungrily, and she felt the warmth of his hand caressing her breast.

"As tired as I've been tonight, I'm going to have a hard time falling asleep." Stone rested his forehead against hers and cradled her face in his hands.

"I know what you mean, Lin. Kiss me again," she said, arching her back.

43

Mill manager Sam Austin slumped into a discarded chair from his own office while at the yard superintendent's shack. He waited to speak with Todd Moore this Friday morning. Moore entered the room shortly and nodded to Austin.

"Good morning, boss. How's everything in the head shed?"

"We're doing fine. Everyone's clocked in. Saws are all running. Lumber's stacking up."

Moore poured himself a coffee and flopped in his chair behind the desk. "Been waiting long?"

"Not long. I stopped in to ask you how the drivers are doing hauling our one-by-four pine with the relaxed requirement."

"It's taking forklift operators ten to fifteen minutes longer to load a trailer. Drivers report they spend more time retightening loads once they're on the highway."

"Haven't lost any lumber, though?"

"So far every stick from down below has arrived here at the mill."

"That's what I hoped you'd say." Austin smiled with satisfaction. "It's going to cost us a little extra in labor, but that's still cheaper than what we were spending on labor, equipment, and materials to band that stuff."

"We're only in this a couple of days, Sam."

"I know that. Keep the pressure on. Every driver must take the time to strap his load the way he's supposed to. And he's got to stop on every run and tighten his load."

"Thomas is a good yard foreman. He'll make sure they toe the mark."

"Todd, the owner was here last Friday with an ultimatum. Either we bring down the costs of finishing the number-two pine or he's pulling the plug on the operation."

"The hell," Moore said.

"He talked about sending four tractors and trailers from here up to Potlatch. According to my estimate, shutting down that part of our operation would throw about a dozen men out of work."

"We can't let that happen, Sam. We'll do our best."

Austin nodded. "I know you will. Listen, I got a tire man coming. I better get back. Keep me posted."

"You got it."

~

At about the same time Moore met with Austin, the McCormick manager at the Cascade Mill was interviewing Jack Duval, a potential new driver.

"Jack, I know you've had a lot of experience pulling steel across country. This job ain't like those over-the-road hauls you've been used to for years." Glen Dustin leaned across his desk and looked the new man straight in the eye.

"I'm looking for a change, Mr. Dustin."

"You'll be hauling lumber from our cutting mill here in Cascade to our finishing mill in McCall. You'll make four or five runs a day, same ole routine six days a week."

"Ah, routine, that's what I'm looking for."

"The scenery won't change much, Jack, at least not for now."

"I need to slow down some. I'm tired of long hauls. I got a woman now in Banks I want to stay close to."

"I'll expect you in here every morning, 7:30 sharp."

"You won't have no trouble with me. I've been getting up with the chickens since my days on the farm."

Dustin nodded his approval and then continued. "We keep to a strict hauling schedule. I don't tolerate drivers coming in late or laying out, for any reason, without first making arrangements."

"I might call in sick once a year," Duval said. "That's about it, though."

"Usually I take a lot more time with new drivers. I'm making an exception with you. Your cousin bent my ear plenty about what a good driver you are."

"I've never been involved in a reportable accident. My record's clean."

"You'll be assigned to the green Peterbilt—number fourteen. It's a good tractor: Cummings engine, air-cushion ride, chrome stacks, and a chrome sun visor. I expect you to take care of it."

Duval nodded. "I will, sir."

"Be here in the morning, 7:30, no later."

"Right, I'll be here."

"I'm going to turn you over to Cheryl. She'll take care of your W-4 paperwork, show you how to clock in, and go over the daily routines. Pay close attention to our work standards. Ask questions as she reviews them. We pay twice a month—on the fifteenth, and the last day."

"Thanks for the job, Mr. Dustin. You won't be sorry you took me on."

The two shook hands, and Duval left the office feeling plenty proud of having landed a new job. Driving home from the mill, his thoughts turned to the night's celebration with Betty and their friends.

44

Brad Summers struggled Friday morning with the same problem he faced all along his trek: heading off thoughts of his dead Helen. As on many previous days, his resolve faded, and he fell once again to thinking about her, convinced somehow that remembering her was good therapy. But it was hard therapy. His mind filled with images of the situations that had likely contributed to her mental breakdown and suicide. Dark memories had haunted him ever since the day he said goodbye to her at the state psychiatric hospital in Warm Springs.

A slight rain had fallen in the predawn hour. Now with a bright sun and a slight breeze, Summers could see little evidence of the earlier rainfall, but he could smell its lingering residue drifting off the fields. Alone with no chance of being heard, he worried the problem partly out loud as he plodded alongside US 95 North.

"Helen always wanted children; she couldn't wait to be a mother. When I was struck with testicular cancer, she knew we'd never have children of our own. We talked about adopting an infant but always put it off until my travel eased up." He halted, threw up his arms, and shouted, "Because of me we ended up childless!"

Another memory soon slipped into his consciousness. Helen had been an excellent college student, and her student teaching supervisor gave her the highest recommendation.

"I knew how badly she wanted to teach school," Summers mumbled. He removed his ball cap and wiped his brow. With his particular line of work, they'd been thrust into remote, foreign locations where it was impossible for her to fulfill her professional ambition. *Because of me, she never experienced the personal satisfaction that comes with a rewarding career.*

Summers left the highway and strolled into a small picnic area bordering the river. He removed his backpack and perched on a bench to rest for a few minutes. Squirrels scampered about and came close, begging for food. Digging into the backpack, he brought out a sack of shelled peanuts and spread some on the ground at his feet. While the squirrels nibbled their treats, he watched the water. Above the sound of the river, he heard voices, and three bright yellow, rubber rafts loaded with teenagers floated around the bend into view. He watched with interest as they passed, waving to him. Over their commotion he heard an adult in the lead raft yell out, "It won't be long and we'll be home"

The word *home* triggered thoughts of Summers' first home with Helen. It had been a wedding present from Helen's father, a modest bungalow that once belonged to her grandparents on the Montana ranch she loathed. *We lived there for over twenty years when we were stateside. Out of the country so much of the time, I never wanted to buy another home.* Helen had often dreamed of a place that was not a family hand-me-down in the cold climate of western Montana, a hundred yards from her mother's backdoor.

He rose from the bench abruptly, sending the nut eaters scampering for the moment. He eased over to the bank of the river, picked up a baseball-sized stone, and tossed it in the water. "We had the money. Why in the hell didn't I buy Helen a nice place years earlier?"

Summers slung on his backpack, positioned his cap, and made for the highway. But thoughts continued to plague him as he plodded along, waving haphazardly to passing automobiles. Mental anguish had tormented his wife over what happened to her older sister—the woman closest to her in the whole world. Stella's three-year-old twin boys had suffocated in a house fire. To make things worse, Stella and her husband, Blaine, separated and eventually divorced. Helen said the couple couldn't go on together after what happened to the boys. There was nothing he and Helen could do about it, yet she struggled for months, perhaps years, sharing her sister's pain. Summers thrust his hands into his pockets and shrugged. He knew his absences during the family trouble had to be another cause of her downward mental spiral.

"Am I to blame for her endless moodiness and depression?" he wondered out loud. She had masked all of it from

211

him with great skill for so many years. Then one day she collapsed, spending the last six years of her life in confinement, ending with her suicide.

Could this long trek be my penance, somehow, for what happened to Helen? Summers shoulders slumped and his gait slowed. The last time he saw Helen, she had confessed a deep, dark secret she'd kept hidden for thirty years. He lowered his head now, shaking it in disbelief. Why, after all those years, did she decide to reveal such scorching news? Her revelation had knocked Summers off his foundation. He pondered over that hospital visit again and again, unable to shake it. "Did Helen hate me that much, want to hurt me so terribly bad, drive me down, and destroy me?"

He wondered if that long-held secret was the root of her illness. All those years, so ignorant, so blinded from the truth. Helen's suicide must have been her warped, screwy way of saying she was sorry for what she had done. Or perhaps closer to the truth, she took her own life as the ultimate revenge, to make him pay for her misery. He'd probably never know for sure.

"Now she's gone and I'm all alone, a sick, miserable old man with nothing, not even memories that make sense anymore."

45

Only a handful attended the early Friday morning graveside service for Calli Mendez. Stone hung back a little in the misty, gray morning and watched the simple casket being lowered into the ground. He thought of Everett Schuster and Tab Johnson's comments about Calli and realized he admired this woman he'd never even met. The previous evening, the county coroner's black Yukon transported the body of Christina Lopez to Toppenish, Washington. Art Sabin's memorial service would take place at 11:00 a.m. that morning. Stone had decided not to attend; he needed to push on with this case.

The sheriff drove to the NAPA store to verify something Tab Johnson had told him the previous day. "I'm working on the Art Sabin case," he told the manager.

"What a horrible thing. Art was a good customer of ours."

"That's why I'm here. Will you please check your Monday receipts for me to verify purchases were made for him on that day?"

"Wait here and I'll be right back."

"Make me a copy of any receipt, please."

The date on the receipt the manager produced was not Monday, but the previous Saturday. Stone reviewed the copy. The scribbling in the customer box was illegible. "Are these Art Sabin's initials?"

"Yes, that's how he always signed our paperwork."

"No receipt from Monday, though?"

"No, Sheriff. You'll notice this receipt shows filters, a gasket set, and a carburetor for an International truck engine."

"Yes, the grandson told me he and his grandfather were rebuilding an International engine. Thanks for your help." Stone turned and left the store, driving to Elam's Crossing to pick up Brenda. When she settled into her seat, he turned to her, a frown mapping his forehead. "Young Johnson lied to us about going to NAPA Monday morning. The parts were actually signed for by Sabin on Saturday."

"Tab must be covering up. If he'd gone to NAPA, as he claimed, the purchases should still be in his Maxima."

"You're right, they would be. I've got to talk with him again."

Stone and Brenda noticed Rusty Gates trotting back and forth in front of the shop door when they pulled into Sabin's yard. Before they stepped out of the car, the sheriff turned to her. "Gates is liable to flirt with you. It's the kind of guy he is. I thought I'd better warn you."

"I know he's a flirt. I won't claw him unless he gets fresh."

Stone grinned. "Try to hold off till after we finish up here."

The sheriff introduced Brenda to Gates. He teasingly looked her up and down and then nudged Stone.

"I thought you said she was overweight? Man, she looks pretty darn good to me."

Brenda just rolled her eyes, but Stone started to crank out a denial.

"It's okay, Sheriff," Gates interrupted "I promise you I won't take her away until you've solved your case."

"Keep this up, Gates, and you won't have to worry about any more work in Columbia County. I'll be calling on Shepherd when I need a criminalist in the future."

"I thought you knew, Sheriff. Leo Shepherd moved his practice to Boise about a month ago."

Stone wrinkled his face. "Damn, that's too bad. Well, come on in, now that you're here."

The three walked into the shop, and Stone flipped on the lights. "I think Sabin may have been in here Monday morning," Stone said. "Someone crept up behind him on his right side and shot him. He fell over onto his left side, and then the gunman fired two more bullets into his chest."

"You could be right, Sheriff," Gates said.

Brenda walked ahead through the center aisle to a truck engine sitting on a pallet. The two men followed her.

"Sabin's grandson told us they were rebuilding a truck engine," Stone said.

Gates knelt on one knee, examining the floor around the pallet for a visible pool or splotches of blood he could sample with a cotton swab. No luck. To one side, he noted that the concrete floor had been wiped clean, disturbing an otherwise thin layer of dust.

"Hit the lights, Sheriff," Gates said. When the building darkened, Gates sprayed the cleaned area with a mixture of luminal powder, hydrogen peroxide, and hydroxide. "As you two know, if blood is present, the iron from the hemoglobin will produce a chemi-luminescent reaction, giving off a pale, bluish-green color. Look." Gates pointed to the area he had sprayed. Small blue spots appeared in a circle roughly the size of a garbage can lid. Gates snapped photographs and outlined the area with a felt marker. The bluish glow lasted for about twenty-five seconds and then began to fade.

"Your theory is confirmed, Sheriff."

"As least now I know where the crime took place," Stone said. He walked back to the doorway, flipped on the lights, and rejoined Gates and Tower. "Let's go into the office where we can talk about the evidence we've collected."

They pulled up metal folding chairs around an old wooden desk. Stone spied a notepad with a Columbia County Grain Growers logo in the corner. Someone had doodled the initials *HJ* several times in various writing styles and sizes on the page. Likely the Johnson boy's scribbling as he daydreamed about a girl, Stone concluded.

Gates reviewed the physical evidence results he'd collected earlier in the week. "I have a print from the house that could match a print on the .22 pistol. I need to get that weapon from you, Sheriff."

"It's in the car. I'll go get it shortly."

"Do you have prints from your murder suspect?"

"We printed him yesterday in the hospital."

"We'll check the suspect's prints against prints from the house and the weapon," Gates said.

Stone turned to Brenda. "Remind me to give Rusty the knife. We also have two slugs removed from Sabin's grandson and the .38 slug taken from Sabin's body."

"The state crime lab can match the slugs to the guns," Gates said.

"We don't have the .38 that killed Sabin, though" Stone said.

"Damn it. That would have helped." Gates shook his head and went on. "I have blood evidence from the upstairs bathroom. The hospital will have a blood sample from your suspect, and a DNA test will validate a match."

"Right." Stone sighed, wishing he had the gun in question.

"I took an impression of a well-worn truck tire from in front of the house. We have a match with Mendoza's pickup. You'll have ample evidence to convict."

Stone nodded. "That's good, Rusty. And I want to ask your opinion about something."

"Sure, go ahead."

"Sabin's grandson lied about his whereabouts Monday morning. Now I'm suspicious the kid may have been involved in his grandfather's murder. You ever run into anything like that?"

Gates rubbed his right ear between a thumb and forefinger. "You know, young people are capable of about anything when they're drunk or jacked up on drugs. It's possible the kid could have done it. In the absence of some mind-altering substance, he'd about have to be a sociopath to kill his own grandfather."

"Tab doesn't fit the stereotypical sociopath," Brenda said. "He's well liked, he's outgoing, has friends. He seems to be quite mature and levelheaded. Every indication we've heard or seen points to him loving his grandfather."

"Aside from his gallivanting around the county with all kinds of girls," Stone reminded her.

Brenda cocked an eyebrow at him. "Okay, aside from that. I can't imagine anything so terrible coming between them that could have caused Tab to shoot his own grandfather."

"Detective, I think you have a soft spot for the kid that's blurring your objectivity."

"I doubt it, Sheriff." Brenda turned away with a scowl. She felt the sting of disappointment at Stone's quick judgment of both her and the teen.

Stone shook his finger at her. "He damn well better explain to my satisfaction where he was Monday morning. I won't tolerate any more lies."

"Ok, so he lied to us. Does that necessarily mean he's a killer?"

"The boy had to have access to a gun," Gates interjected. "It's impossible to know if Sabin kept a .38 where his grandson could get his hands on it. Do you have any other theory about Sabin's murderer, Sheriff?"

"He had his land tested recently for uranium oxide ore. The tests came back positive."

"That's a zinger—a possible uranium mine in wheat country," Gates said.

"Sabin's attorney knew what he was up to."

"You've considered the possibility someone killed him to put a stop to his mining aspirations?"

Stone nodded. "Rusty, could that murder have been a professional hit?"

"I think not, Sheriff. Hit men wouldn't have taken the risks that are evident here."

"Explain."

"Like snipers, hit men prefer distance, and they like high-powered rifles, they like the cover of darkness, and they want obvious escape routes. None of those elements was present in this case."

"But the killer might have entered the property on foot at night, waited in hiding, shot Sabin, and used his pickup to get away," Brenda said.

"Could have happened like you say, Detective, but it was not likely the work of a pro. Loading the dead man in his own pickup and driving him into a field is way too time consuming, too cumbersome, too risky. A professional wouldn't have taken the time to wipe up blood from the shop floor."

"Got ya," Stone said.

Gates went on. "If Sabin had been hit with a high-powered slug while walking from his house to the shop, or while sitting in his pickup in the open, I'd suspect a professional hit. A pro would have stayed out of sight, fired from a distance, and quickly hightailed it."

"Makes sense, Rusty." Stone sat deep in thought for a moment. "Hold on, and I'll go get that blade."

Stone retrieved the large knife from his SUV and handed it to Gates, along with the .22 pistol the car hauler had taken from Mendoza's pickup.

"This is a modified bayonet," Gates said, turning it over and over. He pointed to one area on the weapon. "This channel on the hilt slides onto the underside of a military rifle barrel. This ring fits over the end of the barrel, and the bayonet snaps into place. This is a U.S.-made article for an M1 Garand rifle used in World War II and Korea."

"It looks to me like a blade from a horror movie," Brenda said. "We interrogated two men who were here with Mendoza on Monday morning. They both told us he admitted to killing the Mendez woman. They also witnessed his slaying of Christina Lopez."

"Sheriff, you've got the house murders solved."

"I hope so. Anything else you need, Rusty?"

"Nothing related to the case." He turned to Brenda and smiled. "Want me to pick you up for dinner tonight at six, or would seven be preferable?"

"Rusty, I'm flattered. But no, not this time."

"Ouch! That's too bad." Gates winked at her.

"Gates, I'm going to run you in for unsolicited annoyance," Stone deadpanned.

Gates laughed and winked again at Brenda. "Sheriff, I'm not going to jail over this woman."

"Good." Stone chuckled.

After Gates left, Stone and Brenda stayed to search for the .38. "If the killer didn't take the weapon with him, it could be here in the shop somewhere," Brenda said.

They looked in tool chests and storage lockers, and they

peered along the floor, under the seats, and in the glove boxes of the various vehicles. They searched in the old combine, among the other machines, and even in the garbage cans. No gun. Brenda kicked the bumper on the old International.

"I'll have the deputies go over this shop inch by inch. I need to talk with that Johnson boy again. Want to come?"

"Did you plan on leaving me here?"

46

Stone and Brenda found Suzanna Edwards sitting on the edge of Tab Johnson's bed when they arrived at his hospital room.

"You'll have to excuse my interruption, miss. It's important I speak with Tab in private for a few minutes," Stone told the girl.

Suzanna stood up to leave, placing her hand on Johnson's arm. "I'll be back when the sheriff's finished."

Johnson nodded. "This shouldn't take long." When the girl quietly shut the door behind her, he said, "What can I do for you today, Sheriff?"

Stone folded his arms across his chest and scowled down at Johnson. "Young man, you told me you were chasing auto parts when your grandfather was killed. There's no record of you doing any business with NAPA on Monday. So where were you?"

Brenda watched as Tab's face fell. He looked over at her as though to say, *Can't you help me out with this?*

"I don't like people lying to me, young man. Makes me think they're hiding something. Maybe *you* killed your grandfather?" Stone paused. "It's time you tell the truth about where you were." A long silence filled the room. Stone stood motionless, glaring at Johnson. Brenda felt uneasy for the first time since she'd been with Stone, but she knew better than to interfere.

Johnson finally cast a glance at Stone and said, "I—I did something I shouldn't have done, Sheriff. I was gone when everything went haywire . . ." His voice failed him. Straightening up in the bed, he struggled to continue. "Sheila and I met at the old cottage late Sunday night." He swallowed hard. "I wasn't planning to be gone too long. Sheila brought a bottle of wine. We ended up drinking too much, and we fell asleep. I didn't wake up until after 7:30 Monday morning."

"When did you arrive back home?"

"Sheila's car wouldn't start. Her girlfriend brought us jumper cables, and I helped her jump-start it. It was close to 9:00

a.m. when I arrived back at the house. I didn't know my grandpa was killed until my mother told me yesterday."

"Is this the truth, at last?" Stone snapped. "If I find you've lied to me again, I'll come down on you like a ton of bricks."

"It's the truth, Sheriff, so help me. Sheila will tell you I was with her. I shouldn't have been, but I was."

"Why shouldn't you have been with her?" Brenda asked.

"I didn't have permission to be out."

"Is it unusual for you to sneak out at night?" she continued.

"I knew better, but I wanted to be with her more than I worried about any punishment if I was caught."

Brenda pressed him. "What would your grandfather have done if he'd known you were out all night with a girl?"

"He would have grounded me for the summer, maybe confiscated my car keys—something like that."

"What if he'd told your parents about you and Sheila?"

"Dad would have jerked me back home in a New York heartbeat."

His answer surprised her. She gazed around the room for a moment and then back at him. "Tab, how old are you?"

"I'll be eighteen in a month."

"Ah-hah," Stone croaked.

"You need to get square in your relationships with girls," Brenda counseled. "You're dancing on thin ice, stringing along Suzanna Edwards while you're playing house with Sheila, and others."

Johnson lowered his gaze. "I know. I've been a jerk with Suzanna. Sheila told me I'm just a plaything to her."

"The sheriff is trying to solve a murder, not straighten out your social life."

Johnson's eyes sought Stone's. "I'm sorry for the trouble I've caused."

"You'll be out of here in a few days," Brenda said. "Made plans yet for what you're going to do?"

"Sure. I'm going back to the farm. I can't wait. Grandpa scheduled tractor drivers and combine operators to start harvesting this coming week. My Uncle Tony is taking some vacation time to help with the harvest. Dad and Mom have made arrangements to stay here and help us get started. Grandma has a new dust mask and new asthma medication, so she's coming out."

"It's good your family is pulling together to get the wheat in," Stone said.

"Squeaky—an old friend of Grandpa's —has volunteered to cook for the crew. Tony told me Squeaky cooked for years at the Davenport in Spokane. He told Tony he wanted to help because Grandpa was the best friend he'd ever had."

"I've met this Squeaky—nice man," Brenda said. "Tab, now you think on what I told you about young women."

Johnson pursed his lips and nodded.

After they left Johnson's room, Stone asked, "Think I was unreasonable with the boy, Brenda?"

"You had to go after him to get to the truth." She grabbed Stone's arm and stopped on the sidewalk to the parking lot. "Did you really think he was a suspect?

"Let's just say I'm eager to verify his alibi."

"And you should be."

"Wait a minute." Stone flipped open his cell phone to place a call to Deputy Carver. "Ned, I need to talk with Sheila Wattenburger. Was she at home when you were there this morning?"

"Her little Z car was in the driveway, Sheriff, but I didn't see her."

"Tell me how to get to their place and give me the phone number out there."

47

Stone and Brenda waited in the Wagon Wheel Café for their lunches.

"Excuse me a minute, Brenda, I need to make a call." Stone rose and sauntered out the side door where he tapped in a number on his cell phone. A young-sounding, female voice answered. "Miss Wattenburger, this is Sheriff Stone. I'd like to speak with you sometime today."

"What about, Sheriff?"

"I need you to clarify something related to an investigation."

"I don't think I can help you."

"Maybe I should speak to your father about this instead?" Stone listened to a brief silence at the other end of the phone.

"No, no, that's all right. I'll—I'll talk to you."

"Should I come to the farm, or would you like to meet me in Elam's Crossing?"

"Our place is kind of hard to find. I'll meet you in town."

"Can you be at City Hall at three o'clock?"

"Yes, I'll be there."

"Detective Brenda Tower will accompany me. We'll see you then."

Returning to the table, he answered Brenda's questioning gaze. "I've arranged a meeting with Sheila Wattenburger at three. I hope she'll cooperate."

"Would you like me to question her, Sheriff?"

"It would be less intimidating for her, I think, so yes, why don't you?"

~

Brenda stood with Stone in front of the large, arched picture window at City Hall when Sheila drove up in her red convertible, screeching to a stop. She slunk out from behind the wheel and strolled to the door in white shorts that showed more leg than a Dallas Cowboy cheerleader. Her bright red halter-top required every strand of the sturdy ties to hold things in their proper places.

"No wonder young Johnson can't keep away from her," Stone said.

"Now, Sheriff—," was all Brenda got out of her mouth before Sheila pushed open the door and strutted inside.

"Thanks for coming, Miss Wattenburger. I'm Sheriff Stone and this is Detective Tower. Please follow us to the mayor's office in the back where it's more private."

"I'm not sure what this is about," Sheila said, once the three of them sat down.

"We're investigating a murder that took place this past Monday," Brenda began.

"You're talking about Mr. Sabin, right?"

"That's correct."

Sheila crossed her legs. "It's hard to believe our workers were involved."

"What can you tell us about Joey Valentine and Ken Gear?" Brenda asked.

Smacking her chewing gum, she said, "Both of them worked the harvest for us last year. Dad said they were good workers—never gave him any trouble."

"What do you know about Ramiro Sanchez?"

"He worked at the Sabin farm last year. I remember him telling me he didn't like the man—Sabin."

"When did he tell you that?"

"Ramiro came by our place at the end of harvest last year looking for seasonal work this year. I talked with him in the yard."

"Sheila, I need to ask you, where were you early this last Monday morning?"

"You don't think I had anything to do with Mr. Sabin's murder, do you?"

"No, you're not a suspect. This is just routine questioning to gather information."

Sheila peered at Brenda intently and then turned a skeptical eye on Stone. "Where do the two of you think I was?"

"We haven't talked with your mother, Sheila, to verify you

were home. We may need to do that."

Sheila squirmed in her chair and blurted, "Leave my mother out of this! And don't believe a word Ramiro tells you. You can't trust him."

"What could Ramiro tell us about you, Sheila, related to Monday morning?" Brenda asked.

"I was, uh, with him recently. I don't want my parents to know anything about that."

"We're only interested in where you were Sunday night and early Monday morning. The rest is your business."

Sheila crossed her arms over substantial cleavage revealed by the skimpy red top. "You're wrong, detective, it's *all* my business." Her voice rose. "Look, it's my life, and I'll live it the way I want to!"

"Even if it hurts someone, I suppose."

"I don't hurt other people!"

"You could seriously hurt someone by refusing to tell us your whereabouts Monday morning," Brenda said.

Sheila's eyes narrowed. She uncrossed her right leg and stamped it hard on the bare oak floor. A *boom* echoed through the room. She glared at Brenda. "Why can't you people live and let live?" Jumping to her feet, she started for the door.

"Sheila wait, please come back and sit down. I apologize for threatening you with your mother."

Sheila slid back into her chair. A long silence followed. "Oh fudge, what do you people want from me?" she finally asked.

"All we want to know is where you were on the morning of July fifteenth."

"You're not going to run to my dad with this, are you? If that's your game, you won't get squat from me."

"If we wanted to mess with you, we'd have insisted your father meet with us while we questioned you."

"Or we could've questioned the two of you at my office," Stone added. "We're not trying to give you a hard time. We just need some answers."

Sheila looked at the two of them and her shoulders slumped a little. "Okay. I was with Tab Johnson."

"Where were the two of you?"

"We were at an abandoned cottage on the Sabin Farm."

"What time did you arrive back at the house?"

"Sometime after 9:00 on Monday morning. My parents think I stayed the night with a girlfriend."

"Why didn't you tell me where you were in the first place?"

"Because Tab's only seventeen," the girl answered, her jaw muscles tensed.

"How old are you, Sheila?"

"I'm twenty-one."

"We needed your help to clear Tab Johnson's whereabouts," Stone said.

"We were together, like I said." Sheila stood up and jangled her car keys.

"Your cooperation here is much appreciated, Miss Wattenburger," Stone said.

"If that's all, I'll be leaving now. I'll thank you not to tell my folks what we talked about."

"What we discussed here won't be repeated—you can count on that," Stone said.

Sheila stomped out of the building to her little red sports car and sped off.

"It took some time to get her to confess her whereabouts," Stone said. "You did a good job questioning her." He shook his head and laughed. "That Johnson kid doesn't have a snowball's chance in hell so long as she continues to blow in his ear."

"You wouldn't be at all concerned if she was some plain-Jane country girl, now would you, Sheriff?"

"At least he'd have a fighting chance. With that knockout body rubbing up against him and her breathing sweet nothings in his ear, the kid's going down for the count every time."

"Oh, and what do you know about knockout bodies, anyway?"

"I know what I see, and that one's a knockout, a bombshell, as kids used to say."

"It's pretty clear she likes men and is willing to take some crazy risks to be with them."

"She must have been a handful for her parents when she was a teen," Stone said as they walked to the front door. Stone locked up the building, and then they sat and talked in the Expedition for a few moments before he started it up and drove Brenda back to the B&B.

"I'd like you to come with me to the Blue Mountains tomorrow. Is that something you'd enjoy?"

"Yes, I would—sounds like a fun way to spend a Saturday."

"I'll get Hardesty to cover for me. I'll pick you up in the morning about eight."

"Should I bring my hiking shoes?"

"Yes, we'll do some sightseeing on foot."

48

Following an early supper that evening, Brenda left Huber's Café and treaded north along Main Street in the opposite direction of her bed and breakfast. A short promenade in the countryside would be nice, she thought—it would help her unwind in preparation for a day in the mountains with Lin.

The edge of the village soon became obvious: no buildings, no sidewalk, no traffic. Main Street ended, bumping up diagonally against a recently paved, narrow road leading out of Elam's Crossing toward farmland. Brenda turned left onto the newly surfaced pavement and strolled along, her tan walking shoes and jeans a welcome change from the low heels and skirt she'd worn earlier today. She left the top two buttons of her print, collared shirt open, and the late-day sun warmed her neck and the skin just above her breasts.

Off in the distance, wheat fields covered rolling hills on both sides of the small valley. An azure sky presented an exquisite backdrop to the golden grain fields lit by the early evening sun. Brenda soaked in the calm beauty. In the foreground, lush, fenced pastureland dotted with large trees offered sustenance and shade to grazing beef cattle and saddle horses. Young calves wandered alone in the field for short distances, then hustled to their mothers and nuzzled in, tails wagging. Brenda caught sight of two gray rabbits scampering playfully inside the fence until their ears twitched at the sound of footsteps on asphalt and they raced away. A solitary hawk circled overhead. She hoped it wouldn't spot the cottontails.

The roadside and fence lines were tidy, trimmed clean of weeds and tall grass. White fence posts carried recently strung wire, tight and straight. An alfalfa hayfield rose up on her right side.

"This field is ready for a second cutting," Brenda muttered.

The gurgle of water reached her ear as the road came closer to the Tucanon River, nearing the end of its journey at the shore of the Snake River. It reminded her of the family ranch in Colorado where a hundred acres bordered on the South Platte River. Here, large elm trees lined the road ahead, but the air remained warm.

Brenda could make out a lovely, well cared for piece of property on the right side of the road as she advanced into the welcome shade. A two-story farmhouse appeared with a columned porch and a gabled overhang. Charcoal shutters and a marine-blue front door set off the white paint and gray trim of the rest of the house. A one-story barn tucked behind the house looked as though it had recently been painted red, and a white rail fence outlined the barnyard. An old wooden-handled, horse-drawn plow stood erect in the side yard flowerbed. Someone had recently coated the plow handles, and perhaps other wooden items in the yard, with turpentine. The pungent scent caused Brenda to rub her nose as she drew nearer.

Carefully pruned and shaped shrubs bordered the house. Towering arborvitaes separated the spacious, uniformly green lawn on the far side of the house from the pastureland that spread out beyond. Sunset Maples towered above the under-canopy of dogwoods and flowering cherry trees. Manicured flowerbeds reminded Brenda of photos she'd seen in her *Better Homes and Gardens* magazine.

This is a wonderfully peaceful setting, completely alien to the noise, constant rush, and turmoil of the city, Brenda thought. Mesmerized by this rural beauty, she counted it as a rare glimpse of heaven.

A border collie sauntering onto the road ahead interrupted her serene mood. It didn't bark, growl, or show its teeth, but Brenda stopped and stood perfectly still, not wanting to arouse the animal. Hair standing high on its neck, the dog studied her for a long time without making a sound. Finally it approached slowly and smelled her shoes and the ground around her feet for a few moments. Then the collie cautiously licked her hand. A chill traveled the length of Brenda's body and a wide smile spread over her face. She spoke quietly to the dog as she bent down and stroked it. Following several moments of petting, the female canine leaned heavily against Brenda's leg and looked longingly into her eyes. Brenda had made a friend.

What would it be like to have a little ranch—something like this one? She could have a horse again, she thought. Her sisters and their families would have a place to visit. It would be something she could pass on to her children someday. Children, now there's a concept, she thought. *I'm thirty-five years old, and I don't even have a husband.* To have children, she would want a man, a man who wanted her, who wanted children, and who wanted to live in the country. *I haven't run across too many of those.*

Brenda padded over to the fence, laced her fingers over the top rail, and rested her chin on her hands. *There's so much in life I'm missing. I must make a change.* Brenda knew her confounded rule of not dating men she found attractive was crazy, and she knew she needed to pull the plug on that immediately. She'd met an attractive man, a man she trusted and would like to be with.

Hmm, I wonder if Lin wants children. She felt something warm brush her leg and looked down to see the collie's tail wagging as though in approval.

49

Ed Pearson, a volunteer deputy, arrived at the Dayton Hospital moments before midnight Friday to stand guard over Carlos Mendoza.

"Nurses are here to care for the man," Deputy Weber told him. "The only time you need to go into the room is to release his restraints so he can use the can. Always handcuff him before you let him out of bed. And always keep your weapon drawn when he's handcuffed, understood?"

"Uh-huh," Pearson muttered.

"The rest of the time you can sit or stand here in the hallway with the door open. Hospital staff only is allowed into the room—no one else!"

"I understand."

Mendoza strained to hear the conversation taking place outside his room.

"I'll be relieved at 8:00 a.m., right?" Pearson asked.

"That's correct. Your relief will be here then. This Mendoza will be moved to a cellblock before too long. That'll mean the end of this hospital duty."

"I bumped into Ned today at the office. He was telling me how he and a female detective nabbed those three guys on the highway," Pearson said.

Mendoza held his breath to better hear the exchange outside his door. Pearson tilted his head in the direction of the room. "Carver said two of the prisoners told the sheriff this guy killed the two women."

"He's a bad one, Ed." Weber thumped Pearson on the arm. "You stay alert—be careful here tonight."

"I got your message, Chet."

Weber nodded. "Good." He turned and walked away, eager to get to his car and to his bed.

Pearson settled into the chair in the hallway and waited. Time dragged. He stood and moved around periodically to keep the circulation in his legs alive. About 3:00 a.m., Mendoza yelled out, "I need to pee!"

Pearson entered the room and flipped on the lights, causing Mendoza to squint. The deputy walked over to the bed, unstrapped one of Mendoza's arms and applied a cuff, and then repeated the process with the prisoner's other arm. Pearson stood back to allow Mendoza to throw his legs over the side of the bed. He limped to the bathroom, favoring his bad leg, with Pearson following close behind. Mendoza entered the little room and shut the door. Moments later, Pearson heard the toilet flush. He glanced at his watch and idly surveyed the room while waiting for the prisoner to come out.

Mendoza pushed open the bathroom door abruptly and swung his handcuffed arms hard at the deputy's head. Stunned, Pearson fell to the floor. Mendoza quickly bent down, unsnapped the deputy's sidearm, and slammed the butt of the gun against the right side of Pearson's head. The deputy lost consciousness.

Rummaging through Pearson's front pockets, Mendoza located the key to the handcuffs and quickly freed his arms. He found the deputy's car keys, then hurriedly dressed. Once in the corridor outside his room, he kept his head down and moved as briskly as his bad leg would allow. At one crucial moment, he hid in the shadows of an empty room while a custodian moved along the hall with his cart of cleaning products and a dry mop. When the custodian parked his supplies two rooms down and left for a break, Mendoza slipped out. As he made his way along the corridor, he managed to grab a hospital mask from a nurse's cart outside an occupied room. His mind moved briefly to the painkillers that cart might contain, but the low murmur of voices in the room stayed his hand. The cart would be locked, and breaking into it would take too much time and trouble, anyway. He continued down the hall and around a corner, finally reaching an exit door marked for visitors. Mendoza slipped out into the warm night.

Locating Pearson's car in the parking lot during the day

might have been a challenge, but not at that hour—only a skeleton nursing staff remained on duty. The Chevrolet logo on the car key helped him spot a Malibu in the dim light. He slunk over to the car and tried the key in the lock. A satisfying click rewarded his effort. He opened the door and slid behind the wheel. As the engine hummed to life, he turned on the lights.

"A quarter of a tank. I need gas, and I need cash," he muttered.

Mendoza drove north out of the parking lot toward Main Street, where he turned right. *I hope to hell that gas station at the east end of town is open.* Moments later, he swung alongside one of the gas pumps, grabbed his gun, adjusted the hospital mask over his nose and mouth, and hobbled to the front door. Inside, he found himself alone with a slight-built young man in a NAPA logo tee behind the counter.

Mendoza raised his weapon. "Give me all the bills and be quick about it."

"Don't shoot, mister! I'll get the money." The attendant's hands scrambled through the cash register trays pulling out twenties, tens, fives, and ones. He pushed them across the counter toward Mendoza and noticed the robber was wearing a hospital ID band.

"Now, get me some gas."

"I have to set the pump in here first, okay?" The young man's hands shook as he waited for a nod from the thief.

Mendoza inclined his head slightly and kept his eyes pinned on the employee. After the attendant man filled the tank, Mendoza shoved past him, swung around, and smashed the gun into the man's head. The kid—probably no more than a teenager, Mendoza thought fleetingly—went down hard.

Carlos Mendoza jumped into the stolen car and sped off, tires screeching against dry pavement. The attendant moaned and rolled over in time to see the car enter the highway, traveling east. Moments later, he staggered back into the gas station and dialed 911.

"Sheriff's office, Patty here. Can I help you?"

"This is the night man at the—the Get-N-Go. We've been—

been robbed at gunpoint! The guy is wearing a hospital band."

"Is the man still on the premises?"

"Hell no, he beat it pretty quick."

"Can you describe him for me, sir?"

"He's a heavyset Mexican, somewhere around twenty-five to thirty-five, maybe."

"Could you say about how tall he was?"

"Just average height, I guess. Five-eight, five-nine at the most."

"What else can you tell me about him? Hair color? Eye color? What he was wearing?"

"He had a ponytail. Black hair. I—I don't know about his eyes. He wore a paper mask over his mouth and nose. He was wearing a tee shirt and jeans."

Is he on foot or is he in a car, do you know?"

"Yeah! He made me pump him some gas after he took the money. He's headed east on Highway 12 in a silver Malibu with Washington plates."

"Wait a minute—I'm writing things down, here. Silver Malibu, Washington plates. Okay. I'll send a deputy. Stay on the premises. And lock the place up until our man arrives."

The dispatcher had barely hung up the phone when she received a second, frantic call.

"This is Julie Butler, the night nursing supervisor at the Hospital."

"Oh, hi, Julie. Patty here. I hope everything went all right with our prisoner's move earlier. I sent a second deputy over about 9:00 p.m. to help with that."

"We had to move that nutcase. He was causing an awful disturbance where he was. But we've got a bigger problem now."

"What is it, Julie?"

"Your man has escaped, and the sheriff's deputy is hurt."

"Oh my goodness! I'll have someone there as soon as I can."

~

Stone struggled out of a deep sleep to catch the call before the ringer stopped. He lifted the receiver and noted that the bedside clock showed 3:35 a.m.

"Stone here."

"Sheriff, this is Patty. We've got a problem."

"Talk to me."

"Carlos Mendoza escaped. He robbed the Get-N-Go at gunpoint a few minutes ago. He's headed east on 12."

"Son-of-a-bitch," Stone blurted.

Patty cleared her throat. "There's more, Sheriff. Deputy Pearson's been injured."

Stone sighed heavily. "Oh, no, the new volunteer?" He scratched his head. "Patty, notify the Washington State Patrol and the Idaho State Patrol with a description of Mendoza and the direction of his flight. Do we have a description of the car or a license plate number?"

"I have the make and color of the car."

"Good. I'll get ready and go to the hospital."

~

Stone found Deputy Pearson slumped in a chair in the hospital waiting room, holding his bandaged head. He shot Stone a sheepish look, like a boy who'd just run his father's vintage BMW through the back end of the garage.

Stone placed his hand on Pearson's shoulder. "Ed, are you okay?"

"I've got a whale of a headache, Sheriff, but I'm all right. I screwed up big time—I'm really sorry. The guy knocked me down when he came out of the bathroom. He cold-conked me with my own weapon."

"We can discuss that later, Ed. By the way, I didn't see your car in the lot. Are your keys missing?"

Pearson patted his pants pockets. "Damn, they're gone! So is my gun."

"Looks like Mendoza robbed the Get-N-Go using your weapon. We've alerted the Washington and Idaho State Patrols with a description of your car."

"Someone's gotta catch that bastard," Pearson groaned.

"They will. Let me take you home."

Brenda's phone rang at 6:30 a.m., well before her alarm was set to go off.

"Lin here. I'm sorry to bother you at this hour, but I've got bad news."

Brenda rubbed her eyes and yawned. "Tell me—what's up?"

"Carlos Mendoza escaped. He's on the run in a stolen car."

"Shi—sugar, you do have a problem."

"Yeah, I sure do. I'm sorry, but we'll have to postpone our trip to the mountains."

"Please don't worry about me, I'll be fine."

Silence filled Brenda's ear for a long moment. "Well—but *I* won't be fine, Brenda. I'm mad as hell. I wanted to spend the day with you. Damn!"

"I'm disappointed, too. I was looking forward to our time together. Can I help?"

"Nothing you can do. Not much I can do, either. We have a notice out to the state patrols in Washington and Idaho. My hope is he'll be picked up this morning. I'll call you later today."

"Okay, then, take care. I'll be waiting for your call."

"Goodbye, Brenda."

50

Mendoza raced toward Lewiston, Idaho, in the predawn morning. He had already driven through Dodge, bypassing Highway 127 that would have taken him north to any one of nearly a dozen communities where he could have hidden out. He chose instead to race ahead toward his people in Nampa, Idaho, three hundred miles to the south.

I gotta ditch this car, he thought. Light had not broken in the eastern sky when Mendoza turned into a pull-off along a lonely stretch of road and parked behind a new Cadillac. Leaving the car running, he grabbed the gun off the seat, slid out from under the wheel, and limped to the driver's side window.

"Get out of there!" he yelled. He pulled open the door and waved his gun in a middle-aged woman's face.

"Please, don't shoot!" the woman pleaded, trembling hands flying to her cheeks.

Mendoza grabbed her by the arm and pulled her out of the car while she struggled to keep from falling. "Please don't hurt my father—he's very sick!" she sobbed.

Mendoza hurried around the car to the passenger's side. Shoving the gun in his pants at the beltline, he jerked open the door. Unbuckling the seatbelt, he yanked the feeble old man off his seat and onto the gravel a short distance from the car. He slammed the passenger door and limped back to the driver's side of the car where the woman stood, paralyzed and sobbing.

"Take my car, bitch," he snapped. Sliding behind the Cadillac's wheel, he drove away, stowing the gun under the seat. *No reason to waste ammo on them. I have what I want, and I still got a fully loaded gun.*

Mendoza negotiated the twin-cities of Clarkston, Washington, and Lewiston, Idaho, early enough to miss the Saturday morning traffic. He followed the overhead sign for U.S.

95 south to McCall and Boise and motored on. The pains in his injured leg increased, reminding him he was long overdue for a painkiller. He left the highway at a mom-and-pop convenience store on the outskirts of Craigmont. There he purchased fuel, a cheap baseball cap, sunglasses, scissors, some junk food, and a bottle of Tylenol. With scissors in hand and the use of a washroom mirror, he whacked off his ponytail, throwing the thick hank of black hair in the waste can. After gulping down four of the pain pills, he gathered up his purchases and headed back to the car.

The beautiful scenery over White Bird Pass, the responsiveness of the outstanding automobile, and the exhilaration he felt with his newfound freedom raised Mendoza's spirits. Wide awake now, he noticed his surroundings more keenly. The mountain highway afforded the unexpected thrill of numerous switchbacks. A wind started to pick up, and occasional plump, cottony clouds moved faster. The blue sky gradually took on a dirty, gray cast. *Nothing to worry about.* Reaching his destination was all that mattered.

The highway leveled out and straightened some, allowing Mendoza to pick up speed to compensate for the severe headwind slowing his progress. As the weather worsened, Mendoza noticed most drivers exiting the highway to wait out the harsh winds. But he hurried on—weather be damned.

~

Jack Duval arrived for his first day of work at the McCormick Lumber Cascade yard with a hangover. He didn't have the patience to deal first thing with an engine that wouldn't start, and he breathed a huge sigh of relief when the diesel in Number 14 finally kicked over. He pulled the tractor-trailer near the stacked pallets of lumber as directed and left the engine running. Exiting the cab, he sucked on strong, hot coffee poured from the thermos Betty had prepared. He kept an eye on the forklift operator loading pallets of one-by-four, rough-cut lumber onto his flatbed trailer.

When the front tier filled the bed on both sides, Duval uncoiled three nylon straps housed in the bed frame, throwing one at a time over the load to the opposite side. Walking around to the other side, he secured the straps to their keepers and tightened them. With the use of a come-along, or cheater bar, he ratcheted the straps down until he heard the lumber creak under the pressure. He repeated this process for each of the four tiers along the length of the trailer bed, noticing that the top of the load in the back had slopped over some when the pallets were loaded.

As Duval climbed up into his cab, the forklift operator yelled out, "Stop and tighten your load!" Duval gave a thumbs-up, and Number 14 pulled away from the yard at about 8:20 a.m. The operator had neglected to tell him where the turnout was located, and Duval hadn't thought to ask.

I busted my ass cinching down this load, he thought, once he was on the road. *Where the hell was that turnout, anyway? Oh well I'll look for it on this run.*

~

Strong winds, in conjunction with the suction action caused by passing eighteen-wheelers, rocked Mendoza's stolen Cadillac with each encounter. He gripped the steering wheel with both hands whenever one of the big rigs roared his way. A lumber truck came into view, piled high and approaching fast, pushed by a ferocious tailwind. As it drew nearer, he noticed pieces of lumber flying from the driver's side of the trailer.

The green Peterbilt flashed by, and a deafening roar exploded inside Mendoza's car. Shards of glass flew through the air. Mendoza let out a scream and hit the brakes with his good leg. The car lurched hard to the right, careened off the road, crossed over a dry ditch bed, and tore along a barbed wire fence for a hundred feet before coming to a stop.

A round hole the size of a softball had appeared in the windshield on the driver's side. Inside, the escaped prisoner slumped back in the seat, speared in the chest by the wind-driven, arrow-like flight of a splintered piece of one-by-four pine. The opposite end of the murderous piece protruded almost six feet through the windshield. Blood ran down Mendoza's right side, soaking his shirt and pants, creeping onto the blue leather seat. Laboring to breathe, he slipped into darkness.

Two miles north of the accident scene, Number 14 turned onto the side road leading to the McCormick Finishing Mill. Only then did Duval realize part of his load had sloughed off the trailer.

Less than an hour later, an Idaho State patrolman discovered the battered car and struggled to describe the accident in his report. Putting to paper how a piece of lumber moved through the air with sufficient velocity to penetrate the windshield at just the right angle and imbed itself in a man's body with sufficient force to kill had not come easy.

51

After completing his report on the Get-N-Go robbery, Stone decided to interrogate Ramiro Sanchez with the assistance of Clark, the cellblock deputy, who read Sanchez his rights.

"Why did the sheriff talk to my guys before he talked to me, man?" Sanchez asked.

"You'll have to ask him," Clark said.

The leader of the Sabin burglary bunch echoed his comrades' descriptions of how Mendoza murdered Calli Mendez and Christina Lopez.

"Did you tell Mendoza to shoot the boy?" Stone asked.

"I did not! Joey, Ken, and me were in my car ready to leave when Carlos jumped out of his truck and ran back into the house. He came back out soon, man. It was then he spotted the boy running away. Carlos chased after him. I heard three shots."

"Why did you two move the victim?"

"Carlos wanted the body out of sight from the front of the house, you know. He yelled at me to come and help him."

"Why did you dump the body into the cellar?"

"There were coyotes in the fields last year. I didn't want the kid to get eaten, man."

"The boy isn't dead. He's recovering in the hospital."

Sanchez nodded. "Ken told me. I'm glad he's alive."

Stone's eyes locked onto Sanchez's. "You were the leader that morning. Tell me, why did you allow Mendoza to kill the two women?"

Sanchez sprang to his feet, his chair flying backwards and tipping over. His jaw hardened and his fists clenched. Stone thought the vein in his neck looked like an engorged earthworm. "You don't understand, man! It wasn't like that!" he screamed.

Stone shouted back, "Sit down young man, and behave yourself."

With trembling hands, Sanchez righted his chair and eased himself back onto it. His dark eyes flaming and his voice harsh, but controlled, he continued. "I didn't let him do a damn thing, man. I tried to talk with him, but I couldn't control him, couldn't stop him, you know. He acted crazy, scared me shitless. If I'd tried to interfere with him and Calli, he would've knifed me for sure."

"If he couldn't be controlled, why did you ask him to take part in the burglary?"

"I thought I might need another guy in case Ken or Joey bugged out. I didn't know he was a rapist and a murderer, Sheriff." Ramiro covered his face with his hands and sat motionless. Looking up, he finally said, "Those women would be alive today if he hadn't been along."

"You made some poor decisions, Mr. Sanchez. You're going to need a good lawyer."

~

Stone drove to Deputy Pearson's home to explain to his wife, Anne, what had happened to her husband at the hospital early that morning. But trouble awaited him. Anne started in before he could even say hello. He stood on the third step leading to her front door, receiving no invitation to come farther.

"Why the hell was my husband assigned to guard a killer, Sheriff? Ed came home in bandages, without his gun, and my damn car is gone!"

"I'm sorry about Ed's injury, Anne. And you know we're good for replacement of the gun."

"What about my car?" she screeched. "You know, if it's ever recovered, it'll be beat to pieces."

"Let's hope not."

The woman's hands shook, and her voice rang shrilly in the quiet neighborhood. "You had no business assigning an inexperienced volunteer to a dangerous assignment like that. I'm really pissed at you."

"I don't blame you for being upset, Anne. We had people killed here six . . ."

Anne ignored him and continued her attack. "Ed doesn't get paid a damn nickel for what he does for you. And you give him a dangerous job and get him hurt."

"Wait a minute, Anne. I had a wounded prisoner in the hospital, and all my . . ."

Hands flying to her hips, Anne shouted, "I don't give a flip what you had, Sheriff! I know one thing—you don't have Ed anymore. What if that murdering spic had killed my husband and left me here a widow with three kids?"

"This was an unusual circumstance, Anne."

"Unusual, you say. Well, it won't ever happen again, I can tell you that. Ed will be in soon to turn in his badge." She nodded firmly several times. "Count on it!"

"Maybe you'll feel differently after the two of you have time to talk."

"We did our talking already. It's over. He either gives it up now or he says goodbye to me. Do you understand those apples, Sheriff?"

"I understand, Anne. I'm sorry for what happened." Stone turned his back to her and descended the steps.

"You and your men stay away from him, you hear me? Don't anyone be coaxing him to stay on, unless you want to see him living alone."

Stone kept moving. Without turning back, he raised a hand, signaling he'd gotten the message. Before entering his vehicle, he glanced at his watch. It was early yet for lunch, but he'd been up since three-thirty a.m. with no more than a stale donut and a coffee. To hell with the time, he thought. Stone fired up the Expedition and nosed it toward food.

As he entered the café, an attractive waitress at the Wagon Wheel caught Stone's eye. She batted blue eyes at him and then sashayed toward an empty table. Stone followed. She smiled widely when she handed him a menu and again when she took his drink order. He eyeballed her shapely wiggle as she walked away. Later his gaze again followed the tall, shapely blonde as he devoured his bacon-cheeseburger and potato salad. Stone was working on a slice of apple-cinnamon pie with a coffee and contemplating the eternal beauty of tall, shapely blondes like Sheila Wattenburger and Miss Wagon Wheel when his cell rang.

"I have something for you, Sheriff," Pamela said. "Come in if you're close."

"I'll be over soon."

As he finished up at the café, Stone wondered if Ed Pearson was waiting at the office to return his badge. Or maybe there was a new lead in the Sabin case, or the state police had apprehended Mendoza—he could hope, at least. After driving to the court house, the sheriff parked and walked to his office.

The look on Pamela's face told Stone she had something major. He removed his cap, smoothed his hair back, and slipped into the chair next to her.

"I'm all ears, Pam. Give me the dope."

"Well, Sheriff, your runaway was killed this morning on Highway 95 a few miles south of McCall, Idaho."

Stone straightened up and slapped his right knee. A wide grin stretched from cheek to cheek. "Killed, you say? What a break—this is great news! Do you have any details?"

"The caller told me a piece of lumber flew off a lumber truck, crashed through his windshield, and speared him in the chest. An Idaho State Patrolman spotted the car tangled in barbed wire and fence posts at the edge of a field."

Stone rubbed his palms together. "What a surprise! Pam, you've made my day." He sprang out of the chair and paced back and forth. He rubbed the side of his face, a familiar sign to Pamela that he had more to say. "I normally hate to hear about people dying in accidents, but this is swift, sweet justice for one devil SOB. That Carlos Mendoza was evil through and through, that's all I can say."

Pamela waited for Stone's excitement to cool. When he sat down again, she continued. "There's more, Sheriff. Deputy Pearson's vehicle is in the parking lot at Saint Joseph's Hospital in Lewiston. The woman whose Caddie was stolen drove directly there. Keys are at the reception desk."

"That's more good news! Have Mike's Towing pick it up. It's a silver Chevy Malibu. We won't call Mrs. Pearson until we verify the vehicle hasn't been damaged." Stone paused. "Before I forget, if Ed should come in to resign, don't let anyone try to talk him out of it."

"Problem, Sheriff?"

"Anne is madder than a wet hen over what happened to him this morning at the hospital. She's threatened to leave him if he doesn't quit." He patted Pamela on the shoulder. "Mendoza's dead! What a load off my shoulders."

From his office, Stone called Brenda's room. It was noon, and he worried she might be out. The phone rang and rang. He finally heard her voice at the other end. "Brenda, how about we spend the rest of the day together? We can see some local sights and have a nice dinner in Walla Walla."

"That would be great, Lin, but can you pull away for that long with Mendoza on the run?"

"He's not running anymore, Brenda. Fact is, he's not doing anything anymore. I'll tell you all about it when I see you."

"He's in jail again, isn't he?"

"He wasn't that lucky."

"Don't tell me he's been shot again."

"We'll talk when I see you, Brenda."

"And when will that be?"

"I'll be there between one-thirty and two."

Once at home, Stone made his bed, did the dishes in the sink, and wiped down the counters. He picked up the newspapers from the last few days, swept the front porch, and carried out the trash. Checking around outside, he swept the patio and returned the mower to its assigned spot.

Back inside again, he laid out his best pair of summer Dockers and a medium blue DaVinci sport shirt. He brushed his teeth, shaved and showered, combed his hair, rubbed on deodorant, and splashed on a dash of Polo aftershave. After dressing, Stone slipped into a pair of burgundy Wellingtons. He looked at his reflection in the full-length mirror on the back of the closet door. *I hope she'll agree to come home with me after.*

52

"The berries you served this morning for breakfast were so tasty," Brenda told Carol Wannamaker while awaiting Stone's arrival at the raspberry patch.

"I'm glad you liked them. There've been raspberries on this place ever since I was a girl."

"Someone in town told me your husband has remodeled a few houses on this end of town."

"Yes. He's an excellent carpenter. We're fixing up some old places to rent. By the way, I heard your name mentioned at Huber's yesterday."

"You did?"

"Yes, Melba Townsend said you shot the man suspected of murdering those poor women at the Sabin farm."

Neither woman noticed the blue Taurus stop across the street. Brenda finally glanced in the direction of the driver as he strolled toward her. "I hardly recognize you out of uniform, Sheriff. Have you met Mrs. Wannamaker?"

"Mrs. Wannamaker and I know each other." Stone nodded politely. "Nice to see you."

Carol grunted an inaudible something, and Brenda looked questioningly at Stone. He shook his head ever so slightly in warning.

"Sheriff Stone has agreed to show me some of the countryside and be his dinner guest tonight."

"Have a nice time, Brenda."

"I'll see you later, Carol."

Brenda looked good to Stone in her short-sleeved, taupe pullover and slim-fitting, tailored slacks. A silver peace-sign necklace matched her earrings. Her eyes seemed brighter, more sparkling and alive than usual, and long, dark-brown hair, blue-green eyes, and frosty mauve lip gloss complemented her near-flawless complexion. He leaned a little closer to inhale her perfume—an exotic scent that stirred something deep inside.

The two crossed the road together and entered his car. Stone started the engine and turned the corner onto Tucanon Street, heading out to the highway.

"Lin, why was Carol so discourteous to you back there?"

"She's still miffed at me. I didn't arrest a local boy who beat up her visiting grandson a few years back. The out-of-town kid turned out to be the bully. "

Brenda waited for a moment to ask another question. "Talk to me about Carlos Mendoza, okay?"

"Now that's big-time news. You ready for this?" Stone gazed at her and waited.

"Don't you think I can handle it?"

"Of course you can. Well, a piece of lumber flew off a tractor-trailer, slammed through his windshield, and nailed him. An Idaho state patrolman found him dead behind the wheel."

"Wow, what a way to go! I hate to say I'm glad, but you know, it seems like justice."

"You're right. It's a highly unusual but fitting end for that wacko."

"Where are you taking me, Lin?"

"You'll see."

They soon crossed the Snake River into Adams County. A few miles farther north, Stone swung off the highway onto a gravel road that wound through a wasteland of sagebrush and cheat grass for four miles before ending at a state campground and outlook. Stone parked, and they left the car to take a walk. He put his arm around Brenda's shoulders as they headed toward the outlook.

"Want to hear the old Indian legend about the Palouse Falls?" Stone asked.

"Sure, I'm game."

"An old Palouse Indian myth tells of four giant brothers who pursued a mystic creature called "Big Beaver." Every time the giant brothers speared Big Beaver, he gouged out more of the canyon wall with his claws. See the canyon ahead?"

Brenda laughed. "Will you stop it, Lin? I'm not a school girl here on a fieldtrip."

"It's the Indians' story, not mine. I didn't say you had to believe it."

"Well, okay, Mr. Legend-man, finish your tale."

"The last time the four giant brothers speared Big Beaver, he fought valiantly, tearing out a huge canyon wall. The river climbed over the cliff and became the Palouse Falls. That's it—that's all there is."

Brenda wrinkled her nose. "It's probably good that's all there is."

The two laughed together this time, and Stone's arm tightened around her.

With the falls directly across from them, she said, "This is outstanding. I would never have expected to lay eyes on a beautiful waterfall out here in this wasteland. How far does the water drop?"

"About 190 feet. I flew over it a year ago with a friend in his two-seater. The view from the air is spectacular. The river makes an immediate sharp bend to the right a few feet before the water drops." Stone made a right angle with his left hand to demonstrate. "From some locations, the Palouse River appears to be gushing out of the side of the cliff. Water traveling over solid basalt for thousands of years carved the deep canyon below the falls. The river runs for miles, as you can see, before it dumps into the Snake."

"That's interesting. The falls is so unusual, and the scenery here is remarkable." Brenda turned, placed her hands on his shoulders, and pressed against him, gazing up into his eyes. "Thank you for bringing me."

Stone ran his knuckles softly along the side of her jaw and kissed her. "I'm so pleased we could spend this time together," he said, when the lingering kiss ended.

"Me, too."

~

Stone chose Walla Walla's historic Dacres Hotel, housing the CrossRoads Steakhouse, for dining that evening. A perceptive waiter seated them far enough from the live western music that it didn't interfere with their conversation. The red-checkered oilcloth on the table offered a down-home feeling, and a flickering candle between them added a touch of intimacy, along with the restaurant's soft lighting.

Stone gazed steadily at Brenda in the candlelight.

"What are you thinking, Lin?" she whispered.

He took her hand in his. "I was thinking how beautiful you are."

"Thank you." Even with the dim lighting, Stone could see Brenda blush a little.

"You make me proud when you're with me. I'm lonely now when you're not."

Brenda lifted the menu, partially covering her face. "Oh, Lin. I—I don't know what to say. Could we order now? I'm starved."

Stone hesitated for a moment and ducked his head to hide his disappointment. "Yes, of course."

Following her perusal of the menu, Brenda said, "I'm going to have the fresh trout, wild rice, and asparagus."

"I like how they do prime rib with twice-baked potatoes here. That's what I'm going to order."

Picking up the wine list and glancing over the extensive selection, Brenda inquired, "Will you take wine with your meal, Lin?"

"Remember me telling you I swore off drinking altogether before I moved out here? But you have some if you want to—don't let me stop you."

"Now that you mention it, I do remember. And no thank you, I think I'll stick with water. Alcohol is pretty safe with me, too," Brenda said. "I hate what it did to my father."

A feeling of well-being settled over Brenda, and the two relaxed into the evening, enjoying the conversation and background music. Stone listened attentively when the girl on stage sang the popular Sugarland tune, "Stay," whose lyrics carried a message of specific interest for him. When their plates were empty and talk between them had dwindled, Stone looked at her searchingly.

"What is it?" Brenda asked.

He cleared his throat and looked down at his napkin. Then his eyes met hers again. "I was wondering—if—would you like to see my place?"

"Yes, I would. That would be nice."

"I warn you, it needs paint. And I suppose it could use a good decorator's hand, as well."

"I promise I won't be critical." She paused. "Would you rather wait until another time, Lin?"

"No, no, I'd like you to see my digs. It's a beautiful evening. We could take a blanket out on the lawn, maybe watch the stars together. I mean, if you'd like that.

"You are a romantic, Lin. Look, if a pillow comes with the blanket, I'll stay out with you as long as you like."

While walking to the car, Brenda reached for his hand and nudged his shoulder. "I'm flattered by your sweet words and kindness."

"You must know how I feel about you, Brenda."

"I think I know," she said. "And I hope I'm right."

53

Stone lived on Pittman Road west of downtown Dayton, not far from the county fairgrounds. He parked in front of his garage, walked around the car, and opened the door for Brenda. Arm in arm, they strode along a winding sidewalk. They passed a flagstone alcove displaying a miniature waterfall before reaching a long, wooden front porch painted white. Four rockers and a church bench completed the inviting expanse. Stone released her arm, and they walked up the wooden steps. He fumbled for the house key, unlocked the door, and they stepped into the living room. Brenda glanced about when the lights came on. She clasped her hands below her chin.

"Oh, I just *love* this!" The built-in bookshelves on either side of the fireplace, wide plank flooring, and exposed ceiling beams looked as though they'd appeared right out of colonial America.

"It needs paint."

"You have some great period furnishings. Where did you find this walking spinning wheel?"

"It was here when I moved in. Don't know a thing about how it works."

Brenda moved around the room, letting her hand trail lightly over a walnut display cabinet, a camelback sofa, two wingback chairs, and a granny rocker. "These are beautiful pieces."

"I bought the place furnished. The old couple who owned it previously said they patterned this room and most of the furnishings after a colonial Virginia plantation room."

They moved through the living room into the dining area. Brenda ambled over to a window seat below the bay window and peered out into the tree-covered back yard. She turned and surveyed the roomy kitchen-dining space. "This is something,

Lin!" Standing in front of the sink, she added, "We had a deep farm sink like this on the ranch." Brenda gazed around at red, glass-door cabinets and butcher-block countertops. "This all fits in perfectly."

"Old timey, huh?"

She gestured with a sweep of a hand to indicate a long, plank farm table, six old Windsor chairs, and a walnut pie safe with hand-punched tins. "Those are authentic pieces. I love those hand-punched tins."

"How do you know the tins are hand punched?"

"Come over here and look closely." Brenda touched a tin panel. "Notice, the distances between the punch marks aren't uniform. You can also see slight irregularities from one tin to another."

"What does that all mean?"

"It means the piece is old—the tins were hammered out by a tinsmith in the days before machine stamping. Most pie safes were made of poplar, or pine, not a fine hardwood like walnut. This piece alone would bring several thousand dollars in an antique shop in the city."

"I had no idea."

"Lin, I don't think you know what treasures you have here."

Stone's jaw dropped. "I do know the place needs painting."

"You men!" Brenda sighed and then laughed.

They poked their heads into the two bedrooms down a hallway off the dining area, one of which Stone used for an office. They turned and walked back through the kitchen into a cozy TV room.

"Wait here for a minute," he said, continuing down another hallway and turning left to the master suite. There he grabbed a blanket with a couple of pillows and returned. "Let's go out this side door to the back yard."

A lush green lawn, the result of a recent fertilizer treatment and plenty of watering, greeted them. Stone found the spot he wanted, spread the blanket, and situated the two pillows next to each other at one end.

"Why don't you take off your shoes," he suggested, as he

unzipped his Wellingtons. Brenda kicked off one-inch heels and sank to the blanket.

Stone lay back on the pillow, fingers laced together behind his head. Brenda rolled onto her side, facing him, and immediately started teasing him with the nail of her index finger, gliding it lightly over the contours of his face.

"Hey, you're tickling me." He loved the attention, but the sensation on his skin made him jumpy and a little too aroused, too soon. He interrupted her finger with one hand while rubbing his lower jaw with the other. But the moment his hand retreated, she started in again. The ever-so-light movement of her finger around his mouth, along his chin, and across his lips made Stone a little crazy.

The last of the orange light from a sinking sun had faded from the sky. Before too long, they could make out the stars overhead. Brenda turned on her back and nudged close to Stone as she looked up into the heavens.

"Can you find the Big Dipper, Brenda?" Stone whispered next to her ear. "And what about the North Star?"

"Of course—I can make them out fine." With a finger, she followed the tip of the Big Dipper in a straight line up to the bright North Star.

"You did good."

"What about you, Star Man, can you find Leo, Taurus, or the Scorpion?"

Stone studied the night sky for a while without knowing where to focus his attention.

"Find the pointer stars on the Big Dipper," Brenda told him at last. "Follow them south to that bright, blue-white star. It's called Regulus, and it's located in Leo's chest."

After a moment, Stone took Brenda's hand in his and pointed toward Leo.

"That's pretty good, Star Man. Now find the bull."

After peering into the vast beyond for a couple of minutes, Stone said, "This is getting too hard. Let's do something easier, okay?"

Brenda chuckled to herself and thought for a moment.

"Okay, make a wish upon a star. Just pick one, and make your wish."

Stone rubbed his chin and stared up at the constellations for a few moments. "A wish, a wish—all right, I have a wish."

"Okay, tell me what it is?"

He hesitated for a moment and then whispered "I wish you could stay here for another week."

"Another week, you say—for what purpose?"

His voice rose a little, and Brenda could hear the excitement in it. "You could help me paint the house."

"You are a nut. You'd keep me here and work me to death on your house?"

He placed his arm across her hips. "I'd keep you here any way I could get you. I told you earlier, I'm lonely without you. Now you make a wish."

Brenda chose the star in Leo's chest—symbol of the heart—and took Stone's hand in hers. She closed her eyes and whispered, "I wish we didn't live so far apart, because I want to spend more time with you."

"Ah, seems clear you and I both want to be together more."

"It does, doesn't it?" Brenda turned on her side again to face Stone, and she once more ran her finger along his chin line. She nestled closer and kissed him lightly on the cheek. She unbuttoned the top two buttons of his shirt, and her hand moved underneath the fabric to his chest. Stone's left hand rested on the warmth of Brenda's thigh.

She trailed her hand from Stone's chest slowly along his body to the inside of his slacks, where she traced her fingertips along the seam, up and down several times. Stone felt himself growing hard. Without saying a word, he rose from the blanket and offered Brenda his hand. They slipped their shoes on and walked together back to the house—Stone trailing the blanket over his shoulder—Brenda cradling the pillows under her arm. They went inside the house and down the hall to the master suite. Stone turned on the bedside lamp and closed the door.

54

Up early Sunday morning, Brenda readied herself and packed her belongings, checked over the room, and went downstairs to breakfast. Carol leaned over the counter nursing a coffee while Brenda ate at the table.

"You must have had quite a time while you were here, on assignment with the sheriff's office," Carol said.

Brenda nodded and finished chewing a bite of toast. "I was actually on vacation when I discovered Art Sabin's body. After hearing about his grandson, I felt compelled to stay to help find him. Late Tuesday, Sheriff Stone and I discovered Tab Johnson at the bottom of an abandoned root cellar at the farm. After that, we captured a murder suspect in Hubers' Wednesday night, as you heard. Then Thursday, Deputy Carver and I arrested the three men who burglarized Mr. Sabin's house. So yes, it's been quite a vacation!"

"Is the man you shot still in the Dayton Hospital?

"No, not anymore. Carlos Mendoza has gone to his just reward."

"Did he die from his gunshot wounds?" Carol's eyes widened, and Brenda realized what a treat this must be for her—to hear about a crime from a primary source.

"No. He attacked his guard, snuck out of the hospital early yesterday morning, stole a car, and was on the run when he met with a highway accident in Idaho. It'll be in the papers tomorrow. Mendoza killed two women and shot the Johnson boy."

"What about Art Sabin's murderer?"

"That's a different story. He's still on the loose."

Brenda heard a car pull up in front. "That must be the sheriff now."

"Well, maybe I'll see you again sometime, Detective."

"Maybe—who knows?" Brenda touched Carol's arm and said warmly, "My stay here has been very pleasant. Thanks again for everything, Carol. Goodbye for now."

Brenda strapped her shoulder bag on top of the roll-on bag and left the house, pulling the luggage out to the car. "Wipe that smile off your face, mister," she said in a stern tone. Retrieving her shoulder bag, she watched Stone as he placed the roll-on in the trunk. "You obviously enjoyed last night far more than the law allows."

"And you didn't, I suppose?" Stone replied. He waited to see what look she would give him. She beamed like a woman who'd just won the Publishers Clearing House sweepstakes.

Stone leaned against the open trunk. "I'm not crazy about taking you home, you know. I might hide you out instead—at my cabin."

"Planning on taking me hostage, are you, Mr. Sheriff Man?"

He closed the trunk lid, walked to her door, and opened it. Brenda slid in and he closed the door. Moments later they were on their way out of town and maybe together for the last time, Brenda thought.

Stone cleared his throat. "My smile this morning is all because of you, Brenda. You're a dynamite woman."

"I've been thinking about our first meeting. I keep wondering why I felt so compelled to stay."

"Beats me all to pieces, but I'm awful glad you did."

"So much has happened since I goaded you into taking me on."

"You didn't goad me—it wasn't a hard decision. You had me from 'Detective.'"

"I didn't consciously engineer what happened between us, you know."

"Yes, I know. And neither did I," Stone said.

She shook her head. "You bounder—you've kept me awake nights."

Their route took them to Walla Walla, on to Pendleton, Oregon, and to the freeway. They stopped in Hood River long enough to have lunch. Brenda recommended the 3 Rivers Grill where she selected her favorite quiche with a house salad. Stone ordered a bacon-mushroom burger. Neither said much during the meal, but Stone looked longingly into her eyes more than a few times. Afterwards, they drove south and higher into fruit orchard country for a look at the magnificent scenery. Mount Hood rose to their west and Mount Adams, across the Columbia River, to the north. Stone parked the car at an overlook and they stepped out.

He took Brenda's hand. "What a pretty day, and this countryside is so picturesque."

"It is, for sure. I always like coming up here. Look north—over there—you should be able to see Mount Rainier."

He squinted to make out an outline on the horizon. "You're right. Wow, that's a huge mountain."

"They say it's over seventy miles around at its base."

"This little detour has been nice. We'll have to stay in the lodge at Mount Hood when we have more time," Stone said, his voice hopeful.

Brenda squeezed his hand. "That would be very nice."

It was after two o'clock when they arrived at Brenda's apartment. She unlocked the door and pushed it open, and they walked into a sizable living room. Stone noticed a dining room and a Pullman-style kitchen on his right. "This is very nice. And your place doesn't need painting, either," he said.

She couldn't help smiling. "Feel free to look around while I get us something to drink."

Stone studied framed portraits of Brenda's parents and her two sisters on the living room walls. Brenda carried their drinks out to the veranda, where they sat at a small, wrought-iron table, sipping on their sodas and gazing longingly at each other.

"Now you have to make the long drive back," she said.

"Yes, I'd like to get home before it gets too late."

Small talk continued until Stone at last stood. Head down, he swirled the remaining ice in his glass and then looked at her. "I want you to know I'm in love with you, Brenda. I don't want to lose you."

She stood and moved close to him, laying her hand on his chest and staring into his eyes. "I have very strong feelings for you, too Lin. But I don't want to get hurt again."

Stone pulled her into his arms, kissing her long and deep.

Still holding her close, he spoke softly against her neck. "I don't say things I don't mean—trust me. I love you, and that's it."

Brenda leaned back, peering intently into his eyes. "I know," she said, touching his cheek. "Thank you for being so good to me. We must stay in touch." She laid her head on his chest.

He stroked her hair gently. "Someday, Brenda, I think we'll care so much for each other, we won't be able to say goodbye."

"I hope you're right, Lin. You'd better go now. Call me when you get home?"

Stone nodded, trying not to let the disappointment show on his face.

Brenda stood at the living room window watching as he walked along the sidewalk to his car. He turned and waved up to her, and she waved back. Tears slid onto her cheeks, and she watched the blur of his car until it was out of sight.

Later in the day, Brenda began pacing back and forth in her living room. She worked out on the treadmill in her bedroom so she could pace with a purpose. As she exercised, she pondered over what had happened, unable to shake a persistent feeling that nagged at her. Why hadn't she told Lin she loved him? She felt it, but why hadn't she said it back? *Lin's interest in me will cool. No, it will wither and die, sure as rain.*

She glanced at her watch every few minutes. Mail had been held at the post office for the week, so there was nothing to busy her there. Television couldn't hold her interest. She hardly ever laid out clothes for the coming day, but now it was something to do to pass the time. There were only so many times she could scrub the kitchen sink and wipe down the countertops.

Later, she heated a frozen dinner and ate slowly, more to pass the time than to satisfy her hunger. The ticking of the clock in the dining room marked the long, empty minutes.

Brenda's cell finally rang, and her heart seemed to skip a beat.

"Hello, Brenda."

"Please don't say a word, Lin, okay? I want you to listen."

"All right—I'll be quiet."

"I love you, Lin. I love you. Do you hear what I'm telling

258

you? I'm sorry I didn't say it when you were here. Do you hear me, my darling? I love you."

"Yes, I hear you. You've just made me extremely happy. I love you, too, very much, and I miss you already. This long-distance relationship won't last too long, Brenda. Believe me, I won't let it."

"I'm sorry I was coy with you earlier. I don't want to be that way, believe me. I'll never hold back my feelings from you again. I want to tell you often how I love you. I want you to tell me how you love me." She paused. "Am I making sense—is this—am I sounding foolish?"

"Yes, of course you're making sense, and no, what you're saying isn't foolish. I won't hold back my feelings, either. I'm—it's been a while, Brenda. I'm a little rusty. Be patient with me, and I'll do my best, I promise. I'll get better at all this."

Shortly before their conversation ended, Brenda said, "Lin, after we finish talking, look under the tissue box in your bathroom."

After a long goodbye, Stone found the note Brenda had scribbled in haste the previous night.

Lin, I loved being in your arms tonight. I felt wanted in a way I have never felt before.

All my love, Brenda

55

A lazy evening sun angled its orange light through the maple trees along the eleven-hundred block of Park Street. It was Sunday evening, and as Brad Summers trod along in his slow, steady gait, he glanced at his watch: 7:55. By walking a few extra hours the previous two days, the old widower had achieved his planned arrival time at his sister's front door in Coeur d'Alene. Her cozy bungalow with its metal roof stood ahead on the left.

He shuffled up the walkway, climbed the steps to her front porch, and pushed the doorbell. The Big Ben chimes rang out, yet he heard no footsteps. Pushing the doorbell again brought no response. He shrugged off his backpack and was about to sit on the step to await Margaret's return when he saw her coming around the far side of the house. Summers left the porch and trudged around to where she stood in a brown turtleneck, matching slacks, and a straw sunbonnet, the watering hose still in her hand.

"Bradley, it is so good to see you!" she screamed, dropping the hose and holding out her arms. Summers staggered toward her and flung his arms about her.

"It's nice to see you, too, Sis."

The sixty-five-year-old Margaret Giles stood tall and trim, salt-and-pepper hair in a long pageboy still containing more pepper than salt. She planted a large garden each year and cared for her home and a sizable yard.

"Margaret, you haven't aged a bit in the last ten years. Are you still peddling about town on that five-speed your husband bought you over thirty-five years ago?"

"Yes, my bicycle still gets me around. It's my exercise, and I save a little on gas each month. I'm delighted you're here! I'll turn off the water, and we'll go inside."

Summers carried his backpack into the living room and set it beside the door.

"You know where the bathroom is, Brad. I'm guessing you

might like to use it since you've been on the road. I'll pour us some lemonade."

They sat across from each other in the living room in low-back, over-stuffed chairs with oversized arms. "I hoped you would be here this evening. I cooked a roast and baked your favorite pie."

"That sounds fine, Margaret. I haven't had a good home-cooked meal in a long time."

"Tell me about your trip."

"Doctor told me to lose thirty pounds, so I decided to walk it off. I trekked across northern Idaho on the Lewis and Clark Highway—you know, from Missoula to Lewiston."

Margaret frowned a little. "Oh, you are ambitious, my brother."

Summers pulled the ottoman closer and stretched out his legs on it. "After resting for a couple of days, I decided to go down to the lower Snake River. I wanted to check on one of my old projects. Helen said many times she'd been the happiest of all during the years we lived there."

"I never understood Helen. I couldn't quite figure out what made her tick. But she made you happy, Brad, and that was all that mattered to me." His sister's voice shook a little with her next words. "Oh, I felt horrible when you called this spring to tell me she'd taken her own life."

Summers cleared his throat. "Helen was never the same after she went into the hospital, Margaret. She completely withdrew, you know. Her psychosis deepened—got to the point toward the end she hardly recognized me."

Margaret fiddled with the fabric cording on the arm of her chair. "I'm sorry you two had to go through that—all those years. Why can't people keep things simple, roll with the tide, as they say?"

Summers shook his head. "Helen complained she rolled too much with the tide. She always followed along with whatever I wanted—went where I wanted to go, did what I wanted to do."

"Getting sick in the head wasn't the answer. It only made things worse, and harder than ever on you." Margaret straightened the crocheted coverlets on the arms of her chair and looked earnestly at her brother. "Bradley, do you think—was Helen insane when she threw herself out the window?"

"I don't know, Margaret. She was sane enough to pick up a workman's rope left in the hallway and know where to hide it, too. She was sane enough to know how to tie the rope to the heat register near a window she could open in the hallway. Sane enough, too, to know to jump at a time when no one would be there to stop her. Not long before she died, she told me she'd been keeping a deep, dark secret from me."

"What deep, dark secret?"

"She told me she'd planned to leave me." Summers' voice cracked. He paused, swallowed hard, and continued. "Something happened to change her mind. After that, she hated me, she said. She felt trapped all the years that followed."

Margaret waited a moment, wondering if there was more, but her brother shifted his eyes away from her.

"Now we're both alone, you and I," she finally said.

"How are you coping with Barry's passing?"

"He was the love of my life. Barry could be stubborn as a mule, but there was never a time I didn't want to be with him. I miss him terribly."

"I understand, Sis." Summers gazed out the window as darkness blanketed the yard. "You were lucky; you had a good marriage"

"Well, if I keep the radio or CNN on, I don't feel so alone. I manage."

Later that evening, Summers ate as though there was no tomorrow. Fresh creamed peas and baby carrots garnished his plate, already piled high with mashed potatoes and brown gravy. He could cut the tender slices of roast beef with his fork. Crazy about catsup since he was a kid, he smothered his meat with it. "You always were the best cook in the family, Sis," he said, placing his fork on the empty plate. "This meal was outstanding."

"Did you save room for apple pie and ice cream?"

"There's always room for your apple pie."

After enjoying their dessert and chatting for a while about times on the farm as kids, Margaret showed Summers to his room.

He carried his backpack from the living room into the bedroom and laid it on the bed. After removing the blanket and coat draping the canvas, he untied the opening at the top, turned the pack upside down, and shook the contents onto the bed. Margaret busied herself moving clothes to one side of the closet to make room for his things. She heard a thud and turned to see a pistol lying at her brother's feet. He quickly reached down, snatched it up, and concealed it under the backpack.

She moved quickly to her brother's side. "A pistol, Brad? You always hated guns. Why on earth are you carrying a pistol?"

His face reddened and he fidgeted with a strap on the pack. "It's nothing, Sis. I carry it for protection in the forest."

"I remember well the trauma you went through when Dad shot the family dog for killing the neighbor's chickens. As much as he tried, he could never get you to fire a gun." Margaret sat on the bed and slid the backpack away from the pistol. Picking it up gingerly, she looked it over and then examined her brother's face. "My brother, you've fired this weapon."

"I used it to scare off wild animals. That's all."

Margaret sucked air between her teeth, a childhood habit picked up from her mother. "But I remember how you hated firearms and how you refused to shoot one. Now you're carrying a big revolver—you say to frighten away animals?"

Summers eased down on the bed next to her, and their eyes met. "I have something to tell you about my health."

"Oh, no. What is it, Brad?"

"I have a malignant growth on my brain. The doctors give me maybe four to six months."

"Oh, Brad, I'm so sorry to hear this!" Margaret's voice broke, and they were both quiet for a minute. "Have you gotten a second opinion?"

"I got three opinions, actually. They all concluded that I have an aggressive, inoperable cancer."

"This explains why you're doing things you've never done before, like walking several hundred miles and—and toting a gun."

Hands in his lap, Summers remained silent. Then turning to his sister, he wrapped his arms around her shoulders and sobbed.

56

First thing Monday morning, Anne Pearson barged into Stone's office and started right in. "My car came back yesterday, and it's not all banged to hell. Can you believe that, Sheriff?"

"I'm real glad, Anne."

"I heard the guy who clobbered Ed was killed on the highway Saturday morning."

"You heard right."

"Good, good for him. It couldn't have happened to a more deserving guy. You told me the county would replace Ed's pistol, right?"

"His weapon is being returned to me UPS. I'm expecting it to be here later today."

Anne settled into the chair across the desk from Stone. "I'm sorry, Sheriff, for how I went off on you the other morning. I was scared to death."

"Anne, it's all right. I understand."

"If you still want Ed, Sheriff, he's yours."

"Does he want to work here after what happened to him?"

"Sheriff, he loves being a lawman." Ed's wife picked up a magazine from Stone's desk, rolled it, and slapped it in her hand for emphasis.

"Excellent! He's a good help, and we need him in the department. His working a shift or two a week is a great service to the county, and to me."

As he showed her out, Stone let out the breath he'd been holding. That one's a whirlwind, he thought. She makes me tired. I see why Ed works a second job—even one he doesn't get paid for.

Later on that morning around 11:00 a.m., Tab Johnson and his father, Ron, appeared at Stone's office door. When the two were seated, Tab said, "I told my parents where I was when my grandfather and the others were killed."

"I'm glad for that," Stone said. "You did the right thing."

"Yes, he did," Tab's father seconded.

"I also broke it off with Sheila. Detective Tower was right. I had some serious straightening out to do."

Stone grinned as he thought about how Brenda had scolded the boy on Friday.

"Tab insisted we come see you," Ron Johnson said.

"Will you make sure Detective Tower gets this?" Tab handed Stone a small, brightly wrapped package with an envelope taped to the top. "I'm not going to forget Detective Tower, or you either, Sheriff."

"Thank you, Tab. I'll make certain she receives your gift." Stone set the package on his desk.

"We're on our way to the farm. The doctor released Tab this morning with the promise he'd stay down for a few more days. His work this next week or two will have to be administrative. Tony and I will take charge of the field work."

"I wish you both the best with the harvest. I also wish I could tell you that we have a suspect in your grandfather's death, Tab. Be assured, apprehending his murderer is my top priority."

"Thanks, Sheriff," both the Johnsons said. They shook hands with Stone and left.

In the early afternoon, Stone's office phone rang with a message from the dispatcher that a Mr. Lamarr Treadway from Elam's Crossing wished to speak with him.

Stone pressed the flashing light on his phone. "Mr. Treadway, this is Sheriff Stone. What can I do for you?"

"I go by Squeaky, Sheriff. I may be able to do something for you. I've been thinking quite a bit about Art Sabin's death. I have an idea about who may be responsible. Are you interested?"

"Yes, of course I'm interested."

"Art and me were thick as thieves at one time, see. We knew everything about what each other was doing in those days. I can tell you Art chased the women in three counties after he and Angela split, and not all of them were single, either. Art had more than one scrape with an irate husband."

"Are you telling me, Squeaky, that a jealous husband may

have killed your friend over his wife's infidelity some twenty or thirty years ago?"

"That's my take on it, Sheriff. I've got names of three married women he ran with at one time or another."

"How about I meet you in the morning at the City Hall in Elam's Crossing? We can talk about it then."

"No good, Sheriff. I'll be out at Art's farm, working in the kitchen."

"I'll catch up with you out there sometime mid morning. Thanks for your call, Squeaky"

Stone replaced the receiver and scratched his head. Leaving his office, he strolled into the dispatcher's room and plopped into a chair next to Pamela. The thirty-two-year-old brunette wearing a western shirt, jeans, and cowboy boots let a *People* magazine fall to her desk and turned her attention to the boss.

"Tell me, Pam, what kind of man kills another man over his wife's adultery when it happened maybe twenty or thirty years ago?"

"I don't know any men like that. Why do you ask?"

"That fellow from Elam's Crossing who called believes Art Sabin may have been murdered by a jealous husband."

"Someone told me Mr. Sabin was sixty-five. Kind of late in life to be fooling around with another man's wife, don't you think?"

"The caller told me Sabin ran around with some married women years ago."

"Sheriff, jealous men don't wait to take revenge; no sir, they act right away."

"My thought exactly, Pam. I'll meet with this Squeaky fellow in the morning, but I can't think much will come of it." Stone snatched a pencil from the tray on Pam's desk and began tapping it on the desktop. "Any lead in the Sabin case is better than the current goose egg."

57

Late in the day on Monday, Pamela sat, legs crossed, reading the *Bulletin*'s headline story about Carlos Mendoza's capture, escape, and sudden death. She glanced at the clock on the wall. The second shift dispatcher would be arriving in a few minutes to take her place. She turned back to the Mendoza article. Moments later, the shuffling of feet on the tile floor caught her ear. She looked up from her paper to see two weary-looking, older people, a man and a woman, standing across the counter from her. She folded the paper and laid it aside.

"Good afternoon, folks, how may I help you?"

"I must speak with the sheriff," the man said, his head down and his voice barely audible.

Moments later, the two seniors stood in Stone's office behind a closed door.

Stone approached his visitors. "I'm Sheriff Stone." The two men shook hands.

"My name is Brad Summers, Sheriff. This is my sister, Margaret Giles.

"I'm pleased to meet you both. Pamela said you needed to speak with me."

Summers sighed. "I got to get something off my chest."

"Please have a seat." Stone guessed the man to be around seventy and somewhat frail. "Go ahead, sir, tell me what's on your mind."

"I've always tried to live right, never harmed anyone in sixty-eight years. But I did a horrible, shameful thing."

"What did you do, sir?"

"I couldn't help . . . couldn't help . . ." Summers breathed deeply and started over. "I couldn't help myself, Sheriff." He leaned forward in his chair. "I—I killed Art Sabin."

"You killed Art Sabin?" Stone asked evenly. He couldn't imagine this man being a cold-blooded killer. Yet, Summers' demeanor and tone appeared dead serious. Stone knew he needed another witness. "Please excuse me for just a moment." He pushed the button for his dispatcher's phone. "Pam, have Deputy Clark come to my office."

When Clark entered the office, Stone said, "Mr. Summers, I've asked Deputy Clark in to hear your confession. Before we proceed, he will read you your rights."

"I understand, Sheriff," Summers said. He kept his eyes on Clark as the deputy read the list.

"You told me minutes ago you killed Art Sabin," Stone continued after the deputy had finished and Summers said he understood his rights.

Summers reached over and clasped Margaret's forearm. "Sis here convinced me I should turn myself in."

"Do you want to tell us what happened?"

Summers glanced at Margaret, then Stone, then Clark, and back to Margaret. Finally his gaze settled on the sheriff. "I left Missoula on the twenty-third of June, on foot. I went across Highway 12 over Lolo Pass, on to Lewiston, and then toward Dayton. I turned onto 261 and headed for Elam's Crossing." Summers cleared his throat and looked at Margaret again. She offered an encouraging nod, and he continued. "I arrived at Art Sabin's place after dark last Sunday, and I hid in his shop and waited. He was working on something in there early Monday morning. A young man was with him for a little while, but he left, and I heard his car drive off. My eyes aren't too good, Sheriff. So, I crept up close behind Sabin and shot him. He fell to the floor, and then I guess I fired a couple more times. He was dead." Summers raised a trembling hand to rub his tanned forehead.

"How did you keep the dog quiet when you entered the farm lot?"

"Some bologna left over from my lunch and lots of petting. I like animals—they can sense it."

"Why did you move the body, Mr. Summers?"

"Oh, I couldn't have a family member find him dead in his shop. That would be bad for them."

"So, you put the body in the truck and drove out the back way, is that right?"

"I needed some plan to get away. I figured someone would find him if I left the pickup in the field where it could be seen from the highway."

"Someone did find him, all right. A policewoman from Portland discovered him."

"I'm glad of that, at least."

"Sir, do you still have the weapon you used to commit this crime?"

"I do. It's in Margaret's car."

"Why did you kill Art Sabin, Mr. Summers?"

"Well, I had to, Sheriff. He had it coming. I couldn't just let him go free."

"I don't understand. Tell me what you mean—what did he do to you?"

Summers stomped his foot on the tile floor and his eyes narrowed. "He had to pay for what he did to Helen, to both of us!"

"Go on." Stone sat up a little straighter. Behind the bulk of the wooden desk, his right hand rested on his holster.

"He seduced *my wife*. The thieving bastard stole her heart away from me. What he did to her ruined both our lives."

"We're listening, Mr. Summers. Tell us exactly what happened."

Summers looked down at the floor for a moment, and when he raised his head again, Stone noticed the hard glint was gone from his eyes.

"I was an engineer on the Little Goose Dam in the seventies when the last three generators were installed. Helen and I met Art at a fourth of July celebration. We saw him in town a time or two, and he invited us to a party at his place after he harvested his wheat. There was one other time we were with him, as I recall, and with others on his houseboat. I thought we were friends. But later, when I was away on business, he made moves on Helen. He took her places, bought her things, made her feel special. She told me they spent time together in Coeur d'Alene, and while they were there, he begged her to leave me. Promised he'd marry her."

"But why did you kill him after all those years had gone by?"

"I didn't know anything was going on between Helen and Art back then. Helen confessed to me a few months ago that she loved Art. She told me she'd loved him from the first time they met. She made plans to run out on me, but she couldn't go through with it, didn't have the courage, she said. Sabin didn't make her happy, Sheriff. He made her miserable, horribly miserable for the rest of her days."

"Still, Helen's infidelity thirty years ago is hardly a good reason for killing the man now."

Summers yanked on his hair and moaned. "You don't understand, Sheriff. I'm not finished with this story."

The man's sister started to speak, but Stone held up a hand in warning. He looked Summers in the eye and shook his head. "No, I guess I don't understand. Please go on."

"He *ruined* Helen with what he did. All those years, she plodded on with a broken heart. She was miserable and guilty because of betraying her marriage vows and carrying a lot of terrible secrets. She hated me and wanted him. It got to where she couldn't function outside of the house or even inside, at least not in a normal way. I placed her in an institution six years ago. The doctors said she suffered from some kind of psychosis and depression. She committed suicide in March."

Clark shook his head and glanced at the sheriff.

Stone sighed. "I'm sorry to hear that, Mr. Summers. Really sorry."

"My Helen was so innocent, so loving and caring, so dedicated to our marriage. Sabin changed all that. The longer I thought about what he had done to her and to our marriage, the more I hated him. He'd driven Helen mad, and I couldn't let him go unpunished. I wanted him dead. I bought a gun and some ammunition at a shop in Missoula. I did what I had to do. It's settled now."

"Sir, I'll have to hold you here, you understand." Stone stole a quick glance at the man's sister and noticed her eyes brimmed with tears. "You'll stand trial in the county for murder."

"It doesn't matter much now, anyway," Summers said.

"My brother has inoperable brain cancer." Margaret spoke

quickly. "He has a few months at best."

"Ma'am, I'm very sorry to hear all this and sorry for what you're going through. But I'll need your brother to go with Deputy Clark."

"Bradley, be brave now," his sister said.

"I'm all right, Margaret; don't you worry about me."

The two men stood, and Clark took Summers by the arm and led him out of the room.

Stone turned to Margaret. "Mrs. Giles, you did a good thing, talking your brother into giving himself up."

"Well, I had to do what was right. When I saw the gun, I had a feeling something awful had happened. Once he admitted to me what he'd done, *he* knew he had to turn himself in. I really didn't have to talk him into it."

"Would you let me get you a room for tonight? You could return home tomorrow."

"I'll stay the night if I can spend some time with Bradley."

"I'll arrange it. If you'll come with me to your car, I'll take possession of that gun."

It was after 5:00 p.m. when Stone finished filling out paperwork and finally dialed the woman in the sprawling, white brick rambler on the corner lot in Pinehurst, Walla Walla. "Mrs. Sabin, this is Sheriff Stone. I have your husband's murderer behind bars."

"Oh, my . . . oh, I'm so very pleased to hear that, Sheriff! Can you tell me who he is?"

"He's a Missoula, Montana man, and his name is Brad Summers."

"How do you know he's the killer?"

"He confessed to killing your husband here in my office less than an hour ago. Your grandson mentioned to me this morning that you'll be going out to the farm in the morning. If you want to stop by the courthouse on your way through Dayton, I'll tell you more of what I know.

"Oh, yes, I'll stop by for sure. In the morning then, Sheriff. Thank you—thank you so much for the call."

58

Stone paced back and forth in his home office, glancing every minute or so at his watch. Brenda should be home from work about now, he thought. Excitement streamed through his body when he dialed the number and heard her voice at the other end.

"Hello Brenda, this is Lin. How are you after your first day back on the job?"

"I'm doing fine. It's so good to hear your voice, Lin."

"You couldn't guess in a month of Sundays what happened here today."

"Well, let me try. Hmm, let me see. Lin, did you resign—turn in your badge?"

"No, that's not it. I like my job fine."

"Did the woman in the bra and panties you told me about propose marriage?"

"Hah! No, that's not it. There was a marriage proposal today, but not from her."

Brenda laughed. "Yeah, right, I had a proposal come my way, too. Did it have anything to do with Tab Johnson?"

"No, but that reminds me, I have a gift and a card for you that he left here this morning."

"How nice is that?" Brenda crowed.

"He and his father stopped by the office this morning. Your advice to him took hold. He broke it off with Sheila Wattenburger. I didn't think he'd have the guts to do that once I saw what she looked like."

"She kind of boiled your water, didn't she, Sheriff? I liked the Johnson boy. I hope everything goes well with him."

"You give up?" Stone asked.

"I know what it was, Lin. You got a big pay raise today."

"Don't I wish! Interesting guesses so far, but no Kewpie doll."

"Did you find the murder weapon?"

"I do have the weapon. It's an older Colt .38 Special. But there's more."

"One of the harvest hands in lockup confessed to killing Sabin?"

Stone chuckled. "No, they didn't have a thing to do with it."

"You must have apprehended the killer!"

"Well, let's say I have him in custody."

"Please, Lin, just tell me!"

"Brenda, believe it or not, a Montana man named Brad Summers walked into my office late this afternoon and confessed to killing Sabin."

"Walked in and confessed! That's almost unheard of."

"I know. Anyway, Summers told me Sabin had an affair with his wife some thirty years ago. She kept the affair a secret until this year. The man is convinced Sabin ruined her life—and his—as well. Mrs. Summers had been in an institution for several years. Not long after her confession, she committed suicide. I can tell you more of the specifics soon. For now, I just wanted you to know the mystery's over."

"Quite a story, one old man taking the ultimate revenge on another old man over an affair that took place when I was in kindergarten."

"And me in the fifth grade."

"Lin, remember I told you Sabin had a reputation with the women. But who could have guessed his philandering so long ago would be the cause of his death?"

"Listen to this. I got a call from Squeaky this morning telling me he had the names of three married women Sabin ran with years ago. His theory was that an irate husband killed Sabin. I called him back after Summers confessed and asked him to give me the names of the three women on his list."

"And?"

"One of the names was Helen Summers."

"Were you fortunate or what, having this guy walk in and

confess like that?"

"Boy, do I know it. Anyway, I need to get all this off my mind for a while. Tell me about your first day back on the job, Brenda."

"The chief assigned me to a new homicide case. Lin, It's a nasty affair. A teenager is suspected of killing his girlfriend's stepfather and her mother with a claw hammer."

"You've got a big job ahead of you, don't you."

"I do. But, you know, I've got a good partner. Our suspects were picked up in southern Nevada. They're back here now. We reviewed some of the evidence today, and tomorrow we'll begin our investigative work. Tonight I'm tired, but I feel good."

"I'm glad you're okay. You worked hard last week when it was to be your vacation. Say, I spoke with Chief Lowery about your week here—how you found Sabin's body, recovered young Johnson, stopped Mendoza, helped apprehend three burglars, and gained a rape confession."

"No, you didn't!"

"Lowery wasn't a bit surprised. He told me you're one of Portland's best."

"Lin, tell me the truth. Did you really call him?"

"Of course I did."

"I'm embarrassed you did that, but I love you for it."

"I had to do it. I told him to expect an official letter of commendation from the county. One thing, though. I forgot to tell him I fell in love with you while you were here."

Brenda laughed. "The less you tell my chief, the better off we'll both be."

"You mentioned yesterday how tired you've been for the last couple of months."

"I was afraid there was something physically wrong with me. A copy of the lab results came in the mail while I was gone. Luckily, I'm healthy. My body is within the acceptable parameters for every test my doctor ordered."

"I'm very pleased to hear you say that."

"My problem is emotional stress, Lin. I worry too much: about never getting caught up with the work, about victims of violent crimes, about unfair practices in the department."

"Now you know what's causing your chronic fatigue, you can deal with it, right?"

"Exactly, and I'm going to. You know, a real vacation would've been nice, but then I wouldn't have met you. Dad used to tell us girls a change is as good as a rest. My change last week was better than a rest, and all because of you."

"You're a sweet woman to say that, and you know I feel the same. Listen, I've got something else to share with you."

"Still more?" Brenda asked. "I didn't know what I was in for when I answered my phone!"

"Yeah, listen to this. The Walla Walla Police Chief is posting a new position for a detective this week. I thought you might be interested—you know, just in case . . ."

"Just in case what?"

"In case you decide you don't want to live three hundred miles away from me."

"What would a successful, big-city detective like me do in a podunk place like Walla Walla?"

"It's obvious you haven't been keeping up with the times, Brenda. Mark Fuhrman wasn't the only detective to bail from a metropolitan city to the country in the last decade or so."

"Oh, that Fuhrman, the one who investigated the O. J. Simpson murders and got nailed for perjury, right?"

"Right, and look at me—I left the big city for a calmer work environment."

"True, though last week's work environment missed the *calm* mark."

"You won't have a snowball's chance, anyway, once the word gets out. Walla Walla's a great place to live. There'll be dozens of applicants, maybe even a hundred or more."

"It won't do me much good to apply then, will it?"

"I'll go to bat for you, Brenda. Once Chief Foley hears about your capabilities, he'll want to interview you first. The rest will be up to you."

"Let's say I *am* interested, I apply for the job, get an interview, and I'm selected. Could I come live at your house? I like it a lot. I could commute back and forth to Walla Walla."

"All this time, I thought the attraction here was with me, and now you tell me it's the house."

"I like you fine, Lin, but for different reasons than I like your house."

"Foley might loan you to me to work on a case here from time to time. You could live here then, for sure."

"If I worked for you again, Sheriff Stone, you'd have to chauffer me, and you'd have to pay my room and board, just like before."

"Whoa—slow down, Detective. I'd provide you a car. You could live with me, but that's the only room and board you'll get here."

"You don't say?"

"I do say. One thing, though. My contract requires that I be legally married to any woman I cohabitate with."

"Hey mister, I'm not just *any woman*."

"No ma'am, you're not. You're the woman who keeps me awake at night, the one I want to be with, always."

Stone heard a long, deep sigh at the other end of the phone, and then Brenda said, "In that case, I'd have to marry you, I suppose."

"I love you, Detective Tower."

"And I love you, Mr. Sheriff Man."

20472377R00153

Made in the USA
Charleston, SC
11 July 2013